NOT REGINA

NOT REGINA

by

Christmas Carol Kauffman

MOODY PRESS

CHICAGO

TO OUR OWN BELOVED

MA DONNA LEE

WHO MOTHERED OUR THREE YOUNGER CHILDREN

STANLEE DE VON

JAMES MILTON

MARCIA MARIE

WHILE WE WERE ABROAD

TRUSTING THEY WILL EACH LIVE

IN THE TRIUMPHANT FAITH OF REGINA

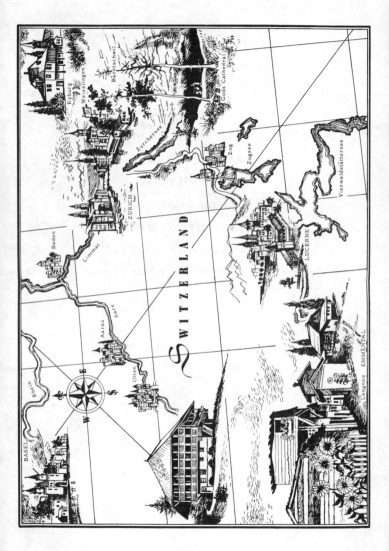

PREFACE

Several years ago John C. Wenger, church historian and professor at Goshen College Biblical Seminary, suggested that I write a historical story setting forth the faith, life, and persecutions of our Anabaptist ancestors. In the summer of 1952 when the way opened for me to accompany my husband to the Mennonite World Conference at Basel, Switzerland, I determined to take advantage of the opportunity to gather firsthand information for such a story.

At this time Paul Peachey was a graduate student of Anabaptist life at the University of Zurich. I am greatly indebted to him and to his wife Ellen, who served as my guide to many places of interest, and who also acted as my interpreter. Ellen spent a week with me at Langnau in the Emmental Valley. We lived in the home of a Swiss family who had a daughter Regina. "Regina" was suggested as a character name as a result of this visit, but the "Regina" of this story is a character of the author's creation and not the Regina of this Swiss family. Among the many places of interest in that area we visited was a cheese factory and the farmstead where the Anabaptists held secret meetings in the barn. We saw the space in the wall between the house and barn where the Anabaptists hid during persecutions.

I also lived one week in Zurich. We stood where Felix Manz' mother stood on the bank of the Limmat River where her son was executed for his faith. We spent several hours in and around Kyburg Castle, studying the prison tower, Lord Engelhard's court room, the torture chamber, and the long steep hill which the Anabaptists had to climb on the way to the castle. We also visited the cave where many Anabaptists found refuge from their pursuers. During a period of prayer in this cave I received fresh inspiration from the Lord to write this story.

Among the actual historical characters in the story are Ulrich Zwingli, Conrad Grebel, Felix Manz, George Blaurock, Lord Engelhard, Felix Manz' mother and brother. Most of the other characters are creations of my own based on stories of Anabaptist life I gathered while in Switzerland.

Never have I worked at any writing that has proved such an enrichment to my own spiritual life and faith. My sincere prayer is that many who read these pages will receive a similar blessing.

August 1, 1954   C. CAROL KAUFFMAN
Hannibal, Missouri

I

It was the year 1525—a beautiful October evening in the village of Weisslingen, Switzerland. As Regina Strahm stepped briskly through the dry fallen leaves she could hear the familiar tink-a-tink of cowbells floating down from the high mountainsides. It was milking time and from each native pine chalet, weathered to a rich golden brown, a boy or girl with a milk can could be seen walking toward a neighboring farm outside the village. This evening Regina with her milk can was on her way to the Rheinhardt barn outside of Weisslingen.

Regina often sang and yodeled as she walked along the bending road to the farm. Her rosy cheeks and quick steps were proof of her love for the fresh mountain air and simple Swiss life. Regina was now seventeen, contented and a bit gay, but unpretentious, and with a brightness about her blue eyes. As she walked along a light evening breeze blew the soft blond hair about her face and high forehead.

This evening Regina was not singing nor yodeling. She did not see the rolling hills toward the north painted in rich autumn reds, golds, rusts, and deep blues; nor the pines and cedars which stood majestic and black and formed an irregular horizon against the blue sky.

When she came to the little rustic wooden bridge, she stopped and watched the rushing water splash against the white stones and twist in little whirlpools.

"Why do they do it and who is right?" This question was constantly turning about in her mind. She had been a member of the Reformed Church at Weisslingen for almost as long as she could remember, the church of Ulrich Zwingli who

1

lived in Zurich, eleven miles northwest. It was the Reformed Church which the government said every one must be a member of. Why were some disobedient to the church and to the government? Why were people being baptized again? Why must there be so much argument over what to believe? Since people were beginning to read the Bible, why must the disagreement be so great? Who really is right? Why is it dangerous even so much as to talk about who the heretics are and what they believe?

Regina wasn't in the habit of loitering; so she hastened across the bridge and soon was near the Rheinhardt barn.

"I saw the young pastor from Kyburg go past the other day," Rheinhardt spoke first. "Was he at your place?" he asked rather seriously.

"He came to order material for a new suit," said Regina.

"A new suit? I see. He chose the best woolen weaver in Weisslingen when he came to your father, Friedrich Strahm. Your father is as thrifty and honest as your grandfather. If only more people were as kind and trustworthy as your father."

"The suit the pastor ordered is to be his wedding suit," Regina said quietly.

"You mean his own?" Rheinhardt asked quickly.

"That's what Father said," Regina replied.

"I thought perhaps the pastor came to question your father." Rheinhardt looked sharply at Regina.

"Question my father?" Regina asked with a start. "My father is the most faithful member of the parish in Weisslingen. He's troubled about this confusion just as you are. Why can't somebody do something about it?"

"I ask your pardon," Rheinhardt answered with a smile and took the milk can from Regina's trembling hand. "I should not speak of these troubles to one so young. This Anabaptist doctrine has a way of spreading, but I know your father is faithful."

"Thank you, Rheinhardt," Regina said.

"But none of us know what to expect these days, with whole families suddenly becoming Anabaptists and disappearing overnight. We never know who next might become heretics. No one knows who next might be questioned by the pastor. When he passed here, he seemed quite friendly and bade me the time of day. So the young Pastor Hofmeier is going to get married."

"He will be coming for the cloth next week," Regina said as she stepped back to let each cow take its stall. "You seem to be as much surprised as Father was."

"He's not the first priest to marry and I suppose many more will be doing the same. I think it is all right, too."

"He told Father that Pastor Zwingli encouraged him to get married," Regina said.

As Rheinhardt picked up the milking stool he said, "Then it must be all right. Give me your can, Regina. I'll fill yours first. Either I'm slow tonight or you came early. Who will the bride be? Or is that a secret?"

"He told Father it will be Catri Landwirt."

"Well, Landwirt is a good name in these parts. It must be one of Caspar's daughters. I'm really glad he did not come to question your father, Regina. I don't want my good neighbors to become heretics. I could hardly wait to find out."

Regina quickened her steps as she hurried homeward. It was difficult for her to understand how the strong ties of friendliness and neighborliness between the people of her own country of Switzerland could become so strained. Their closeness to the mountains, their dependence on nature, their love for beauty, and their appreciation for each other had made the people deeply religious and earnest.

But this evening Regina thought little of her homeland—the fir-clad slopes that hemmed in lush valley pasture lands, and blue mirrors of Alpine lakes that nestled peacefully between glittering snow peaks always pointing sharply heavenward.

3

At the top of the gentle slope which led from the lower edge of the garden to the back door of the Strahm cottage, Regina stopped abruptly. Then she ran quickly up the steps, and setting the milk can on the kitchen table, dashed through the house to the weaving shop adjoining the cottage.

"Father!" she called.

"Yes, Regina?" Friedrich Strahm looked up and smiled and then finished the left run of the shuttle.

"Father, you must stop your work and come outside to see something beautiful. You can see the Jungfrau if you come right now."

Father Strahm got up immediately from his bench and followed Regina to the spot by the back door where, between two clusters of pine trees on a hill in the far distance, the snow-capped Jungfrau glistened pinkish-white in the setting sun.

"Isn't it beautiful, Father?" she exclaimed, clasping her father's arm.

"I have seldom seen the Jungfrau as clear from here."

"It's fifty miles, isn't it?"

"All of sixty. Call Mother. She must see this, too."

"She's not here, Father."

"Not here?"

"Didn't she tell you she was going to take a fresh loaf of bread over to Granny Sankhaus this afternoon?" Regina asked.

"She told me, of course. But I thought she'd be back by this time. It won't last long. She should be coming."

Friedrich Strahm and Regina stood quietly admiring the beauty of God's handiwork. Suddenly he trust his hands deep into his trouser pockets and said solemnly, "I only hope—" The sentence was not finished.

"Hope what, Father?" asked Regina, her large blue eyes looking into her father's.

"I hope our future will be as bright as that," he said.

"Our future? Father, why do you say that? You mean your future and my future? Do you really think it might not be?"

4

"Of course it will be," he answered quickly. "We won't allow ourselves to become confused about the heretics and what they believe. We must be more careful what we say to others—even our friends. I do hope Mother is careful about what she tells Granny Sankhaus. I hope they didn't talk about the Anabaptists."

Regina glanced toward the distant Jungfrau only to see it almost hidden in the magic colors of the evening sunset.

"I must go back and work a while before it gets dark, but I'm glad you called me. It may be a long, long time until we see the Jungfrau again."

Regina followed her father into the shop. For several minutes she stood beside the loom watching his face and the shuttle passing swiftly between his hands.

"I know I shouldn't bother you when you're so busy, Father," she said hesitatingly, "but why have you been so quiet and serious since the pastor from Kyburg was here to see you?"

"Since Heinrich Hofmeier was here?" Her father's voice betrayed a note of concern. Every day Regina surprised him with new questions. As he rested his hands on the loom, he looked at his daughter.

"Yes. Mother noticed it, too," she said.

"That I looked serious?"

"Yes. Did he question you, Father?"

"Question me?" His forehead wrinkled.

"Yes."

"What makes you ask?"

"Rheinhardt asked me when I went for the milk this evening."

"Rheinhardt? Rheinhardt asked you if Hofmeier questioned me!"

Friedrich Strahm clutched both sides of the loom and rose halfway to his feet.

"Listen, Regina." He looked grave but his words were strangely tender. "Everything will soon be all right. I've told

5

you and Mother many times this heretical teaching won't last long. It can't. The pastor and I discussed some things, but I told him firmly where our family stands. Don't worry, Regina. Rheinhardt should not be asking you such questions. He should come to me if he wants to know. What did you tell him?"

"I told him the pastor came to order material for a new suit."

"Of course, that's what he came for," said her father. "And he did not come to question me. I've told you and Mother over and over, Regina, we'll not allow ourselves to be deceived. Rheinhardt is too inquisitive. Don't let him disturb you."

"It always makes me feel better to talk with you. There are many things I just can't understand. It doesn't seem right that the Wittmers had to leave. I lay awake every night thinking about them. I loved Ann, Father. I loved Ann with all my heart."

Friedrich Strahm saw her lip tremble.

"After supper we'll talk. You should go now and cut the bread and cheese, and make the tea so that when Mother comes we can eat."

Friedrich Strahm turned toward his loom, and Regina walked to the house to prepare supper. It was times like these she missed her brother Hans. She looked down the road he had taken seven months before when he left to begin work in his uncle's cheese factory at Langnau in the Emmental. She wished she could talk to him now. They always seemed to understand each other.

He had understood why she had tried not to cry when they said good-by. She had walked beside him with his horse to the edge of the town.

"Sixty-five miles is too far to be away from home," Regina had said sadly, holding out her hand.

Hans held it as he planted a kiss on each cheek.

"I'm really proud of you, though," she added quickly, smiling through a few tears. "It will be wonderful when someday

6

you can make a cheese yourself and own a factory. Think of it, Hans!"

"Yes. Good-by now. Don't be sad."

"You'll try to come home at least once a year, won't you, Hans?"

"I'll try. I'll miss you more than you will me, Regina."

"Hans, that could never be. I'll miss you terribly. I hardly know what I'll do with you and Michel both gone."

Now Regina still remembered the parting words of Hans. She was now alone at home and she could no longer depend on Hans to answer her questions, especially about the Anabaptists and their teachings.

II

Regina was cutting the cheese when her mother came in.

"Did you think I was never coming, Regina?"

"Father has been anxious."

"Anxious? About me?"

"Yes. And you missed seeing the Alps! They were never more beautiful, Mother. We saw them only a short time."

"Is that why Father was anxious?"

"Well, yes; but he was also hoping you weren't discussing the Anabaptists with Granny."

"Oh, she did most of the talking, as usual. Father is so afraid someone will draw me out and I'll say too much. I was very careful."

"Did she tell you anything new? I hope if she did it's good news."

"I'm sorry, Regina," she said sadly. "It's the opposite."

"What now?" Regina dropped the knife.

"Another family has turned Anabaptist."

"Who?" Regina asked cautiously.

"The Brohens over the hill." Mother took off her head scarf and woolen shawl and hung them on the hook behind the door.

"Oh, no! Mother! And does that mean they too will leave?"

"Yes, Dear, it means they had to leave the canton. Granny's son saw them leaving yesterday."

"No! Mother, they were some of the nicest people we knew."

"Yes, Dear, I know—but you see," she spoke sadly, "it's like Father said. When people you know deliberately disobey the government—oh, I know it's unbelievable; but they're gone."

"But, Mother!" Regina lifted her apron and covered her face.

"If it makes you feel like that, Regina," her mother said, "I—I can't tell you any more. Don't cry. Please." Mother wiped her eyes quickly. "Sh-h, I hear someone coming."

Regina darted into her room and closed the door.

* * *

"You stayed quite a while, Mother."

Melka looked up. "Yes, yes, Friedrich, I know—but it was hard to leave. Granny wanted to talk. She's there alone so much during the day and never gets out. Just listens to Jacob bring home things that upset her."

"What's the matter? Did you get into any dangerous discussions about the heretics?" he asked quickly.

"No, Friedrich, not dangerous. But she told me that Brohens have become victims and—" Melka's voice broke.

"What? Not Heini Brohens?" Friedrich Strahm stepped back.

"Yes. Yes. They're gone now—too."

"Gone?" Friedrich reached for the back of the chair.

"I guess I shouldn't have told Regina. It hurts her worse each time."

Friedrich shook his head. "She'd find it out sooner or later anyway. We can't keep these things from her; I've decided that today. She's no child any more. Regina will soon be eighteen. Where is she? I told her to have supper ready."

"She's in the bedroom, Friedrich, and I am afraid she's badly upset about this. She might even be crying."

"After supper I'm going to talk to her."

"Come, Regina, let's eat." Gently Father rapped on her bedroom door.

"Did someone come, Father?"

"No, Regina. There's no one here but us three. Come."

"Then I'll be out in a minute."

After supper Regina washed the few dishes while her mother

sat by the candlelight with her knitting. Her fingers which usually worked with magic swiftness seemed tired or clumsy. Every now and then her hands dropped to her lap and she looked long at Regina and Friedrich.

Father brought in an armful of wood and built a fire in the fireplace of the living room. The three sat close by the fire—Regina on a low wooden stool beside her father. Every now and then the wind blew a branch of the apple tree against the window, making an unpleasant, scraping sound. Father arose and closed the shutter. Then, returning to his chair, he said,

"Now, Regina, it is my duty as your father to tell you as best I can about the heretics so that you will not be so disturbed, and so that you will be true to the holy Christian church you were baptized into as an infant. I hope you will never listen to the teaching of a stranger or a heretic. We must all put our whole faith in the laws of the church and not become troubled over what's happening to the people who refuse to listen to advice." Father cleared his throat. He seemed out of breath. He crossed his legs and rubbed his knee.

Regina sat in deep thought, her chin resting on one hand.

"These are foolish decisions the Anabaptists are making," Father continued. "Someday they will see the terrible mistake they have made. I'm sure the Wittmers wish they were back."

"But, Father," asked Regina, "why are more and more people believing the Anabaptist way? Some are the best people we ever knew, like the Wittmers. And now the Brohens."

"It's just like Granny said today." Mother tried to help Father by adding to the discussion. "This doctrine is like a dreaded disease or plague. It overcomes people we would least expect it to. It makes me shudder even to think of it. Who will be next?"

Father continued, "We must band ourselves together as a family, Regina, and condemn this strange doctrine and not allow anyone to talk to us about it. We've got to take every precaution."

10

"I hope you don't think I would even think of being disobedient, Father," said Regina, looking at the flames rising in the fireplace. "But I can't keep from wondering about things when people like the Wittmers and now the Brohens accept this teaching. We've been such good friends all these years. I just don't know what to think."

"But, Regina, aren't you satisfied that we have brought you up right and have taken care of your spiritual welfare by having you baptized as an infant?" Father cleared his throat again. "You are safe, Regina. Be satisfied with what we did for you."

"Yes, Father," said Regina, "I thank you for everything you've done for me. I couldn't ask for better parents or a better home. It's not that, Father. I just can't understand; I mean, why all this trouble ever had to start. Why can't people live in peace and love each other? It's so beautiful here. I love it. The trees, the sky, the mountains, everything. We've always been so happy here. I'd never want to leave. The Wittmers and Brohens were happy here, too, I thought. Then why did they have to leave? Something must have made them feel as if it was worth leaving. This new faith—maybe I can't make you understand what I'm trying to say, Father. Haven't you ever wondered?"

"Yes, Regina, I've wondered about all that—but—but I know this: If I would go to an Anabaptist meeting now when we've been warned not to, and allow myself to be baptized again, I would only be inviting trouble, punishment, or persecution. Heinrich Hofmeier gave me some things to think about. He is smart, too. If I'd deliberately, knowingly disobey the government, I wouldn't expect anyone to pity me if I'd have to leave. I would expect to go and I'd take what I deserved."

"Maybe that's what they did, Father. Surely they were not compelled into being rebaptized. Of course," she added, "I know there are a lot of things about all this I may never understand. But I can't help wondering what they thought about

11

before they made their final decision. Wittmers chose not to have their baby baptized, didn't they? Don't you think they did a lot of serious thinking about it first, Father?"

After a long silence, Father spoke as though he had discovered a good idea. "I know, Regina, what we'll do. When Pastor Hofmeier comes for his material next week, I'll have you ask him a few questions for yourself. He will know what to tell you to set you straight on this whole matter. He is well educated and knows the situation from beginning to end."

"But would he want to take time to bother with me? I doubt it."

Friedrich Strahm sat thinking.

"That isn't what I'm wondering about," he answered. "Maybe after all that would not be the thing to do. He might wonder why you even consider spending so much thought—wait, let me think this through first. We've all got to be more careful what we ask or say to anyone or we will be suspected. Right now the best fatherly advice I can give you, Regina, is this: Stay by the decisions and rules of the church, our church, the state church, and remember, a man as sincere and as educated as Ulrich Zwingli and as learned in the Scripture as he, wouldn't lead anyone astray."

"Father," she said softly, "wouldn't it be wonderful if we had a Bible all our own and could read it for ourselves?"

"I intend to get one sometime," answered Father, "but that may not be very soon. And if I ever can afford to get one, I wonder how much of it we will be able to understand."

III

The controversy between the Swiss Brethren or Anabaptists and the Zwinglian Reformers became more serious each week. The three principal leaders of the Anabaptists, in the face of prosecution by the civil authorities, had held a public meeting in an open field near Hinwil. The story of the arrest and imprisonment of these three leaders, Conrad Grebel, Felix Manz, and George Blaurock, had spread far and wide. Everyone in the canton was listening, watching, wondering what would happen next.

Many people became afraid even to discuss their opinions with their neighbors, their friends, or even their closest relatives. Threatenings, mandates, punishments authorized by the lords, the council of Zurich, were terrorizing hundreds over a large part of northern Switzerland. Every day someone stopped at the shop with more startling news about what was happening.

Why were there such great differences in Biblical interpretations among distinguished scholars of the best theological schools? Is it possible to obey the teachings of the Bible and discard what cannot be established by the Scriptures? Are there not some things the Scriptures teach that are impracticable?

These questions perplexed not only the commoners but also the doctors, scholars, businessmen, and even some of the council men themselves.

Michel, Regina's oldest brother, was twenty-two, and an apprentice in Mathis Bartsche's print shop in Zurich. One Sunday when he came home on horseback to visit with Regina and his parents, he brought news about his work in the shop and about the alarming happenings at Zurich.

Regina listened eagerly to the report Michel gave.

"The situation in Zurich is worse than ever," he began. The four, Michel, Regina, and their parents, were seated around the kitchen table. "Zwingli has just brought us his fourth book against the Anabaptists. We are working on it now, but truthfully I can't see that it will accomplish more than his others. The Anabaptists claim their doctrines are based on Scripture."

Father stared in astonishment. "Michel, why do you say that?"

"Because, in spite of all Zwingli has said, done, and written, more and more people are turning Anabaptist. Great crowds have been listening to the Anabaptist leaders speak at many places. Hundreds have already been baptized again."

"But, Michel," asked Regina, "why would anyone even want to listen to those men when they know Zwingli is working so hard for our good? Father says he is the most powerful teacher and the greatest Bible master living. The pastor from Kyburg was here just recently and said it is marvelous how he can quote Scriptures from memory. He says he is actually an orator as great as Cicero. That's saying a great deal, isn't it?"

"He is a very learned man, Regina, but his opponents are learned, too. Conrad Grebel and Felix Manz are both well educated. So is George Blaurock and some of the other Swiss Brethren. They are as able speakers as Zwingli. Their arguments against infant baptism and in favor of baptism upon confession sound as reasonable as Zwingli's for infant baptism. At least, I mean to say many must think so," he added. "They quote Scripture to support their arguments. That's what makes the situation so confusing. They say they are willing to change their position if they can be convinced from the Bible that it is wrong."

"Michel," whispered his mother. "You shock me. Why, Michel!"

14

"And you shock me," added Father. "You argue for the Anabaptists."

Regina caught Michel by the coat sleeve. "You surely don't mean the Anabaptists are beginning to convince you with their doctrine! Michel!"

Michel laughed dryly, as he leaned back in his chair. "Of course I'm not being convinced," he said. Don't get excited about me. It's such a relief to come home where I can express myself without being afraid I'll be suspected or lose my job. I'm only talking. Just talking to show you what's going on. There are two sides to this controversy. In the shop I've got to be tight-mouthed all the time. Of course, I read everything I can that we print. What I don't get to read for myself I hear Bartsche discussing with someone; so you see, I hear quite a bit. I know pretty well all of Zwingli's arguments in favor of infant baptism and maintaining the state church and all that he teaches against the mass, images, fasts, pilgrimages, indulgences, purgatory, and saint worship. But I know pretty well, too, what the Anabaptists have to say. I'm only trying to give you an honest picture of what this is about. That's all."

"How do you know so much, Michel?" asked Regina, bending forward.

"Because I've heard for myself. That's how. There are some smart Anabaptists, I tell you. They know the Scriptures. They say if we teach that the mass is wrong, then why not stop having it? The Bible is authority on spiritual matters, not the city council."

Regina, and her mother and father were very quiet. She could feel the situation being very tense. But Michel went on. "Yes, I heard them twice, once in the town hall in a public debate, and once in a home."

Friedrich Strahm stood up suddenly and put his face close to Michel's. "Michel, you frighten me. You stun me," he moaned. He grabbed Michel on the shoulder. "You—went to a home to hear—Conrad Grebel speak!"

"Come, Father," Michel pulled on his father's coat. "Don't be frightened. Please sit down, Father. I simply went out of curiosity. They can't both be right; we all know that. And—well, we know Zwingli is. Do sit down, Father. Grebel is smart—but Zwingli is right and smart both. Yes, indeed! Zwingli is a great reformer. He is nothing less than a Swiss Luther, and he even goes beyond Luther in his reform movement; for he wants to follow only the New Testament, not church tradition. Grebel and Zwingli are both brilliant men, but what astonished me is the way that young Blaurock can speak. He doesn't have the education Grebel has, but he is positively eloquent and has great power to sway the people. I could feel that. But," Michel added, stepping closer to his father, "Zwingli has experience politically. He can and will outdo any Anabaptist any day. Zwingli is right and we all know it. Sit down, Father."

"Yes," Father said emphatically, "we all know Zwingli is right. Stay by that." But Father did not sit down. He ran both hands into his pockets. His one foot tapped the floor.

"Of course," continued Michel, thoughtfully, "Zwingli has to be right—he is a scholar and pastor of the Great Münster. All should respect his teachings. The Anabaptists surely will finally give up. We are already convinced of that."

"Well, Son, I'm glad to hear you say so," said Father sitting down with a sigh of relief. "Maybe you'd better quit your job in the print shop, Michel, and come home and help me." Father looked up at Michel with consequential seriousness on his face.

Michel sat thinking. "But I love my job," he said presently. "I meet a good many prominent men who come in the shop. It's all very interesting. I'm learning new things every week. I hear lots of talk."

Father Strahm looked out the window a moment, then back at Michel. He reached over and put a hand on his shoulder. "Maybe too much, Michel."

"But, Father," exclaimed Michel, "there is something in me that wants to know everything there is to know. I don't want to quit now. I want to know how this is going to turn out. I—well, I can't quit now."

"You're just like I am," added Regina. "I wonder and wonder about things, too. And I want to know why about everything. For instance, why Wittmers were driven away from their home. I loved Ann, and I can't think that she or her parents were so wicked."

"Come, come, don't let that trouble you so," Father's voice was kind and very gentle. "I've tried to tell you before, Regina, that such things only happen to those who disobey the government. Can't you see that?"

"But did they really disobey government, Father?"

"Regina, I wasn't going to tell you all this, but I happen to know that that crippled bookseller, Castelburger, who is reported to be a rank Anabaptist, held a service in their home one night and by their invitation. This was an act of disobedience. They knew better. Besides, after that they refused to have their new baby baptized. That was another deliberate act of disobedience."

"How did you find out all that, Father? You never told me before about the meeting in their home."

"What you don't know you can't tell; so please don't ask, Regina. Please don't tell anyone either. This is in strict confidence. You are not to tell a soul that I know this. Never, never tell Rheinhardt."

"You told me about the baby's not being baptized, but not about the meeting. But is there no other way to get people to obey the government besides driving them out of their homes and putting them in prison?"

"If there was, you may be sure Zwingli or the lords would have thought of it before now."

"Well, I loved Ann." Regina turned her face and bit her lip. "I can hardly believe she or her parents deliberately did

17

anything so dreadfully wrong. They wanted to obey God and the Bible."

"But they knew when they were rebaptized that they were violating the law," Father said.

"And they really did that, too?" asked Regina. "But, Father, you hadn't told me that either."

Michel put one hand on his father's arm. "Listen, Father, the Anabaptists contend they do not satisfy the laws of God unless they are rebaptized upon their own confession. They say no baby can confess his own sins or have faith in God; so that's why—I'm just telling you their belief, Father."

Friedrich Strahm got up and walked back and forth in front of the kitchen stove.

"Listen to me," he began stopping abruptly. "The pastor from Kyburg told me when he was here how dangerous this whole Anabaptist teaching is. We see examples every week of how our neighbors are being deceived and blinded. Three years ago when Conrad Grebel, the nobleman's son, came back from school abroad, Zwingli fully expected him to work with him in this reformation. And Grebel almost worshiped Zwingli. Yes, and he admits that it was Zwingli who led him to evangelical faith in Christ. And Zwingli even used Grebel for a while as his principal reader. Now the whole thing is terribly confused. As soon as Zwingli saw it was best to keep the church and state united young Grebel started opposing him. He claimed to have new light on the interpretation of the Scriptures. He said he had a religious awakening." Father paused to take a breath. He walked over to the window and back again.

"Well, Zwingli had an awakening first," he continued. "He's been working hard to reform the church against enough opposition. Young Grebel might not have got very far, but then Felix Manz started helping him oppose Zwingli. I feel sorry for Zwingli. Now these Aanabaptists want to establish what they call an evangelical church. That's what Heinrich Hofmeier told me. Yes, we talked about it, and he knows both sides, too. But look at all the trouble they are making. I mean the Anabaptists. They can't be right. It's a dangerous and deceptive doctrine in many ways. Good people like the Wittmers were simply misguided."

"And listen to this," Michel stood up tall and strikingly handsome beside his father. "Next week there's going to be another debate in Zurich about baptism, and Grebel, Manz, and Blaurock will speak again. It's not settled. It looks as if each side is becoming more dogmatic."

"Oh, I wish—" whispered Regina. Then she pinched her lip.

"Listen, one hundred Anabaptists were given a hearing before the court in Zurich this past week," continued Michel.

"One hundred!" cried Regina. "Michel, that's a lot of people, isn't it?"

"That's why I say the situation is getting worse. Hundreds in different cities and towns west of here have already been baptized. It's not just hearsay. The magistrates, particularly in the Gruningen area, are greatly disturbed and I heard yesterday that the Anabaptists are gaining their sympathies."

"No! Not the sympathies of the magistrates!" exclaimed Father. "Then the situation is really serious."

"Are you going to the debate?" asked Regina, catching Michel by the coat sleeve again.

"I would like to well enough," he said softly after a brief pause.

"You'd better not," suggested Father. "Michel, you'd better not."

"Why not?"

"It might be risky."

"Risky? It's going to be a public debate. Anyone may go."

"Are you positive you know where you stand and what and who you believe?" Father asked.

"I think I stand exactly where you do Father," answered

19

Michel calmly. "You and Mother," he pointed to each in turn, "and you, Regina. We all stand together, don't we?"

"Michel," suggested Regina, looking at the clock, "it's time for me to go for the milk. Why don't you walk along with me?"

IV

The gray stone church with stained-glass windows and tall spire stood in the center of Weisslingen. Those who faithfully attended the Sunday morning services were accepted and acknowledged by civil authority as good people, loyally abiding by the religious laws of the country and supporting the evangelical reformation introduced by Ulrich Zwingli. Those who absented themselves were first missed, then spotted, and finally branded as Anabaptists or Anabaptist sympathizers.

Ulrich Zwingli, former parish priest and student of the New Testament, now pastor of the Great Münster Church in Zurich, had six years previously separated independently from Martin Luther, the noted scholar and reformer who created an uproar throughout Germany. Zwingli was now advocating other reforms such as the right of priests to marry and the reduction of tithes. He also preached against traditional forms, ceremonies, and the highly organized church. He vehemently pleaded for a church that would uphold only the doctrines and practices of the New Testament.

This sixteenth-century movement touched the lives of everyone, from lords to peasants. It plunged men and women, and parents and families into a conflict between the spirit of the individual and the spirit of unity. Those living in the Zurich Canton could not escape the controversy.

Then, too, the translation of the Bible for the first time into the language of the common people and the newly invented art of printing small portions of the Bible for distribution paved the way for the spread of any kind of Reformation doctrine. Zurich, the New York of Switzerland, was not only the

21

financial and commercial center of Europe, but the very seat of religious and historic beginnings. To complicate matters further, the young religious scholar, Conrad Grebel, disagreed with Ulrich Zwingli on certain points of the Scripture. Grebel preached against the baptism of infants and advocated baptism on confession of faith. Grebel's doctrine was enjoying good acceptance and gaining converts, causing such confusion and divisions that throughout northern Switzerland the graveness of the situation was alarming.

The Strahm family regularly worshiped at the Weisslingen Church. The elderly pastor, Reuben Ziegler, had appointed a petty government man to record carefully the names of those who entered his church, and then the pastor carefully checked the records. His sermons, which he usually read, were dull and meaningless. Sunday after Sunday Regina listened for something satisfying, enlightening, or convincing. She wanted to pledge her allegiance to something she could understand. Each Sunday she went home more confused than the Sunday before. She found herself wondering more and more about Ann and her family, and the other families who gradually, one by one, failed to appear at the services.

Comments about the contention between the reformers and the Anabaptists, which Regina overheard from men who stopped in the shop, only added to her confused thinking. Then, too, each time her father came home from one of the weavers' guild meetings in Zurich, she knew without asking that he had heard something that deeply disturbed him. Unmistakably the situation grew more apprehensive.

Secretly Friedrich Strahm hoped the young pastor from Kyburg would call for the material for his suit when Regina had gone for the milk. Long before the week had passed, Regina and her parents agreed that it would be unwise to ask Heinrich Hofmeier any questions about the problem. If any one of the family discussed anything with the pastor, it should be Father Strahm himself.

One evening Regina met Pastor Hofmeier on the road as she was going for the milk. He drew his slick black horse to one side and spoke in a low, pleasing voice. "Good evening."

"Good evening," she answered timidly.

"You needn't be frightened," the pastor said kindly. "I'm not an Anabaptist; you don't need to be afraid to speak to me." He chuckled.

"Oh!" Regina smiled faintly and fastened her coat collar.

"You're Friedrich Strahm's daughter, aren't you?"

"Yes, sir."

"I thought so. Do you know whether or not your father has my material ready?"

"Father has had it measured and cut for several days."

"Thank you. Then I'll be going on. Good-by."

"Good-by," answered Regina politely.

Although the late afternoon sun shone red on the distant hills, the strong November wind was chilly. It set the naked tree branches waving back and forth. Regina stepped briskly to keep warm.

"I guess I really have no reason to fear the pastor," she said to herself, and before she realized it, she was humming softly.

* * *

Heinrich Hofmeier examined the material, smiled, then opened his money bag.

"I met your daughter down the road," he said.

"Regina?" Friedrich Strahm asked.

"So her name is Regina? She's a lovely girl."

The pastor took out his money.

"You look surprised." The pastor smiled. "Has no one ever told you that you have a beautiful daughter?"

"Well. no one needed to tell me that," Friedrich replied. "I—well, I just wasn't expecting such a frank remark from you. She's not only beautiful, Pastor, but she is a good girl."

"I believe that. And she is the loveliest girl I have seen in Weisslingen. And I suppose the young men know it too."

"She has not yet met many young men. Regina seems to have ideals of her own, and does not seem interested in young men right now."

"How old is she?"

"She'll be eighteen on her next birthday."

"Take my advice, Strahm," the pastor said, stepping closer, "and keep her close home, if you can, until every Anabaptist is dead or recants."

Friedrich Strahm's face twitched. Had Regina talked to the pastor in spite of the warnings given her? "How are things—I mean over at Kyburg, by this time? Any better?"

"I can't honestly say," answered the pastor. "I never heard of anything so baffling. One day we think we've got those Anabaptists conquered and the next something new crops up. It's like trying to get rid of a poisonous weed. You think you've got it killed, roots and all, and before you know it, it's coming up some other place. I've had to report several of the best farmers near our village. They were sent up to Kyburg Castle for questioning. One was released, but two men are in prison yet. I don't know what the council will decide to do with them!"

Friedrich Strahm stood rigid a moment, then asked a second question. "Do you know how the debate turned out? My son Michel works at Bartsche's print shop and usually comes home on Sundays and tells me the news."

The pastor laughed. "The three young heretics got what they deserved. Felix Manz, George Blaurock, and Conrad Grebel are in the witch tower again, on bread and water. No one is allowed to speak to them except the guards! This time they may be in there for months or years or for life. Three other young men who have been doing as much damage, or maybe even more, were banished from the canton."

"How do you decide who should be reported for questioning?" Friedrich asked carefully.

"That's not difficult," answered the pastor. "In the first place, if persons in my territory miss church, I go and find out

24

why. If they can't prove to me they were sick, I ask what they believe. Then I watch them.

"If I know of parents who have a new baby and fail to bring it to church to be baptized before or on the eighth day, I report them to the court. If I see two or more men talking with each other on the road or in the field, and I think one of them might be an Anabaptist, I make it my business to find out.

"I'm watching continually for suspicious-looking gatherings or groups. It's not a pleasant job. It's not an easy job, either, but if we all work together, Strahm, we'll get them conquered in due time. But," and this the pastor added as he walked to the door, "the worst thing about this Anabaptist doctrine is—" he stood with his hand on the door latch—"it is saturated through and through with what they call Christian love. An Anabaptist won't fight. I have not met one yet who resisted me or even argued with me when I told him he might have to go up for questioning. Those who use daggers or swords or curse or talk back I always know are not Anabaptists. I can tell them almost without fail. Oh, here, I almost forgot to pay you."

* * *

Regina and the pastor met the second time that evening.

"Your father did a nice piece of work, Regina." He smiled and nodded as before.

"He always tries to please his customers," she answered. "I hope the tailor does a good job for you, too."

"Thank you." The pastor smiled and tipped his hat as the horse pranced to go. "Now take care of yourself, Regina," he called to her over his shoulder.

* * *

As Regina came closer to her home from getting the milk, she saw her father watching for her through the shop window. He opened the door and called before she reached the gate.

"Come in this way, Regina."

"What is it, Father?" she asked. "You look worried again."

"Did he talk much to you?"

"You mean the pastor?"

"Yes."

"No, only a few words."

"Then—you didn't get into any discussion about the heretics or ask him any questions?"

"No. You told me not to, Father, and I've tried to be very careful, especially when I go for the milk. Are things no better? Or didn't you discuss that with him either? You look troubled, Father."

"I really did not intend to. I—I was not going to, but he brought up the subject first."

"You mean to question you?"

"No, no. He just told me to keep you close home until this trouble with the Anabaptists dies down."

"Me? Does he think I go away a great deal? Why did he say that?"

"I don't know exactly. It may be he had a double warning in those words, inferring that I should stay close home myself. You just never can tell—you never can tell what people might mean these days."

Slowly Friedrich Strahm returned to his work at the loom. "I was not going to ask him any questions, Regina, but I couldn't help it."

"And you are sure he knows where you stand?"

"I think so. Yes, I'm sure he does. And we all stand together."

During the four long months of winter, Friedrich Strahm's sales of woolen materials dropped considerably. A number of his best customers had been exiled. Some of them had large families. The peasant's revolt of the previous summer had failed to obtain a tax reduction. Many of the well-to-do farmers around Weisslingen had no money to buy woolens. Friedrich was distressed.

Regina offered to work somewhere for her board and room,

but the very thought of this was out of the question now. Where could she find work if her parents would consent? Where would it be safe for her to go? Friedrich looked troubled and serious.

"We'll skimp and stick together," he said one evening after taking another inventory. "I will sell my own shoes, Regina, to buy food before I'll let you work out. And I'll hardly have money to buy a Bible very soon if this keeps up."

One forenoon in March, while Regina was sweeping in the shop, a stranger knocked. A young man greeted her father with a friendly voice.

"I'm a linen weaver from Baretswill," he announced. "My name is Johann Ferlinden."

"Johann Ferlinden?" asked Friedrich.

"Yes. I heard about you and I came over to ask if you'd be interested in exchanging some thread. I would like to weave some woolens and I thought perhaps you would be interested in some of my linen thread. I brought some along to show you what I have. If you don't mind, I'd like to look at some of your patterns, too."

Friedrich Strahm pondered. He had never made a trade like this before.

"You say you're from Baretswill? I thought I knew all the weavers in our canton. I don't recall seeing you at the weavers' guild."

"I was at a meeting in December."

"That's the meeting I missed. I wasn't feeling well that day."

"I visited the guild because I thought it would be a valuable business association. But I do not intend to go to more guild meetings," the stranger said. "I learned that night that I could never conscientiously participate fully in what goes on there. I have decided not to attend any future meetings. I have been in Baretswill only about seven months and I haven't much business yet. I used to be a monk in St. Francis Monastery."

27

Friedrich stared. "You mean—you left the monastery? And now you're a weaver?"

Regina stopped sweeping.

"Yes, I was not happy in the monastery. For months I tried to make myself believe I was—but I was wretched. I went through soul agonies that words couldn't describe. More than once I was punished because I let my thoughts wander from my books. But I could not help it. I was without a minute's peace of mind or soul. One day I got word my mother was seriously ill and I persuaded the abbot to let me go home to see her before she died. I see now it was God's leading. He knew I was unhappy. I was crying to God for peace of soul as I walked along. In the road I noticed a little pamphlet. I picked it up. It was written by Ulrich Zwingli against the Anabaptists. I wondered what this all meant and I soon found out. That's my story in a few words; but there's more to it than that, a lot more. Yes, I gave up the monastery to preach Christ and the way of true discipleship."

Regina stood motionless. The stranger did not seem to notice her at all. Her father's face looked pale.

"The way of what?" Friedrich Strahm spoke roughly.

The man smiled. "I've been very careful what I say to strangers about what I believe, but somehow," he hesitated, "I feel I can't keep still today. Conrad Grebel, Felix Manz, and George Blaurock are not afraid to speak boldly."

"You mean—," Friedrich Strahm spoke sharply, "you're an Anabaptist! Don't you know you put me and my family in great danger?"

"Don't be afraid, Friend," the man said kindly. "There are things in this world worse than being in bodily danger. I will not hurt you. I have only love in my heart for you."

"But please, sir, there's my daughter, my only daughter standing there." He pointed to Regina, leaning on the broom handle. "I also have a wife to protect. It's not myself I care about—but—must I tell you to leave?"

The young man turned and looked at Regina, and she saw a warmth and kindness in his eyes. He smiled at her, then turning, spoke to her father again.

"I will leave, my friend, very soon, and when I do, I'll pray God's comforting blessing on you and your daughter, and you need not fear. Perfect love casts out fear. The Bible says that, and it's true."

"Perfect love?" asked Friedrich. "Who can have perfect love with all this trouble going on?"

"The three young men who were in prison for life did not fear what men could do to them. They loved God and feared only Him. I feel the same way. I may be picked up and put in prison, too; maybe on my way home, but I am not afraid. I am now a transformed monk. A happy love-disciple of Jesus Christ, and I'm born again, thank God. Thank God forever my blinded eyes were opened and I found peace for my troubled soul before it was too late."

"You mean to tell me—you mean—you speak out boldly like this everywhere? And you—are—not afraid?" Regina wished her father would not ask the stranger any more questions.

"I have not spoken so boldly to a stranger for a long time, but on my way over here I heard the news. Haven't you heard the three young prisoners have escaped? And Grebel, instead of grieving because of his punishment, read the Scriptures to the other prisoners admonishing them to be true to God no matter what comes. It made me feel like giving my testimony, too, no matter what happens to me. The minute I saw your face the Spirit told me to be bold. You look troubled, Friend. I used to look that way, too. Please do not be frightened at me. I will leave presently. Shall we exchange threads?"

"Yes, but quickly, sir," he said. "And, if you please, don't ever call again. I'm sorry, but please leave at once!"

Regina stood fixed until the visitor had gone outside the gate. "Father," she whispered. "What did he mean and what will we do now?"

V

The strange visit of the converted monk from Baretswill added more anxiety to Regina's troubled mind. Her father seldom mentioned the incident even when the three were alone in the house.

"You heard what the monk from Baretswill said, Regina," he finally managed to say the morning after the man had gone, "but you must never, never tell a single soul. If Rheinhardt saw him go by and asks you any questions, tell him he came to exchange thread; nothing more. Understand?"

"Yes, Father."

Regina noticed from that day on that her father sat by the fire longer after supper in deep meditation and with troubled countenance. Mother, too, was unusually quiet. Regina wondered what they were thinking. Whenever customers or neighbors came into the shop, her father tried to act undisturbed.

Almost every day Melka lay down her knitting, looked across the snow-covered valley, and with wistfulness said, "I wonder how Hans is. I wonder what Michel is doing. I wish both boys could be with us today."

When Michel came again the last Sunday in March, he brought news more startling than ever.

"A new mandate has been issued which demands that anyone who rebaptizes another must be drowned without mercy," Michel said.

Father leaned hard against the wall and a stifled moan escaped his lips.

"And what do you think of such a mandate, Michel?" Regina asked.

"I don't know what I think," answered Michel. "At least I won't attempt to say what I think. In the shop, opinion has to be in favor of it, but even so one of Bartsche's leading printers left us Thursday."

"Left?" asked Father. "What do you mean?"

"He disguised himself to attend an Anabaptist meeting over at Zollikon. He thought no one would ever find it out, but he was caught."

"And then what?" asked Regina.

"He's being held in prison, to be sure. Bartsche warned all of us more than once not to attend these meetings. If he gets out of prison, I doubt if Bartsche will take him back. He's strong for Zwingli and his movement."

"It's another example of deliberately disobeying the law," exclaimed Father, shaking his head. "The man went against better knowledge and defied authority. If things get much worse," he added, "and very many more families have to leave the canton, my business will be less than ever."

The four sat in silence. Cold rain beat against the wooden shutters. Father stirred the fire.

"Michel, did you go to that debate?" asked Regina at length.

"Yes, and Bartsche went, too. But that was open to the public."

"And the three Anabaptist debaters? They lost, didn't they? What was it like, Michel?"

"It was very dramatic, I'll say that."

"And what did Bartsche say about it?"

"He said he wasn't—" Michel stopped short at the sound of horses' hoofs on the frozen ground. The gate was opened and closed—there were steps up to the door—then a knock. Before Michel was halfway across the room the latch was lifted, and there in the doorway, dirty-faced, cold, wet, dagger in one hand, stood Hans. His eyes were bloodshot.

"Hans!" cried Regina, running to him. "Why—Hans!"

The other three stood wide-eyed with surprise.

Hans's voice was husky. "Is there anyone here?" he asked.

"No one but us," said Father, stepping to the door. He put one arm around his son and drew him into the room. "Come," he said; "come in where it's warm. You look cold, Hans."

"I am. It's raining hard—a freezing rain, too."

"Then come close to the fire," said Regina. "Take off your wet coat."

Hans dropped to the floor beside the fire and sat leaning against the wall. Regina sat close beside him. She took the dagger out of his hand and handed it to Michel.

"Hurry, Hans," she said; "tell us why you came like this." She helped him remove his coat.

"I came to see if you were all right yet," he panted.

"Yet? What do you mean?" asked Father.

"And why are you here, Michel?" Hans looked at his brother with genuine fright in his eyes. "Were you sent home, too?"

"This is nothing unusual. I often come home on Sunday. Did you come from the Emmental today?"

"No. We came yesterday."

"Who did?" asked Michel. "Who is *we*?"

"Uncle Rudolf and I. We came to Zurich together. Uncle Rudolf had some business to look after and he told me since I hadn't been home for five months, I should come along and come on out here to see you while he looked after his business. But then near Ruschlikon yesterday afternoon we met a man on the road that Uncle Rudolf recognized. He had heard him preach once in a neighbor's barn."

"Where?" asked Father, pulling a stool close to Hans.

"Over in the Emmental a few miles from his home."

"Go on," said Regina; "talk faster."

Hans rubbed his hands over his dirty face. "I'll talk as fast as I can. One time last year in November when Uncle Rudolf came to Zurich, he said he listened to a debate in the Great Munster Church where three Anabaptists debated against Zwingli and his associates."

"But how did it happen he went there?" demanded Father huskily.

"He went to Zurich on business, and while in the city he said he heard there was to be a debate in the city hall. He was just inquisitive and went. But the crowd was so large they had to go over to the Great Münster."

"Say, were those three young men Conrad Grebel, Felix Manz, and George Blaurock?" asked Michel.

"Those are the names, I'm sure. Uncle Rudolf came home all excited and talked to us until morning."

"Who do you mean by *us*?" asked Regina.

"Aunt Margrit, Mary, and I. Elizabeth went to bed. But Uncle Rudolf was really full that night. He couldn't get done talking about that debate."

"But what about this man on the road whom you met yesterday?" Father asked.

Hans took a long, deep breath.

"I'm just trying to tell you that ever since Uncle Rudolf heard that debate, he's been wanting to go to more Anabaptist meetings. This man we met yesterday was Johann Ferlinden, an Anabaptist preacher who used to be a monk."

Regina looked at Father. Father looked at Regina. Neither said a word.

"He's the same preacher Uncle Rudolf heard speak in that secret meeting in the barn," continued Hans.

"Hans! You mean Uncle Rudolf talked to that man, that Anabaptist, right out on the open road, Hans!" asked Friedrich Strahm.

"Why, Father, yes. I'm telling you the truth. We were both on our horses, but the preacher was walking. Uncle Rudolf acted very glad to see him. He told him he had even been praying that he might meet him or one of those three young debaters on this trip."

"But why?" inquired Father. "I can't understand this. Why would Uncle Rudolf say such a thing?"

"He said he wanted to be baptized."

"Uncle Rudolf said that? Hans!" said Mother, as she covered her face with her handkerchief. "I can't believe it! My own brother, Rudolf! Why he's going against better knowledge! Didn't he know?"

"Go on," whispered Regina. "What next? Hurry, Hans!"

"Well, the preacher told Uncle Rudolf he remembered him and had been praying for his soul ever since he met him in the barn meeting. That night when Uncle Rudolf came home it was nearly morning. He has never been the same since."

"How do you mean?" asked Regina; "never been the same?"

"He's just been different." Hans hesitated. He cleared his throat. "I always did like Uncle Rudolf but after that he was— I don't know how to say it to make you understand, but he was kinder than ever and full of love, some way. One of his very best customers turned Anabaptist, too. Other farmers in the Emmental have turned. Lots of things have happened since I left home. More than I could tell tonight. But last evening that preacher told Uncle Rudolf there was going to be a secret meeting in a certain house near Ruschlikon where he could go and get baptized if he wanted to."

"And you mean," exclaimed Father—"you mean he went there!"

"That's exactly what he did."

"Last night?" whispered Mother.

"Yes."

"And where were you last night?" asked Michel, still holding the dagger in his hand.

"I went along with him."

"You?" chocked Father. "You went to that house! Hans Strahm!"

"He asked me to go along. Uncle Rudolf has been like a second father to me since I went there. I didn't want to go into Zurich alone and leave him. We stopped in Ruschlikon first and got some supper. Then after dark we made our way to that house. No one along the way seemed to pay particular attention to us, but all the while I could see Uncle Rudolf was praying silently. He prays many times. Several other people came to the house to be baptized, too. A man and a woman and one young girl about your age, Regina. Every one of them was happy. I can't explain it. I mean, truly happy. After the meeting, they told Uncle and me to sleep in the barn all night and this morning the woman of the house invited us in for breakfast. She was very kind. Then we started out for Zurich. We hadn't gone a mile until we knew we were being followed."

Regina felt goose pimples cover her arms.

"Two men on horseback came out from behind a hedge and followed us closely until we got to the edge of Zurich. Then they demanded that we stop."

"No!" whispered Regina.

"They asked us where we were from, and where we'd been the night before."

"Oh!" gasped Regina.

"Uncle Rudolf never acted a bit excited. He simply told the truth. They asked him if he had been baptized and he said he had been. His face didn't even get red either. They tied ropes to our horses and led us into the city and notified the council. Uncle Rudolf is in prison."

"No!" sobbed Mother, "not Uncle Rudolf! My brother!"

"Don't cry, Mother," said Hans. "He wasn't scared or mad. They might not keep him there long since he's from Langnau. Don't cry, Mother, please."

"But the man who baptized him and those other people," Regina said. "They'll be drowned without mercy. Uncle Rudolf didn't know that, I am sure."

"Drowned?" asked Hans. "Why drowned?"

"That's the new mandate. Michel just told us today, didn't you, Michel? Anyone who baptized another must be drowned?

"That's true. Yes, But how did you escape- Tell that quickly, Hans," said Michel. "That's what I'm anxious to hear."

"Well, after they took Uncle Rudolf away and locked him up, they asked me more questions. I told them again where I was from and that I had not been baptized since I was an infant. I didn't know for a while what might happen to me. I thought they never would get done questioning me. It was past noon and I was getting worried. But when I thought of Uncle Rudolf and how happy and brave he'd been, I felt better. Then a preacher came in to talk to the council about something, and he noticed me and asked them who I was. They said, 'He's the son of Friedrich Strahm, the woolen weaver from Weisslingen.' He suggested letting me come on home. He told the council he knew you well and you were all right, and I was too young to be punished anyway."

"The preacher said I was all right?" asked Father. "Who was he?"

"I don't know, but he was a little larger than I am and had black hair. He told them you were a noble man and stanch in your faith. He had purchased a suit from you and knew where the family stood. But before I could go they made me swear I'd never go to another Anabaptist meeting as long as I live, or allow an Anabaptist to talk to me any time or anywhere. They gave me this dagger and told me to carry it all the way home to prove I was not an Anabaptist nor an Anabaptist sympathizer." Hans covered his face with his hands. "I feel terrible." he cried brokenly. "I feel wicked."

"Why do you say that?" whispered Regina, "Hans, tell me."

"Because," he cried, "because I know I am. And, well, I'm a liar, too. You can't imagine how awful I feel. I did not mean I'd never talk to another Anabaptist as long as I live. How could I mean that? I want to go back to Aunt Margrit as fast as I can and tell her everything."

"Go back!" exclaimed Mother, her face drawn with fear. "Go back alone? All the way to Langnau? No! No!"

"Hans," whispered Regina, putting her lips close to his ear. Tears blinded her eyes. "Hans, I think I know partly how you must feel. I can't bear to think of you going back alone, but I'm proud of you for wanting to, Hans. You're so brave."

"This is what we can do." Michel said with a mixture of triumph and big-brother love. "Since it's raining, I'll stay here overnight. Real early in the morning we'll start out together. A good many of the council men know Bartsche, and if we meet an officer I will tell them I work for Bartsche. Let me do all the talking. You keep still, Hans. I'll escort you beyond the other side of the city, and return the dagger without saying that you went back. If we all pray," he added softly, "I somehow believe God will help you get back safely. It's not exactly right for you to go back, but what else can you do?"

Regina looked at Michel standing there, handsome, erect, a head taller than Hans. Suddenly she clasped her hands over his. "Michel," she exclaimed, "I think you're just wonderful to help him."

Hans had a difficult time convincing his parents it was his duty to go back to Langnau. After eating a simple supper of bread and tea, the family talked for more than an hour, sitting around the fire.

"Someone has to go back and tell Aunt Margrit. What if Uncle Rudolf has to stay in prison for a long time?" pleaded Hans. "I've got to go back."

"But it's another case of disobeying the law if you go," insisted Father. "You swore you'd never talk to an Anabaptist again. You'll be putting yourself in danger."

"But I'm not afraid of that kind of danger, Father," answered Hans. "And besides, someone has to take care of the cheese. Aunt Margrit can't do it alone. I'm sorry and ashamed I swore to all that. I lied to them but I thought I had to. What will Uncle Rudolf think of me, if I don't go back? He'll think something worse than going to prison has happened to me, and if I stay here I'm not sure but what it might happen."

"Then go." Mother said brokenly. "And God go with you, my boy."

"I'll start out early in the morning," he said.

"And you'll take the dagger with you?" asked Regina.

"I don't know. It's a borrowed one. It's a broken one at that. The worst of it is, I promised to return it sometime."

"I know," suggested Regina. "Let Michel return it for you. He has to go back to Zurich tomorrow."

"But surely you won't start out without it, Hans, not now after what they told you," remonstrated Mother.

Evidently none of the neighbors had seen Hans coming home in the dark, for no one, not even Rheinhardt, asked any questions, and to be sure, none of the Strahms made any comments outside the family circle.

A moment of silent thanks was always observed before the meal in the Strahm home, but Regina had never heard either of her parents offer an audible prayer. She often wondered if they ever actually prayed. It had been only a few years since the pastor of Weisslingen had been given the liberty to teach against the Roman Catholic practice of praying to images; so family prayers were unheard of.

"I'll ask God to protect you both," said Regina. "Tonight when I go to bed. Good night, Hans," Regina eyes filled with tears. "Good night, Michel." She hurried to her own room and dropping on her knees beside the bed buried her face in the pillow.

"Dear Virgin Mary," began Regina. She caught herself, remembering that the pastor had only recently reminded his parishioners that Zwingli had said that prayers to Mary or any of the saints were ineffectual. "Dear God," she began again, "please protect us all, and do please take care of Hans and Uncle Rudolf. Help us to know the right things to believe and to find that perfect love that casts out this terrible, this awful fear."

VI

It was springtime in the year 1526 in the Swiss village of Weisslingen. The last snow, except that on the mountaintops, had disappeared and again the valleys were a bright new green. Regina loved the springtime when she could work in the garden. The tension between the Anabaptists and the followers of Zwingli had not subsided. Fear, dread, and uncertainty hung over northern Switzerland like a heavy cloud. There was also real danger of war between the Catholic and Protestant cantons because of their strong religious differences.

In spite of the Zwinglian movement, there were still those who held tenaciously and resistingly to the old Catholic faith. They would kill before they would compromise. Regina saw the growing concern in both her parents. She never felt like singing. Three months had passed since Hans returned to Langnau, and not a word had been received concerning either him or Uncle Rudolf. Michel did learn, however, that a man from the Emmental had been released after three days of imprisonment in Zurich. He hoped it had been Uncle Rudolf but did not inquire, however, for fear of being questioned about Hans.

In vain the family waited for Michel to bring home the report that the worst was over. But one Sunday in July, Michel came home and was greatly alarmed.

"Another large number of Anabaptists were placed in the witch tower, and the Kyburg castle prison is full," he announced. "The more they are punished, the larger their group becomes. I can't understand it. I am beginning to wonder what is going to come of all this, and so are a lot more folks.

Yesterday a man from Basel stopped in the shop with a pamphlet on baptism written by Conrad Grebel. Grebel had tried to get it printed here more than a year ago, but Zwingli warned Bartsche not to do it. Now if that pamphlet is circulated and read, as I suppose it will be, it won't help matters any. Already too many are convinced Grebel is right."

"Say, Michel, you wouldn't have one, would you?" inquired Father, hesitatingly.

"Why, no, Father, I didn't even read it. I only overheard the man talking to Bartsche and I saw the pamphlet in his hand. Bartsche read it, I think. I do know he's going to tell Zwingli about it, and Zwingli will try to do something to counteract it. He is getting desperate now. We all know that many things have changed here because of Zwingli's teaching, but Grebel wants more changes. He thinks the church today should be just like the church of the New Testament."

"If you ever get hold of one, Michel," Father said, "you bring it home and let me read it, will you?"

Surprise spread over Michel's face. Regina listened, wondering what her father was thinking about.

It was a warm day in August when Regina looked over the wash line on which she was hanging up clothes and saw the pastor from Kyburg coming up the road on his sleek black horse. Although she had not seen him for months, she recognized him at once. Surely he would not be coming to buy new suit material already. Was he coming this time to question her father? If he needed to be questioned, why couldn't the pastor at Weisslingen do it?

Regina watched the pastor tie his horse at the gate and walk toward the shop.

"Dear God," she breathed, "help Father to tell the truth, for he cannot say that no Anabaptist was ever in his shop. And he cannot say now that he isn't interested in what they teach, and for some reason he has missed the last two guild meetings. O God, help Father." Regina then ran into the house.

"Mother," Regina called, as she entered the kitchen. "Mother," she repeated. She went through the house calling. "Mother."

No answer. Regina listened. Mother was in the shop with Father and the pastor. She heard Mother's voice and she heard her mention her name. What could it mean!

Slowly she walked to the garden. The fragrant scent of shrub roses filled the morning air, but as she drew a deep breath, she wondered again why there had to be this contention, dread, and fear—always fear. For ten minutes she stayed in the garden, nervously pulling a weed here and there. What could the pastor be talking about? The minutes seemed hours.

"Regina." It was her father's voice from the shop door.

"I'm out here in the garden, Father."

"Come here. We want to talk with you."

Gathering courage, Regina hurried to the shop.

"Good morning, Regina." The pastor bowed when Regina appeared in the doorway. "I've been discussing something with your parents that I hope will interest you. We have twins at our house and need a girl to help us. I could think of no one but you, Regina."

Color crept into Regina's cheeks. "Oh!"

"I realize this is a surprise," he said, "but I think your parents are willing for you to come. You'd be only three miles away; so you could come home occasionally when we could spare you."

"I'm indeed very much surprised. How old are the twins?" asked Regina.

"They came yesterday. Catri's mother is there now, but she can't stay long. Do you think you would enjoy helping take care of them?"

"Oh, yes. I'm quite sure I would." Regina looked first at her father, then at her mother. "I'll do whatever they say. Father has been having rather a difficult time financially, but I wouldn't do it without his consent, of course."

"Under the circumstances," her father nodded, "Mother and I think it would be all right."

"You—you do? When could I go?"

"Whenever you can get ready."

"If you feel you can't come today, come tomorrow," the pastor suggested. "I could walk home and leave my horse here for you."

"That is not necessary," said her father. "We have a horse and I can come after it and bring it back."

"Very well," answered the pastor. "I'll be going." He stopped short. "I know you will be glad to hear this, too. Things will be better now," he said, arching his eyebrows, "now that Conrad Grebel is dead."

"Dead?" asked Friedrich Strahm. "Conrad Grebel is dead?"

"Haven't you heard? I hope it's not a false report. I heard he died of the plague. So we see what happens. Those that spread a plague such as he did shall likewise die of the plague. This should convince everyone now that he was a false leader and we'll see his wicked work shall come to an end. Good-by. I'll be seeing you soon, Regina."

Regina's father knew the question in her mind, and as soon as the pastor had gone, he hastened to explain.

"This is different," he said. "We will have no fears for you, if you go to live with Heinrich Hofmeier. It will give you a chance to earn a little and besides you will have many interesting experiences in his home. You surely will be a lot safer there than here with us. Then, too, you see, Regina, if you keep your ears open you may learn the answers to many of your questions. We have been hoping and even praying about this very thing, and—" he hesitated and cleared his throat, "perhaps, this is the answer."

"Maybe so, Father," answered Regina.

VII

It was a beautiful morning. The sun shone clear and bright on the mountains. The pleasant breeze and the sweet fragrant scent of shrub roses gave Regina an invigorated feeling. Since her bundle of clothes was neither large nor heavy, she decided she'd rather walk than ride a horse to Kyburg to begin serving in the pastor's home.

"And remember," her father told her the second time, "if anyone along the way asks you where you're going, you don't need to fear. Tell him you're going to work in Pastor Hofmeier's home. Be brave, Regina. You're eighteen now."

"Somehow I am not one bit afraid, Father. I am sure I'll get there all right," answered Regina. "Mother, please don't worry about me and don't work too hard. I'll be thinking about you every evening when it's time for you to be going for the milk. Won't Michel be shocked when he comes home and finds I'm not here?"

"I won't be surprised if he'll be coming to Kyburg to see you some Sunday instead of coming home," answered Mother.

"Oh, that would be wonderful. I hope he does." Regina kissed her parents good-by, and they both smiled and patted her on the shoulder.

Along the way she stopped to say good-by to one of the neighbors, Paul Specht, an elderly man who was cutting hay.

"And to think," said Mrs. Rheinhardt, over the yard fence, her plump arms akimbo, "you are going to take care of the Hofmeier twins. You're a lucky girl. I'm surprised they couldn't find a maid in Kyburg. Why did the pastor come 'way over here after you?"

43

"I do not know why," answered Regina. "I wondered that myself."

"Unless I'm badly mistaken, some girls around Kyburg will soon be jealous of you. And you say it's a boy and a girl? Too bad they couldn't have been alike."

"But I think it will be ever so much more interesting this way, Mrs. Rheinhardt."

"And just to think," continued the woman stepping closer to the fence, "you'll be near those Anabaptist prisoners in the castle tower. You'll probably even get to see the officers taking them up the road unless this nonsense will soon be a thing of the past."

"Oh, do you think?" asked Regina. "You think I'll have to see that?"

"Well, the pastor's house and church are at the foot of that long hill below the castle, aren't they?"

"Yes, but—"

"Well, then you're likely to get in on a lot of what goes on there. You've heard Conrad Grebel is dead, I suppose," went on Mrs. Rheinhardt.

"I heard the pastor tell it yesterday to Father."

"Let's hope that the other ring leaders of his party will lose heart and recant. That's what they ought to do, don't you think?"

Regina stood thinking. Must she answer? The Rheinhardts always asked too many questions. "You see," she began carefully, "I really do not know enough about the situation to say what I think about anything, Mrs. Rheinhardt. I only hope for the best. I must be on my way."

"Well, after you've lived with the pastor and his wife for a while, you will know what's what, I am sure. I'll be asking your mother about you, and I suppose you'll be getting home once in a while. If I were you, I'd be all excited."

As Regina neared Wittmers' empty house, her eyes filled with tears. When she reached Wittmers garden fence, she walked faster. She looked in the opposite direction and hurried until she reached the corner.

Not until she was in sight of the castle did Regina feel a sense of frustration. She stopped. At the top of the steep, winding road, beyond two large weeping willow trees, towering above the deep mote and stone wall, passable only by an iron drawbridge, stood the great Kyburg Castle. Regina had seen it before, but it had never looked so cold and massive as now.

On the one side dipped a yawning gorge; on the other, far below, stretched rich pasture lands, glistening in the morning sun. The castle tower was pierced in three places by very narrow barred openings. She could not help wondering if by chance an Anabaptist prisoner was inside looking down at her. Slowly she walked on, still looking at the castle.

Stopping at the village crossroads a moment, she looked in every direction. A bird in a tree somewhere was singing vigorously. The clouds in the deep blue sky were white and fluffy. The hills were a rich green; the trees in summer foliage, the brook, even the pebbled ground under her feet seemed to be trying to rebel against the spiritual tensions which she felt but about which she knew so little.

Suddenly she heard a man's voice. "This way, Regina." Then she noticed the pastor standing in the open door of the parsonage.

"You did not walk, did you?" he asked reaching for her bundle with one hand and shaking her hand warmly with the other.

"I wanted to. It's such wonderful morning and it didn't seem far at all."

"My wife is anxiously waiting to see you. Come in."

Regina followed the pastor into the house. "Catri, this is Regina Strahm," he announced, placing her bundle on a chair inside the door. "You'll excuse me, Regina," he said. "I have to go up to the castle on business."

45

The pastor's wife, lying on her bed, greeted Regina with a smile and extended her hand. "How glad I am that you came, Regina! Sit down and rest yourself."

"But I came to work, Mrs. Hofmeier," smiled Regina.

"'My dear, there will be plenty to do, if you want to work, but since I heard you telling Heinrich you walked from Weisslingen, you must first rest a while. Sit down. Heinrich has often told me what an attractive young lady you are."

Regina was quite surprised, for she had expected nothing of' this sort. "May I see the twins?" she asked. "I can hardly wait to see them."

"Certainly. My mother has just finished giving them their morning bath. She has them in their basket in the other room. She will stay for several days and help you get started with the work. You don't know how glad I am you were able to come, Regina. We think the twins are very sweet, of course, but they will make considerable work, more than I had counted on. That's why we sent for you."

"I'm not afraid to work. What have you named the twins?"

"Frieman and Frieda. You may call me Catri, Regina. Mother," she called, "come meet Regina and show her the babies."

Catri Hofmeier had a gracious way of making Regina feel at ease. She was only three years older than Regina, and treated her more like a sister than a servant.

In contrast to Regina's blond hair, blue eyes, and gentle features, Catri's hair was black, her eyes a dark brown. Her features indicated keenness of mind. She was attractive, kind, talkative, and refined.

The five-room stone house was comfortably but not lavishly furnished. Hand-braided rugs brightened the floors of the living room and both bedrooms. There was a fireplace in each room. The kitchen and dining room combined was inviting with its fireplace which extended the width of the room. Bright-colored plates, pitchers, cups, and teapots decorated the long mantel. Through the kitchen window at the opposite end of the room salmon-colored geraniums could be seen in full bloom in an outdoor window box. Off the living room was the pastor's study, a small room furnished with two simple pieces of furniture, a homemade wall desk and stool. On the desk lay a large stiff-backed Bible.

"Regina," said Catri kindly, "you are to make yourself at home here. We will do our best to help you enjoy your work. The house is your home now. Only never go into Heinrich's study without knocking. It's just a place he partitioned off where he can be alone when he wants to. You see, he goes there to meditate and sometimes to read the Bible or fill out his records. He is very particular that no one disturbs his papers and no one else is to handle his Bible, not even I."

Regina nodded understandingly. "I want you to be perfectly free to tell me what to do and not do, and how to do things the way you want them done. I never before worked for anyone but Mother; so I'm anxious to learn."

"I'm sure we're going to get along fine, Regina. You've never helped take care of a baby either, have you?"

"No, but I know already that I love them both. They're very, very sweet. I'll do my best. You tell me how and I'll try to obey."

"Well, I'm young and inexperienced, too, Regina; so we'll learn together. I never took care of a baby either."

That night Regina was tired. She had assisted with the dinner preparations, washed the dishes, hung up baby clothes, swept the porches and the stone walk, and baked custard.

"You'll be sleeping with my mother until she leaves," Catri told her.

Quickly Regina replaced her sudden look of disappointment with a smile. Just as she was about to say good night, the pastor stepped from his study.

"Regina," he began in a friendly tone, "how is that brother of yours?"

"You mean Michel, my brother who works in Zurich?"

"I mean the one that was held by the council for questioning one Sunday morning and I helped him out. Didn't he ever tell you?"

Regina held her breath a second. "That was Hans," she said. "Yes, he told us."

"What's he doing since he's home?" ask the pastor.

Regina hesitated as she lifted her clear but troubled eyes. "He's not home now," she answered.

"Where is he?"

"He had to go back and tell Aunt Margrit what happened. He had to."

"Go back where?" asked the pastor.

"Back to Langnau to the cheese factory."

"You mean to tell me," demanded the pastor, looking straight at Regina, his dark eyes glistening, "that that little rascal went back to Langnau to his uncle's place after he swore to the council he wouldn't speak to another Anabaptist! And he's still there?"

In spite of herself, Regina's eyes got misty. She stepped back a little. Her lip trembled as she spoke, "We've not heard from him since he left. It's five months now."

"Don't make her feel bad, Heinrich," called Catri, who could hear distinctly and see from her bed. "She can't help what her brother did, Heinrich."

The pastor turned and faced Catri. "I'm not blaming her, Dear," said Heinrich, tenderly. "I just happened to think about him tonight. There's a young man up there in the prison that reminded me of him."

"Oh," exclaimed Regina. "But it's not Hans, is it, Pastor?"

"Cheer up, Regina," he said smiling. "This fellow's name is Baffler. No, it's not your brother. But I'm wondering what my duty is now since I know—" The pastor stood a minute as though in thought, then returning to his study abruptly, he closed the door softly.

"Come here, Regina," called Catri. "Do not let this worry you," she said with tenderness. "Heinrich is very conscientious about his responsibilities, and, you know, Lord Englehard is always having interviews with him about new reports. You must learn how to take Heinrich. It was very unfortunate that your brother got mixed up with the Anabaptists. Don't feel bad. Now go to bed and sleep well."

Regina swallowed hard and tried to smile. "If there is nothing else for me to do for you, I believe I'll go to bed."

When Mrs. Landwirt, Catri's mother, went into the room a few minutes later, Regina was on her knees beside the bed, her face buried in the circle of her arm.

"I beg your pardon, Regina," said Mrs. Landwirt as soon as Regina got up from her knees. "Do you often have to do that?"

"I don't do it because I have to," answered Regina, brushing back locks of blond hair. "No one ever told me to. I just feel better when I ask God to take care of Hans and the rest of my family."

"And I'm sure they need God's help to protect them from these heretical Anabaptists. Maybe we all do."

"You should pray every day," went on Mrs. Landwirt, "that your brother will be enlightened about this Anabaptist foolishness and that he will help get rid of it instead of being overcome. Of course he won't be influenced, I'm sure."

Regina made no comment. She unbraided her hair, brushed it, rebraided it, said good night, and crawled into bed. It was a long time before she fell asleep.

VIII

The crying duet of the twins wakened her early in the morning. Without being told she hurried to give them attention.

Regina did enjoy her work in the pastor's home very much. The twins with their tiny soft heads, their delicate pink faces, and their tiny hands and feet fascinated her. She liked to cook and bake, and best of all, Catri was not hard to please. Heinrich, too, seemed satisfied with Regina's meals and occasionally made remarks of appreciation about some tasty dish she had prepared. There was no part of her duties which she did not do with real enjoyment. It was even more interesting than she had anticipated.

But almost without fail, Heinrich and Catri discussed the Anabaptists at mealtime. Regina listened, trying at the same time not to appear concerned or alarmed. She often remembered what her father had said to her in the shop the morning after the pastor left. "If you keep your ears open, you may learn the answers to many of your questions." To be sure, Regina kept both ears open, but as yet her questions were still unanswered. More than once the pastor was just a little perplexed at the expression on Regina's face during the table conversation.

"Catri, is Regina always so quiet?" he inquired one afternoon while Regina was in the flower garden. "She seldom says a word at the table. Sometimes I wonder what she's thinking. Do you think she is happy here?"

"She seems free to talk to me about anything—I mean anything except the Anabaptists. She has not once committed herself on that subject."

"Sometime I'm going to ask her what she thinks about it all."

"Do be careful. You remember how you made her feel when you asked her about Hans. Regina is all right, Heinrich. She is such a sweet, sensible girl. Don't embarrass her again. She's just naturally more reserved when you're around. Mother just loves her and she's simply wonderful with the babies. By the way, Heinrich, Mother wants to go home tomorrow. Regina thinks she can get along all right now without her. But we wanted to have the twins baptized before Mother leaves."

"Then I might as well do it this afternoon. I have to go over to Sennhof on a little business, but I'll do it when I get back. Have them ready around four o'clock."

* * *

Regina was in the garden picking a fresh bouquet.

"Working hard?"

Regina looked up in surprise. On the other side of the garden fence stood a tall young man about the size and build of Michel. His ruddy complexion and brown wavy hair reminded her of Hans. He smiled and stepped closer to the fence. Removing his hat, he spoke in a low, pleasing voice, "I hope I didn't frighten you. My name is Peter Reimann. I'm a nephew to the pastor's wife, Catri."

"I'm Regina Strahm."

"Yes, I've heard about you."

"About me?"

"Uncle Heinrich comes up to the castle every day. Sometimes twice a day. He told me about your coming to work here. I wonder where he is now. Do you happen to know?"

"I could not tell you."

"Is Aunt Carti in the house?"

"Yes, she is."

"Tell her Andreas is sick and won't be able to come down and work in the garden today."

"The garden? This garden? I do not understand, but I will give her the message."

51

Peter smiled. "Andreas is the gardener for Lord Englehard, you know." He pointed to the castle.

"I've been here only six days and I haven't met anyone from the castle yet."

"Pardon me. You said your name is Regina?"

"Yes."

"I suppose no one has told you yet, Regina. You see," he continued pleasantly, "Andreas comes down here one day each week to work in the pastor's garden. He was going to come today, but since he is sick, he won't be down. You didn't suppose you would have to take care of all this, did you, besides all the other work?"

"I didn't know."

"Andreas sent me down to explain. I thought maybe Aunt Catri would be resting and since I saw you out here, I decided I'd just come and—and meet you and tell you, since I have but a minute."

"Then I'll tell Catri her nephew Peter was here," Regina smiled and nodded.

"That's right, and thank you. How do you like your work here?"

"Very well. Catri is a lovely person to work for."

"I suppose the twins keep you plenty busy."

"Not as busy as I imagine they will in six or seven months from now." Regina's eyes shone. "They're very interesting."

Peter laughed heartily. He put both hands on the fence. "I see you sometimes when you're hanging up the clothes, really almost every day."

"See me?"

"Yes."

"Why—where are you that you see me?" Regina's cheeks felt suddenly warm.

"I take care of the Lord's horses and I see lots of things from up there. You'd be surprised. It's a wonderful view down here and all over Kyburg Valley. I sleep in a room above the

52

stables. See, 'way up there?" Regina's eyes followed his finger as he pointed.

"You must have an interesting job. I'm quite fond of horses myself. How many does the lord have?"

"He has twenty right now. We never know when he might have to make use of them all. I also polish the armor."

"What armor?" Regina looked attractive to Peter, standing with a bouquet of red, purple, and white asters against her pink dress, cheeks flushed, blue serious eyes uplifted.

"There are two large rooms in the castle full of armor," he said. "But I much prefer working with the horses. The prettiest horse I ever saw was the one Conrad Grebel used to ride."

"Conrad Grebel? Did you know him?"

"Of course I knew him. He used to come to Kyburg Castle often. I always took care of his horse while he was here. It was a beauty. He called him Spike."

Tell me," ventured Regina, "is it true that Conrad Grebel is dead? I heard he was."

"Yes. He died several weeks ago."

"And why did he come to the castle?"

"He was related to the lord. They were cousins. I always liked young Grebel, even though he came from a noble family. Nothing ever surprised me like his opposing Zwingli and turning Anabaptist. Of course after that he never came again. I don't know whether Lord Englehard ever will forgive him or get over it, even though he's dead. Now he is very bitter against the Anabaptists. Before he changed, the lord thought a lot of Conrad and so did the lord's sons. They had great times together. I used to envy Conrad coming over here from Zurich on his fine horse. Too bad Conrad had to turn out like he did. I guess he lost every friend he had except those followers of his. Even his wife turned against him. But the strange thing about it is that the prisoners up there who have taken up his doctrine won't recant now, even though he's dead. You'd think they would."

"You mean—" Regina looked toward the castle. "You mean there are prisoners in the castle now. It seems awful to me, like it really can't be."

"The prison is full today," he said. "They brought in two new men last night. The board of trustees and Uncle Heinrich had a consultation with the lord, I understand."

"Why?" Regina bit her lip. "I really shouldn't know why," she said. "I have no right to ask you these questions. You don't need to tell me why. I am only a servant here."

Peter laughed softly. "Of course you have a right to ask if you want to," he said. "You can ask me anything and I'll answer it if I can. The prisoners absolutely won't tell who baptized them. That's why. The lord is determined they shall tell. They are talking now of trying the torture chamber next."

"Oh!" Then she had not misunderstood what the pastor was telling Catri and his mother-in-law in the living room the evening before when she was in the kitchen.

"Regina!"

She turned. "Someone's calling me. I must go."

"Well, good-by, Regina," Peter said. "I'm very glad I got to meet you, and no doubt we'll get to see each other again sometime before long. At least, I hope so. I used to come down often before we had all this extra work."

"Did you call me, Mrs. Landwirt?"

"Yes, Regina. But you didn't need to hurry. You look frightened. Nothing is wrong. Catri wants us to take the twins over to the church to have them baptized as soon as Heinrich gets home. Were you working hard?"

"No."

"You look hot. Your cheeks are red."

"I was just picking a fresh bouquet of asters, that's all."

"I didn't know where you were. That's all right. Go back and finish picking your bouquet. Just so we plan our work and are ready when Heinrich comes home."

"What do you want me to do?"

"I'll carry one baby and you'll carry the other. Catri will not be going along over. The twins will be eight days old tomorrow, and I'd like to go home. That's why we decided to have them baptized today. Will you help me to get them ready?"

"Of course, Mrs. Landwirt."

The stone church was dark and chilly. Heinrich entered first and lit two white candles on either side of the stone baptismal font below the chancel. Carefully, he laid two small white robes on a brass table beside the font.

As Grandmother Landwirt and Regina walked down the aisle, each carrying a tiny blanketed infant, their footsteps on the stone floor echoed in the empty church. They stood before the infant baptistry, while Heinrich hunted for the Scripture passage in the large stiff-backed Bible. Looking down at his mother-in-law and with the palm of his left hand on the open Bible, he said solemnly, "In the name of God, Amen. Our help is in the name of the Lord who made heaven and earth. Is it your desire that the child in your arms be baptized into the baptism of our Lord, Jesus Christ?"

"Yes," answered the child's grandmother.

"Name the child," said Heinrich.

"Frieda Hofmeier."

Heinrich drew from beneath the Bible a small black book and opened it. "Let us all pray together," he said. "Almighty, eternal God! Thou who through the flood didst doom the unbelieving world in accordance with the firm judgment and didst, in Thy mercy, preserve the faith of Noah and the eight souls in the ark, and didst drown the obstinate Pharaoh with all his host in the Red Sea, and didst lead Thy people through with dry feet, whereby this bath of baptism was prefigured. We pray Thee, according to Thy fathomless mercy, that Thou wouldst behold in mercy this, Thy servant, Frieda Hofmeier, and wilt grant her the light of faith in her heart; in order that she may be incorporated into Thy Son, may be buried with

Him in His death, with Him may rise in newness of life, that she may daily follow in the bearing of His cross with joy, may cling to Him in true faith, firm hope, and fervent love; that she, Frieda Hofmeier, may leave this life, which is nothing other than death, for Thy sake, and may appear on the last day at Thy common judgment without fear. Through our same Lord, Jesus Christ, Thy Son, who lives and reigns with Thee in the unity of one God and the Holy Spirit, Amen."

The pastor then slipped the little black book under the Bible and read from the Holy Book, "And they brought young children to him, that he should touch them: and his disciples rebuked those that brought them. But when Jesus saw it, he was much displeased, and said unto them, Suffer the little children to come unto me, and forbid them not: for of such is the kingdom of God" (Mark 10:13, 14).

Heinrich dipped his hand in the font and sprinkled a few drops of water on the sleeping child. As he picked up one of the baptismal robes, and draped it over his tiny daughter, he prayed, "God, grant that as thou art now bodily clothed with this white garment, thou mightest appear before Him on the last day with a pure, unblemished conscience. Amen. The Lord be with you. You may now present the other grandchild."

The pastor held his tiny daughter until her twin brother was transferred from Regina's arms into the arms of his grandmother, then he handed Frieda to Regina and the same ceremony was performed for the infant son.

Slowly Heinrich Hofmeier closed the copper lid of the baptistry and pinched out the candles with the tips of his fingers.

As the three walked out, the pastor leading the procession, their footsteps echoed again in the empty church. Something echoed in Regina's heart, too—snatches of things Michel, Hans, and the converted monk had said: "I feel so wicked"; "Infants can't believe or confess sins"; "Perfect love."

Catri was sitting in the living room when they came in.

56

"Are you home already?" she asked.

"There's not much to it," Heinrich remarked. "But the recording, that's what's important and I'll do it right away." He went directly into his study and closed the door behind him.

"I wonder," thought Regina, as she put tiny Frieda into the basket on the chair by the window, "if that's all that needs to be done to have salvation. Father said he had my spiritual welfare taken care of and I need have no fears. But Uncle Rudolf was not satisfied. I wish I knew. The Wittmers decided for themselves not to have their baby baptized."

Bending over the basket, she looked into the sweet face of the tiny sleeping baby girl. "You dear little innocent thing," she whispered. "You don't even know you were carried over to the church. You don't know your father baptized you. You don't know what sin is. You don't even know you exist."

IX

At daybreak the morning after the twins were baptized, Mrs. Landwirt started her four-mile walk home to Kollbrunn. She had told Regina the evening before that she wanted to get home before the day got warm, and also in time to go to church.

"Good-by, Dear," said Mrs. Landwirt as she kissed Regina on the cheek. "I'm so glad you are here to help Catri. No, don't get up. It's not necessary. I told Catri last night I'd make myself a cup of tea and slip off quietly. I'll try to come back sometime before too long and see how you're all getting along. Now go back to sleep."

But Regina did not go back to sleep. Birds in the cherry tree not far from her bedroom window began their early morning chorus, and as she lay listening to their happy songs her eyes filled with sudden tears.

"Dear God," she breathed, "somehow show me what's wrong and help Hans and Father and Mother. If there is such a thing as perfect love, help us all to find it. I know I should be happy here, but—"

Regina listened. She sat up in bed and leaned forward. Through the thin partition she could hear quite distinctly the voice in the next room.

"But God, who is rich in mercy, for his great love wherewith he loved us, even when we were dead in sins, hath quickened us together with Christ, (by grace ye are saved;) and hath raised us up together, and made us sit together in heavenly places in Christ Jesus: that in the ages to come he might shew the exceeding riches of his grace in his kindness toward us through Christ Jesus. For by grace are ye saved through faith—"

The voice stopped abruptly. Regina sat motionless. She could hear heavy breathing, then a stifled moan. Then she heard the rustling of the pages in the large Bible.

"We have heard with our ears," she heard after a short pause, "O God, our fathers have told us, what work thou didst in their days, in the times of old. How thou didst drive out the heathen with thy hand, and plantedst them; how thou didst afflict the people, and cast them out." He cleared his throat and continued, "For they got not the land in possession by their own sword, neither did their own arm save them: but thy right hand, and thine arm, and the light of thy countenance, because thou hadst a favour unto them. Thou art my King, O God: command deliverances for Jacob." There was a short pause.

"Through thee will we push down our enemies: through thy name will we tread them under that rise up against us. For I will not trust in my bow, neither shall my sword save me."

The pastor cleared his throat and she could hear him walking back and forth across the room. Then Regina heard the pages being turned and once more he read: "And they led Jesus away to the high priest: and with him were assembled all the chief priests and the elders and the scribes. And Peter followed him afar off, even into the palace of the high priest: and he sat with the servants, and warmed himself at the fire. And the chief priests and all the council sought for witness against Jesus to put him to death; and found none. For many bare false witness against him, but their witness agreed not together. And there arose certain, and bare false witness against him, saying, We heard him say, I will destroy this temple that is made with hands, and within three days I will build another made without hands."

The pages rustled again. "In the beginning was the Word, and the Word was with God, and the Word was God." His voice sounded almost weary. "The same was in the beginning with God. All things were made by him; and without him was not any thing made that was made. In him was life; and the life was the light of men. And the light shineth in darkness; and the darkness—"

One baby started crying, and then the other. Regina got out of bed and dressed quickly.

When she opened her bedroom door, she stopped short. The pastor was in the kitchen pouring wine from a jug into a small wine glass.

"Maybe this will steady my nerves," he said, holding it up and looking at Regina.

"Are you ill this morning?" she asked. She crossed the room and picked up one of the twins.

"I never feel as well on Sunday morning as I do other mornings." Heinrich took a sip. He leaned against the table and looked out the window.

"Why is that?" asked Regina.

"Sunday is the hardest day of the week for me since all the trouble with the Anabaptists started." He took the second sip. "It's very difficult to know what Scripture to read or what is appropriate to say in church."

"I think it would be wonderful to be able to read the Bible," said Regina. "I wish I could."

The pastor shook his head. "You are better off as you are, Regina," he said. "Too many who are able to read the Bible get radical ideas. That's the trouble up there in the prison. One of them can read, but all the rest listen to him as though he had some divine authority. Conrad Grebel would have been far better off if he had never gone to school. His knowledge carried him away and made him dissatisfied. Then the trouble started." Heinrich took another long sip, set the glass on the table, and stepped over to the basket. He picked up the other baby and walked back and forth across the room patting her nervously.

60

"There, there, don't cry, Frieda," he said. "Your mother wants to rest, and I have my Scripture to select. Hush now, you naughty girl."

Regina had never seen the pastor act like this. She drew back in astonishment, as he came close and said, "Say, Regina, have you ever heard an Anabaptist talk?" He looked her straight in the eyes.

She waited. "Once," she said softly. "Only once."

"Where?" he asked.

"A man stopped at my father's shop," she said. "Father had never seen him before and he never came back."

"What did he want?"

"He came to talk about exchanging thread."

"Thread?"

"Yes."

"You mean he was a weaver?"

"Yes." Regina's voice was almost a whisper.

"Was he by any chance from Baretswill?"

Regina held the baby boy close to her. Her legs trembled a bit.

"Yes," she answered.

"And was it Johann Ferlinden? Can you answer me that?"

"Yes," she answered feebly. "He said that was his name."

Heinrich laughed. "He's the man up in the prison who can read and thinks he knows the Bible better than Zwingli does. He's in solitary confinement now."

"Oh," she looked away and held the baby still more closely.

"So he was at your father's shop? And did he try to persuade you to believe his doctrine, Regina?"

"No. He didn't talk to me. He only talked to Father a little while, then left."

"And did he try to convert your father?"

"Father was frightened when he found out he was an Anabaptist. But the man was not unkind. He said he was happy, but Father told him—"

61

"Told him what?" The pastor moved closer to Regina, so close she could smell the alcohol on his breath.

She drew back. "Well, he told him not to come back until this trouble was ended."

"He told him that?"

"Yes, he, well, he didn't know what else to say I guess, but Father—"

"God be thanked," said the pastor. "Well, I thought your father was firm. And I doubt if Johann Ferlinden will call at your father's shop again. You see, Regina, it's all this on my mind that makes Sunday a hard day for me." Nervously he patted the baby in his arms. "It's extremely difficult for me to get into the spirit of worship and find a suitable passage to read with all this going on. You have no idea what trouble these Anabaptists are causing us. I'm a bit upset this morning."

Heinrich Hofmeier laid the quieted baby in its basket and returned to his study. Presently Regina heard him reading aloud again. She listened, standing in the doorway of the living room.

"Turn us, O God of our salvation, and cause thine anger toward us to cease. Wilt thou be angry with us for ever? wilt thou draw out thine anger to all generations? Wilt thou not revive us again: that thy people may rejoice in thee? Shew us thy mercy, O Lord, and grant us thy salvation."

Catri tiptoed into the living room, her beautiful black hair hanging around her shoulders. "Regina," she whispered, "Mother left, didn't she?"

"Yes."

"I might as well get up. I heard both babies. Thanks for getting up. Heinrich seems very nervous this morning," she whispered. "I heard him talking to you out here. I feel sorry for him. He has so much on his mind. I don't think he slept a bit all night. You know Heinrich was never stern or severe and now it seems he must put forth all his energy to work against the Anabaptists. It is very trying. Of course, he knows they're wrong, but it's hard on him anyway. I've never seen Heinrich quite so upset. He must do everything in his power to be loyal to his position and work with Lord Englehard and the state. But this trouble is doing something to his personality. I can see it. Hear him! He's still in his study trying to find a Scripture to read in church this morning. I don't know enough about the Bible to help him. I hope the wine settled his nerves."

"Why is it so hard for him to find a suitable Scripture?" asked Regina. "Of course, I don't know the Bible either, and maybe I shouldn't ask."

"I don't know, Dear. Just think, Regina. Oh, I hate to say it, but Heinrich told me last night he almost wished he were only a dirt farmer until this church difficulty is ended. When we met, he was so happy in his office. I thought it was going to be so wonderful to be the pastor's wife. But don't ever tell a soul what I've told you. Since he is pastor of Kyburg, he will be brave, of course, and conscientious and faithful. Heinrich wants to be, too. Don't ever let anything he says disturb you, Regina. I'm going to comb my hair now and come and help you get breakfast. Remember Heinrich thinks you are a wonderful girl; so don't ever be distressed at him or what he says. Thank God it's only on Sunday morning he acts like this."

"Are you going to church today?" asked Regina.

"Not today. I might go next Sunday. Regina, you go this morning."

"But I shouldn't leave you here alone with these two babies. What if they both cry at once like they did a while ago? Please, Catri, let me stay with you. I am sure Heinrich would expect me to."

"You're very considerate, Regina."

X

As the days turned into weeks Regina was becoming more and more attached to the growing twins. Their morning care was more fascinating each day. Their plump soft bodies, their baby smiles thrilled her. She enjoyed working with Catri. They spent many pleasant hours together. Except for his nerve-racking Sunday mornings, Heinrich was congenial and treated Regina with kindness and respect. She did her work cheerfully and thoroughly in a quiet unassuming manner, and they readily agreed she more than earned her four shillings a month.

Regina liked the little stone house with its cherry fireplaces and braided rag rugs. She enjoyed the spacious lawn, the cherry tree outside her bedroom window where the birds held their daily morning concert.

She liked the rose bushes, the columbines, the flower garden, the geranium box outside the kitchen window. She liked the vegetable garden and Andreas, the gardener, his round, plump, pleasant face, his quick step, and magic touch with plants. They often exchanged words at the clothesline in the yard, or when Catri sent her to the garden with a basket for him to fill with fresh vegetables.

"Never saw a garden do so well as this one," Andreas said to Regina one morning. "Looks like the good Lord has blessed the pastor since you came to live with them."

Regina smiled modestly. "I'm sure the good Lord blesses the garden, Andreas, but I think you have a lot to do with it, too. It seems you know exactly how to make a garden grow." Andreas beamed with delight.

64

Each Sunday morning Regina insisted Catri should go to church and she would stay at home with the twins.

"I'm willing to take turns with you," Catri would say.

"But I'm your servant, Catri. It is my duty to stay here and let you go. Please, Catri, for your friends want to see you and ask about the babies."

"But you must go sometime, Regina. Don't you know anyone who misses going to church must have a good excuse?" Catri smiled pleasantly.

"But the twins are excuse enough, don't you think? And every Sunday morning I listen very carefully while Heinrich is reading the Scriptures. I can hear ever so well when I'm in my bedroom and he is reading in his study."

Catri laughed. "Then I suppose you feel like you've already been in church and that will satisfy?"

"Well," Regina hesitated. "Well—yes, Catri. I do feel very serious and reverent while he is reading and while I listen I hold a service right here in my own heart. You understand, Catri, I hope. I'm not trying to be stubborn or disobedient— but if anyone stays at home, it should be me, I think. Don't you?"

"Very well, Dear. I'll explain to Heinrich."

Catri did explain. And the pastor accepted the explanation. In fact, he was glad and even proud his wife could be in the service every Sunday morning. "True," Heinrich told Catri, "it's rightfully Regina's place to stay with the babies. That is one reason we hired her, isn't it?"

One Saturday afternoon the pastor said to Regina, "Catri and I have decided that you may have tomorrow off to go home, if you like. You have been a faithful worker."

"You mean it? Thank you. I'd be glad to go home to see the folks."

"Catri said she could manage for one day without you. But I'd like to ask a favor of you before you go."

"What is it?"

"I'd like you to go over and dust the chancel of the church. Old Mary Barben who has been cleaning the church for years must be losing her eyesight. She did such a poor job of dusting last week, I was actually embarrassed. How about it?"

"Of course I will."

"Then I want you to see if you can find enough flowers in the garden to put a fresh bouquet in the vase by the altar."

"Very well."

Regina left the door wide open to admit some sunlight. She had not been inside the church since the afternoon when she carried tiny Frieda in for baptism. Her footsteps echoed again on the stone floor. She placed the flowers at the altar. Carefully she dusted everything—the ledge, the window sills, the chair, and last of all the pulpit and the large stiff-backed Bible. When she had finished, she rested on one of the front chairs for a while, and folding her arms, sat in meditation, looking intently first on the Bible and then on the stone baptistry. Finally her lips moved in a whispered prayer that broke the stillness. "I wish, dear God, I wish I knew for sure." Slowly she walked out and latched the door.

It was a beautiful fall Sunday when Regina set out from Kyburg for her home three miles distant in Weisslingen. Before Regina had gone half a mile, she met Michel coming toward her on horseback. She almost ran to meet him.

"Michel," she exclaimed, "you haven't forgotten you have a sister, after all. I've been expecting you the past two Sundays. Michel, it's so good to see you."

"Are you on your way home, Regina?"

"Not to stay. I must be back before dark. I have the day off."

"Do you want to ride my horse? I can walk."

"Oh, no, Michel. Let's both walk. It's such a grand morning, and we'll be there almost before we know it."

Michel dismounted and they started down the road together.

"Now tell me about yourself and your work, Regina," began Michel. "How are you? You're looking very well, I'll say that."

"Michel, I am. My work is taking care of twins, washing, cooking, and everything that goes with housework where there are two babies. I couldn't find a nicer place to stay, Michel. The pastor and his wife are both nice to me. The twins are so dear and sweet and interesting. Of course, I have a terrible time hiding my feelings sometimes when the pastor comes in with news about the Anabaptists. That's the hardest part. It worries me. I'm so confused about it all, too. More than ever, I think, I just have no desire whatever to attend the Kyburg church."

"Did you know the pastor came in to see me one day about Hans?"

"No." Regina looked up at him, startled. "What about Hans?"

"He wanted to know what I knew about him and why he went back to Langnau after the scare they gave him."

"O Michel! What did you tell him?"

"What could I tell him? I tried my best to protect him without lying. I said he felt an obligation to Aunt Margrit, and he had to go back to take care of the cheese."

"What did he say to that?"

"He didn't like my answer very well, I could tell that. He said in the sight of the law that would be a mighty flimsy excuse, but since Hans was your brother—"

"My brother?"

"Yes. Since Hans was your brother, and since he thought a lot of Father and you, too, and since Langnau isn't in the canton, he'd drop the matter."

"Oh! And you haven't heard anything from Hans yet?"

"Not a thing."

"And the folks haven't either?"

"They haven't heard a thing from him or Uncle Rudolf. The folks are almost frantic sometimes."

They walked on silently, Michel leading the horse. Regina broke the silence, "It's so good to see you, Michel!"

"Something is happening to Father," Michel said abruptly.

"Happening to Father? What do you mean, Michel?"

"I think he's very unsettled."

"About what?"

"About who's right. That's why I went home every Sunday instead of coming over to see you. Father and Mother both wonder all the time about Hans and Uncle Rudolf, too; so I felt it was my duty to go home and try to cheer them up. And they miss you, Regina."

"I suppose. But tell me why you think Father is unsettled."

"Regina, didn't you think Father wasn't quite himself before you left home?"

"Well, who can be with all the fear in people's hearts? Can you always?"

Michel did not answer.

"Listen, Michel. I got to carry one of the Hofmeier twins into the church the day the pastor baptized them. I've wondered an awful lot since that day. More than ever. I've never been able to forget the things you said the Anabaptist believe about being baptized upon their own confession, and that infants can't have faith or confess their own sins when they never sinned, and all that. You remember, don't you? If my baptism was like the Hofmeier twins was, well, if my baptism is enough, then—why do I feel so uncertain about it? Why can't I be completely satisfied? Why are more and more people asking to be rebaptized even though they have to go to prison?"

Michel made no answer.

"Surely no one would allow himself to get locked up in Kyburg Castle just for the fun or thrill of it, would he?'

Michel gave no answer.

"Would they?" whispered Regina.

"That's the way Father talked last Sunday when I was home. Exactly like that."

"You men—why, Michel! He told me my spiritual welfare was taken care of when I was an infant."

"I know. I'm just telling you Father doesn't act like himself ever since I took one of Zwingli's latest booklets along home and read it to him."

"What was it about?'

"About predestination."

"Predestination? What's that, Michel?"

Michel sighed. "Well, in his argument for infant baptism, Zwingli says that every person who believes in God is a son of God, but the Bible talks about some people being elect."

"What's that? Tell me, Michel."

"It means chosen of God. So, since some are chosen of God, the only safe way is to baptize all infants. See?"

"And that's what you read to Father?"

"Yes."

"And he couldn't see it? I mean, he couldn't agree with Zwingli?"

"Regina, we talked all afternoon. I'm sorry, but he was quite upset when I left. I wasn't able to help him one bit."

"Poor Father! And what about Mother?"

"She sits and listens. Of course, she believes everything Father does. You know Mother. Yes, she's unsettled now, too."

"I know just how they feel then, because every Sunday morning while I'm still in bed, I can hear the pastor reading from the Bible. He always practices reading aloud what he's going to read in church. I can hear, but, of course, I don't know what it all means. For some reason he has an awful time finding what he wants to read. And he is always so nervous and unhappy on Sundays. It puzzles me. Why does the same Bible make some people happy and others so miserable? Michel, if I could only have one and read it for myself. When I hear it, it makes me feel quite upset for some reason. I don't want Hofmeiers to know it. Sometimes it makes me feel so—Michel, how shall I tell you—so warm inside. The converted monk talked about a perfect love that casts out fear. He was so happy. I can't forget him."

69

"What monk?"

"Didn't Father ever tell you?"

"No."

"His name was Johann Ferlinden, a weaver from Baretswill. He came to exchange thread with Father one morning when I was in the shop sweeping. Strange, Father never told you."

"Then what?"

"I heard what he told Father that morning about his conversion to the Anabaptist faith. It wasn't much, but I can't forget it."

"Johann Ferlinden? That name sounds familiar. That's the preacher Hans and Uncle Rudolf met on the road, wasn't it? Say, that's the man the authorities are hunting. I'm positive."

"Hunting? No! He's up in the prison at Kyburg."

"But I'm certain it's Johann Ferlinden they are hunting. The city council has promised ten pounds to anyone who will capture him. Zwingli was in the shop yesterday and said a horseman from Kyburg Castle, named Peter, reported his escape."

"His escape!" exclaimed Regina. "What more did Zwingli say?"

"He said there's no use passing a mandate unless it's put into effect. He often comes in to explode to Bartsche. He was pretty well worked up."

"Michel! What does that mean?"

"That's plain," answered Michel. "It means if he really has rebaptized anyone and he's caught, he'll be drowned."

"Michel! Do you think they will capture him?"

"Yes, of course they will."

"Oh! Michel, tell me what you honestly think of all this. Michel, he seemed so brave and happy that day in the shop. Not one bit afraid of the prison. Tell me what you think of all this."

Michel groaned. "I'm not to say what I think, Regina. And I'm not even to think twice," he whispered. "What I think, I think. I know that sounds absurd, but you can't imagine the tight place I'm in, Regina," he continued, still whispering. "I'm positive I'm being watched all the time in the shop. I don't like to tell you and Father you're silly for being upset about this, but Ferlinden will be caught. Let's talk about something else now."

Regina ignored his suggestion. "Once you said you think just the way I do. Remember? Do you still say that? Can't you just tell me that, Michel? If you still think and believe as Father does, do you mean you, too, are somewhat upset now?"

The two walked on in silence for a quarter mile.

"What are you thinking about, Michel?" asked Regina at length. "You don't answer my question."

"I wish Hans would come home today and tell us what he knows," Michel answered. "But I wouldn't want him to come in as he did the last time and give us a scare. He was running a risk to go back the way he did, but if— Look, Regina, church in Weisslingen is over. Look. There go Father and Mother toward home."

The two quickened their steps.

"Won't they be surprised to see us coming home together, Michel? But if Father and Mother are so unsettled, what good do they get out of going to church?"

"What else would they do?" questioned Michel.

XI

With shoulders erect and hat in hand, Peter stood facing Lord Englehard on the inner castle court steps. The sun shone on his wavy brown hair.

It was not in Peter's place to make suggestions to any of his superiors—least of all to Lord Englehard. But with the intensifying conflict, Peter and the lord had had occasion to converse quite frequently. Little by little, the lord assigned responsibilities other than the horses to Peter.

"So you think you ought to go to Heinrich Hofmeier's church this morning?" asked Lord Englehard, deepening the furrows in his high forehead and folding his arms.

"My lord, I only asked to see what you think," Peter answered. "There might be a slight possibility of getting some clue, if I go. It just occurred to me."

"A very slight possibility," replied Lord Englehard. "But you may go. There is plenty of help here, if I need it while you're gone. Tell the pastor to come up immediately after church is dismissed. We've got to try anything and everything to capture Ferlinden. This is the most disgraceful thing that has happened since young Conrad lost his head. Go, if you think you can find anything. Before you go, Peter, bring up my horse. No, I'm not going to leave; I just want to ride around the grounds for a little exercise and see what I can find."

It was unlike Peter Reimann to ask permission to attend the church at the foot of the hill. In fact, the only times he had been inside Heinrich Hofmeier's church were when he had been given special orders by Englehard to go. It was understood that no one living at the castle left the grounds without permission or commission. Furthermore, it was taken for granted that everyone at the castle, from the lord himself to the lowest servant, was a loyal member of the state church; and the fact that they obeyed the lord was proof of their obedience to highest church authority.

Peter delivered the white horse to the office entrance, bowed when the lord appeared, and hurrid back to his room above the stable.

Carefully he brushed his best suit and, with extra pains, combed his wavy hair.

As he started down the hill he looked almost constantly in the direction of the pastor's house. He did not catch a glimpse of anyone in the yard, not even when he passed the gate. At the entrance of the church he combed back his hair and fastened his coat.

Inside the door he hesitated a moment, scanning the seated crowd, then took a seat close to the center aisle near the rear of the church.

He felt a hand on his left shoulder. Peter looked up.

"Good morning, Peter."

"Good morning, Uncle Heinrich."

"What brings you here this morning, Peter?"

"I'm on the lookout for clues," whispered Peter under his breath. "You know, Ferlinden."

Heinrich Hofmeier took his place behind the pulpit and opened the large Bible. For a moment he stood with bowed head. Solemn-faced, but with a strong, clear voice, he read Psalm 5, then offered a short prayer.

Peter never turned his head to the right or the left, but out of the corner of his eye watched occasionally in the direction of the door for a possible late-comer. It struck him forcibly how morose, depressed, and dissatisfied everyone in the congregation looked that morning. In vain he searched for a happy face. In vain he looked over the group for a certain beautiful

73

girl with fair complexion, blue eyes, and blond hair. Neither could he find Aunt Catri.

"Friends," Heinrich Hofmeier was saying, "please give me your attention for a few minutes while I admonish you to be faithful to God and to the church. By coming to church you will find mercy and freedom from fear of our dreaded enemies, the Anabaptists. We know they are full of wickedness, and deceit is in their mouths. I regret that so many of the neighbors we thought were truly settled in the faith have made such drastic departures and have so grossly sinned against higher authority. I fear for their souls. Unless they recant, I see no hope for their escape from punishment. We know God Almighty will bless those who are faithful and obedient, but there is no blessing, no protection, no hope for those who rebel.

"Before you leave today, I wish to get the names of everyone present. If any new babies have been born in this territory, please report them after the service. If anyone present knows anything of the whereabouts of Johann Ferlinden, the Weaver from Baretswill, please give me the information at once. You would be doing the church a great favor at this time, if you could give me any information about this enemy of righteousness.

"Now peace and goodness be upon you, and may you continue to put your full trust in the holy Christian Church as promoted and protected by the civil government. May your full allegiance, without any question or faltering, be placed in the laws of the church and the government, knowing they are first sanctioned by the Word of God, as Ulrich Zwingli has so clearly taught us."

Peter lingered at the door, shook hand with a few people, and then crossed the yard. Gently he rapped on the front door.

"Good morning, Peter." Catri greeted him with a glad smile. "Where are you going, all dressed up? Come in. I haven't seen you in those clothes for a long time."

"I've been to church. Why weren't you there, Aunt Catri?"

74

"I had to stay with the babies."

"I thought you had a nurse to do that." Peter looked through the house in the direction of the kitchen.

"She went home this morning."

Peter cleared his throat. "You mean Regina went home?"

"Not to stay, Peter. We'll keep her indefinitely, if we can. We let her have the day off. She'll be back before night. You've met Regina, haven't you?"

"Out by the garden fence once. I thought I'd drop in and see the twins."

"I'm glad. It's about time, too." Catri ushered her nephew across the room to the basket by the window.

"You'll have to tell me which is which," laughed Peter. "They certainly do look alike to me. And my, so tiny!"

"This is Frieda," Catri removed the blue blanket. "Frieman, you see, has a slightly rounder face and a little more hair. Can you stay and eat dinner with us?"

"Thank you, Aunt Catri, but I'd better not today."

"Some other time?"

"I'd be very glad to. I'd have to get permission, however."

"I think Heinrich could arrange that, sometime. You stand in pretty good with Lord Englehard, I understand."

"How do you know?"

"Don't you think Heinrich finds out such things as often as he goes up there?"

"By the way, Aunt Catri, I'm to give him a message to come up to the castle. I'll have to go tell him at once. And you're sure you want me to come for a meal sometime?"

"Why not? Of course. I mean it, Peter. If there's any possible chance of your getting away that long I know everything is abnormal now. Isn't it awful?"

"I haven't eaten any of your cooking for a long time," laughed Peter. "It would taste mighty good."

"If you come," answered Catri, "you will very likely have a chance to eat Regina's cooking instead of mine. She's excellent

75

at that; in fact, she is very good at everything I put her to. We're fortunate to have such a fine girl with us. She is wonderful with the babies, too. So you were in the church service? How did Heinrich get along, Peter? Tell me about it before he comes in."

"What do you mean, Catri?"

"He was so worn out and nervous this morning, he said he was afraid he couldn't collect his thoughts enough to have much of a service. Now since Johann Ferlinden has escaped, he is more upset than ever. He was awake all night. I hate to see him so tired. But don't tell anyone, Peter. Heinrich tries to hide it from Lord Englehard and the trustees as much as possible. This trouble hasn't upset you yet, has it?"

"Upset me? No, I don't think so. What do you mean, Aunt Catri?"

"I mean physically. I know you're not upset spiritually. Of course, not. Neither is Heinrich. But it's nerve-racking to see how our neighbors, our friends, our once good church members are being so deceived. Don't misunderstand me, Peter, about Heinrich. He's got to do his duty, and he will do his duty as you will do yours, but I wish for many reasons this trouble were ended and we wouldn't have to be talking about it all the time. And by the way," Catri said confidingly, "if you come for a meal keep in mind that Regina doesn't—"

"Well, did you find any clues, Peter?" Heinrich asked before he crossed the threshold.

"No, I didn't, Uncle Heinrich. Did you? Lord Englehard will be very much disappointed, I'm afraid. You are to go up to see him at once. He told me to tell you."

"What now?"

"I don't know. What were you saying, Aunt Catri?"

"We'll finish that some other time, Peter."

XII

The day passed swiftly.

It was six o'clock before they realized it.

"I'd offer to go for the milk, Mother," said Regina, "but I know if I'd go, Mr. and Mrs. Rheinhardt would both ask me too many questions. I think I should be starting back anyway right now."

"I'll walk with you to the crossroad," said Michel; "then I'll cut back and strike out for Zurich. Let's go."

It was much harder for Regina to leave home this time than the first. She kissed her father and noticed the quiver in his voice when he said good-by. Mother laid her head on Regina's shoulder and cried softly a little.

"Don't cry, Mother dear. I pray for Hans every night and I pray for you, too."

"If it wasn't so far," said Father, "I'd be tempted to go over to Langnau this next week end and see them, but then someone would likely report me, if I did."

"Remember the Alps that evening, Father? You said you hoped our future would be that bright. Remember?"

"Yes, Regina, I remember."

"I think of that every evening and wonder."

* * *

Friedrich and Melka watched their two children until they were out of sight. Friedrich drew Melka close to him. "I'll never be able to forgive myself, Melka, if it's my fault their future isn't bright."

"But you've done the best you know, Friedrich, haven't you?"

"But that doesn't always make a thing right, Mother. I'd give a whole lot to be able to talk with Wittmers or Brohens or Rudolf a few minutes. What if after all, I've not taught the children right."

* * *

"Michel," said Regina, before they reached the crossroad, "did you notice how gray Father was today?"

"That didn't strike me as much as the expression on his face. He looks tired, and I'm sure it's not that he works too hard."

"Tired wondering what to think, I guess. You'd better go home to see them whenever you can, Michel. Don't forget you have a sister over at Kyburg, but look after them first. I'll try to get home again before cold weather. You were right. He is disturbed. Poor Father! Don't you pity him, Michel?'

"Of course, I do. But who isn't a little disturbed if he's honest?"

* * *

Andreas laid down his hoe and walked over to the well just as Regina was coming out of the house, pail in hand.

"Let me draw the water for you," he said, taking the pail.

"Thank you," Regina smiled.

"That's more than Lisette says," remarked Andreas, opening the well.

"Who's Lisette?"

"She's the kitchen maid at the castle. I often draw water for her, but she never says thanks. Not that I expect her to, but it sorta makes the pail just a little lighter when it's coming up, see." Andreas' smile stretched across his whole round face. "There you are, Miss Regina, and what will you take for a few swallows on a warm day like this?"

"What will I take?" she said. "I'll take just what I gave you."

Andreas laughed good-naturedly. "Very well." He unhooked the gourd which hung by a string on a post beside the well and dipped some fresh cold water out of the pail and drank. "Thank you, Regina."

"You're quite welcome, Andreas. And since you said thanks, I believe the pail will be just a little lighter for me, too. Maybe no one ever taught Lisette to say thank you."

Andreas laughed again. "She can say it all right when she feels like it, and she always feels like it when Peter Riemann draws water for her." Andreas chuckled.

"Peter?"

"Haven't you met Peter, the Lord's horse tender? He said he talked with you."

"Oh. Yes, I know who Peter is."

"Lisette breaks her neck to go for water whether she needs it or not whenever he's near the well."

"And isn't he often near the well to help her?"

Andreas wiped the perspiration from his damp forehead with his handkerchief, and from his big strong body rolled a long deep chuckle. He ran one hand back across his graying hair. "I'm not supposed to know, and I don't let on I know much, but a fellow dumb as I am can use his eyes and ears and what little brains God has given him. No, I'd say Peter isn't at the well nearly often enough to suit Lisette. He's a busy man, Peter is. He does more than tend the horses these days. Of late Lord Englehard seems to think Peter can do anything. He's gone out again to fetch in some Anabaptist for questioning."

"Oh, no!" Regina put the full water pail on the ground. Her eyes widened. "Not another Anabaptist, Andreas. Does Peter have to do that?" she asked.

"He brought one in this forenoon, Miss Regina."

"How many prisoners do they have up there now?" Regina asked.

"I couldn't say," Andreas answered. "Some swore off and they let them go, otherwise they wouldn't have room for them all. One got away Friday night."

"Which one?"

"The one they thought they'd have to drown."

79

"You mean Johann Ferlinden, Andreas?"

"That's the one, Johann, the converted monk. No one knows how it happened unless someone on the outside helped him out in the night."

"But how could they?"

"I don't know, Regina. It's a mystery. But from now on, Peter and I are to take turns acting as night watchman besides our other work."

"And will you like that job, Andreas?"

"It's not a case of liking or disliking a thing these days, Miss Regina. I do what I'm told and ask no questions. Since my wife, Elsie, died five years ago, I've been taking orders from Lord Englehard. I was told to come down here and clean the pastor's garden; so I'd better go do it right now. Look who's going there!" Andreas pointed toward the road in front of the pastor's house.

She turned. "Oh!" Regina pressed her lips.

On horseback, Peter was closely following a middle-aged man and woman. Meekly, with heads slightly bowed and hands folded as if in prayer, the couple trudged up the long steep hill toward the castle. Peter looked over and, seeing Andreas and Regina, lifted his hand. Andreas answered.

"Didn't you see Peter wave to you?" asked Andreas.

"He wasn't waving to me," she said quickly. "He was waving to you, Andreas. And anyway—when I see something like that—I—I—don't—" Regina picked up the pail of water and hurried toward the house without another word.

Regina almost stumbled into her bedroom and, closing the door, stood with her back against it. She covered her face with her hands. "I dare not let anyone hear me. Never! But that poor, dear couple going to prison! Being actually driven up to prison by Peter! By Peter Reimann! How could he!"

Heinrich dropped his goose quill pen. He opened his study door, and looking across the living room, saw Catri busy making the bed.

"Where's Regina?" he whispered, walking over to her.

"I don't know, Heinrich. Why?"

"Is she in her room?"

"I don't think so. I think she is washing in the yard."

"Very well then."

"Why, Heinrich?"

"I thought I heard someone crying."

"Crying?"

"Look. Her bedroom door is shut. I think she's in there."

"She's not in there, Heinrich."

But presently Regina's door opened. Quickly she walked through the kitchen and resumed her work in the yard.

"She was in her room," said Heinrich "And I'm confident that she had been crying. I heard."

"I would know of no reason for it, Heinrich."

"Nothing happened this morning?"

"Not a thing that I know of. Go back to your work. I'll find out after a while."

"You don't suppose she's homesick since we let her go home yesterday?"

"I haven't the slightest idea. She seemed happy last night when she came back, didn't she? I'll find out."

Catri did not rush out to the yard where Regina was washing, but kept on with giving the twins their baths. There would be plenty of opportunity to find out later.

* * *

From the garden, Andreas watched Regina busy at the wash-tub. Almost cautiously he approached her while she was hanging up clothes.

"This will be the last of the garden vegetables," he said pleasantly. "Winter is on the way, and you won't be washing outside many more times, either. Shall I take these things up to the house for you, Regina?"

In his arms Andreas held a squash, a few carrots, and two heads of cabbage.

"Please, Andreas," Regina answered; "and thanks. Catri is in the house. Just call her and she will tell you where to put them."

"I didn't want to offend you, Miss Regina," faltered Andreas, awkwardly. "I was only teasing."

"Offend me? Why, no, Andreas, you didn't."

"Well, when you left so suddenly, I thought I'd said the wrong thing for sure about Peter waving to you. Pete's pretty much inter—"

Regina blushed. "No, Andreas, that was not what hurt me. It was nothing you said."

"Well, I wouldn't want to make you sad, if I could help it, and I'm sure Peter Reimann wouldn't want to either." With that Andreas went toward the house.

"Good morning, Mrs. Hofmeier," he called, tapping lightly on the door casing with the toe of his shoe. "Are you there?"

"Yes, Andreas," came her answer from the kitchen.

"Your maid is busy; so I brought up the vegetables. This will be the last. I'm cleaning off the garden today. Where shall I put them?"

"I'll bring a basket, Andreas. Just a minute."

Andreas put the vegetables into the basket and, placing his hands on his hips, shifted from one foot to the other.

"I'm awful sorry she took it like she did, Mrs. Hofmeier," he stammered. "I wouldn't offend that young lady for anything in the wide world. I want you to know that!"

"Hurt who, Andreas?"

"Your maid, Regina. She's a mighty fine lady, Mrs. Hofmeier. I didn't mean to upset her, for Peter, he—" Andreas swallowed and pulled his double chin.

"I don't understand, Andreas. What's this you're trying to tell me?"

"Well, Peter was going up the hill—" Andreas stopped abruptly, for Regina was coming across the yard with the empty clothes basket in her hand.

XIII

"Heinrich," said Catri Hofmeier that same afternoon while Regina was in the yard taking down the clothes. "Since you have to go to Zurich today, I wish you would try to find time to buy some linen material so I can make Regina a new dress. Nearly every dress she has is either worn or faded."

"You mean we'll take it out of her wages then?"

"No, I mean I'd like to surprise her. She really earns more than we give her. You've agreed with me on that."

"Yes. You must think a lot of her."

"I do. I believe I love her almost as much as my own sister. She's always sweet and patient with the babies and does her work well. And if Peter or you can get permission from Lord Englehard, Peter's coming down for a meal sometime. It's been all of three or four months since he's been here to eat with us, Heinrich. He wants to come sometime."

"Yes. But what has that to do with getting a new dress for Regina?"

"Well, I want her to look her best when he comes."

"You mean?"

"I don't mean a thing, Heinrich—not one thing, except that I want Regina to have a new dress. She needs it and she deserves it. Listen, I know this much, it was something about Peter that made her feel sad this morning."

"About Peter? Did she tell you that?"

"No. Andreas did."

"Andreas? What does he know?"

"He was starting to tell me when she came across the yard."

"And you haven't tried to find out?"

"I had no chance yet. Regina acts perfectly happy around me, and I hate to let her know that I knew she was crying. I mean, if she really was."

"Why didn't you ask Andreas, if he knows?"

"I said I had no opportunity. Heinrich, it was something about Peter's going up the hill. That's all I know."

"Up the hill? I can't imagine. He often goes up the hill."

"I'll be glad if you bring home some dress material. Will you, Heinrich?"

"How much?"

"Get enough for a dress. Ask the storekeeper."

"What color?"

"She looks very pretty in blue."

"In blue?" Heinrich patted Catri on the arm. "If I bring blue for Regina, what color shall I bring for you?"

"I really don't need a dress, Heinrich."

* * *

A dozen officers appointed by Lord Englehard and the Zurich council combed the country for miles around without success. Johann Ferlinden was nowhere to be found. One by one the hunters returned without even a clue. A reward of ten pounds was offered now to anyone who could tell of his whereabouts. Two weeks passed and the search continued.

Peter stood before Lord Englehard in his inner office. "Your honor," he said, bowing and holding his hat behind him.

"Speak, Peter," said Lord Englehard.

"Perhaps if we'd all lay off hunting for Ferlinden for a while, he might come to light. It could be he knows he's being hunted. If he finds out we aren't trying to capture him, he may expose himself."

Lord Englehard tapped his fingers on his table top.

"You might have a point there, Peter," he said, after due consideration. "I'll talk it over with the pastor and the trustees. But whatever you do, don't slacken your night watching. Who is on duty tonight?"

"I am."

"Have any of the prisoners resisted?"

"None whatsoever."

"Most harmless bunch of prisoners I've heard of. You've never had to strike any of them?"

"Never! Some of them even sang while I was bringing them up the hill."

"Strange, indeed." Lord Englehard tapped the table top again and shook his head. "But most aggravating, I'd say. It would be easier to deal with them if they would resist once in a while, at least."

Tall and handsome, Peter stood before the lord's table.

"Your honor," he said.

"Speak, Peter. What's on your mind this evening?"

"Would there be any possibility of my getting permission to go down to the pastor's house for a meal sometime? Aunt Catri would like to have me come, but I told her I'd have to get permission from you first."

"You are right, Peter. You should ask for permission. You may go this evening. I suppose, of course, the horses have been taken care of."

"This evening?" Peter looked at the clock on the wall. "Thank you Lord Englehard. I'll feed and water the horses at once. I'll tell Andreas I'll be back to take over the job at ten o'clock. If you need me before then, you know where I'll be. Thank you." He bowed and walked gracefully to the door.

Peter dressed and combed his hair. He hurried down the steps and saddled his horse. The cold November wind whipped around the north side of the castle and set his black hat wheeling across the stone courtyard. Lisette at the well saw it coming and caught it. Holding it above her head she laughed in her characteristic high shrill voice.

Peter ran after it.

"For drawing two pails of water for me, you shall have your hat, Peter Reimann," she said, still laughing.

"Very well, Lisette," answered Peter. "Give me the pail, for I'm in a hurry, and I need my hat."

"And where are you going in such a hurry, Peter?"

"Somewhere by special permission of Lord Englehard."

"Special permission?" laughed Lisette. "You mean by special command." Quickly Peter lowered the pail and drew it up.

"No, I mean by special permission. Here's your water now. How about my hat, Lisette?" Peter's voice sounded impatient.

Lisette held it behind her in teasing delight. "I said two pails, Peter," and with hat in hand, she dashed across the courtyard to the castle kitchen.

Peter frowned. He had a notion to go on without his hat, but he certainly did not want Lisette to have it in her possession. He put his hands on his hips and scowled.

"Here it is, Peter," she laughed, holding out pail number two. "And where did you say you are going in such a rush by special permission of Lord Englehard?"

"You are entirely too insistent this evening, Lisette," Peter remarked, rebukingly. "I'm going to the pastor's house for supper, if you must know." He lowered the second pail.

"Oh!" Lisette's countenance fell. Her black eyes became slits. "And I've made fresh bread and hash just especially for you tonight. Shame on you for running off."

"Especially for me?" questioned Peter in a disapproving tone.

"Of course. I heard you tell Andreas once that's what you like on cold evenings." With reluctance she handed Peter his hat, as she saw his look of disgust.

"I don't recall saying that, but maybe I did. If I'm not here you and Andreas can eat that much more." As Peter ran back to his horse. Lisette called out in her shrill voice, "Thanks for drawing the water, Peter."

* * *

Andreas came in late. All the other servants had eaten. Lisette edged up to him and eyed him inquiringly.

86

"What's the big attraction down at the pastor's house to-night?" she asked.

"Big attraction?"

"Yes, why did Peter go down there to eat?"

Andreas laughed. "I guess he wanted to get some good cooking once."

Lisette put her hands behind her and thrust out one foot. "Huh! Good cooking once? Well, I like that, Andreas. You look like you fare pretty well on mine, and Peter eats like he's always satisfied, too. I made fresh bread and hash especially for him tonight, then he goes off down the hill to eat."

"There might be other attractions down there beside the good meal," chuckled Andreas, walking over to the table.

"What attractions?" came Lisette's determined voice.

Andreas screwed his lips and stroked his double chin with his plump hand. "Well, maybe he and the pastor have things to talk over, and maybe he and his aunt have things in common, or maybe he wants to see the twins or the twins' nurse."

"Nurse?" snapped Lisette, and the corners of her mouth dropped. "You mean that blond-haired, slim young thing from Weisslingen?"

"She's blond, yes," replied Andreas "and she's slim; but she knows how to work all right."

"I'll bet. How do you know?" Lisette's face was sullen.

"I've seen her."

"Close up?"

"Yes."

"I've seen her, too, from the road; and sure, she knows how to hang up baby clothes. That's not hard work. And you'd call her pretty, would you, Andreas?" Lisette's tone changed. It was almost sad now.

"Pretty?" Andreas sat down at his place at the table and took a drink of water. "No, Regina is more than pretty, Lisete. I'd say she's plain beautiful. She is a very fine young lady, too, if I know anything about judging ladies."

Lisette handed Andreas the bread. "Here, Andreas, take some. It's cold now. Do you really think—?" she stopped abruptly. An awkward pause followed. "Who's going to feed the prisoners tonight?" she asked.

"I will after a while."

"Bread and water again?"

"That's the orders. Bread and water. You haven't had to spend much time cooking for them, Lisette; so you shouldn't be worrying about that."

"I'm not. I just wondered who was going to do it tonight since Peter is gone."

XIV

Catri put the last stitch in the collar and held the dress out at arm's length. "How about trying it on just once more, Regina," she said smiling. "I'll mark the hem, then, and finish it tomorrow. Or," glancing across the room to Heinrich, who stepped from his study at that moment, "if he will help take care of the twins for a little while [and Catri gave Heinrich one of her irresistible smiles] I might even finish it tonight while I'm in the mood for sewing. Step in your room and slip into it, Regina." Then turning again to the pastor, she said with a wistfulness in her voice, "I do hope you're in for the night once."

"I hope so, too," returned the pastor. "Bring the babies over to me. I'll hold them here on my lap." He pulled the rocking chair onto the rug. "And I'll watch you sew."

Catri's face brightened. "And you won't even mind if supper is a little late tonight?"

"No. We had an extra big dinner. I won't even mind."

"Why the big sigh?" Catri looked at Heinrich inquiringly. She placed one baby in Heinrich's right arm. "Don't you really want to after all?"

"Of course, I do. Bring the other one. Let me see, this one is Frieman, isn't it?"

"You don't hold them enough to know them apart yet. Think of it!"

"It's not that I wouldn't like to well enough, Catri. They are getting brighter, aren't they? See, I believe he recognizes me."

Catri laughed. "You should see how they respond when

Regina talks to them. She has such a way. Look, Heinrich. Isn't the dress pretty? And doesn't she look nice in it?"

Regina stepped from her bedroom, a delicate smile playing around her lips.

"Yes, indeed," admitted Heinrich. "Catri's a pretty good dressmaker, isn't she, Regina?"

"I hope before long I can sew as nicely as she does."

"It fits her perfectly, doesn't it, Heinrich?"

"Except for the length."

"Yes, and we'll take care of that tonight. Stand over here closer to the light, Regina. That's better. It won't take but a minute."

Catri dropped on both knees and started folding up the bottom of the dress. The lamp flame sputtered and flickered as the wind whistled through a crack in the windowpane.

"It must be getting colder," Catri remarked.

Heinrich sat rocking the twins, looking down over their soft little heads. "The Eichers haven't brought in their new baby yet," he said with a tired but concerned tone.

Catri's hands dropped. "Oh, Heinrich! I just can't understand why some people are so divided against such a little thing as the baptism of a baby. Why can't they obey the church and the government, and save themselves and the rest of us all this trouble? It makes you feel awful, doesn't it?"

"I'm disappointed in Simon, to say the least. We grew up together. Eicher's farm and ours touched. Simon and I often went fishing, swimming, nutting, skating, kiting, mountain climbing, hunting, and what not. We did everything together until I went away to study. I always thought Simon Eicher was about the finest fellow on earth, and now—"

"I thought something special was on your mind, Heinrich."

Heinrich looked at the floor a long time. "Well," he said at length, "it's not so hard to turn in someone you don't know very well—or someone you never liked anyhow—but Simon. Well, I just can hardly think of it."

90

"And his wife, Heinrich? Lucia is so sweet. Will you absolutely have to report them?"

"If I don't, you know what might happen to me."

"Can't someone else besides you do it?"

"I guess I could send Peter."

Regina tried to keep from blushing and seem uninterested.

"Heinrich," said Catri thoughtfully, looking at the same time at her contented babies in their father's arms, "if they wouldn't bring the baby in for baptism and he would die—" She hesitated. "Do you honestly think," she looked at Heinrich earnestly, "he would be lost forever? You don't really, do you, Heinrich?"

Heinrich looked frightened, bewildered.

"Please, Catri," he exclaimed. "That's not the major point of contention. It's disloyalty to civil authority that has to be punished. I'm tired tonight, Catri," he added wearily. "Let's not talk about babies dying and being lost now. We might even get Regina disturbed talking like this." Then looking up at Regina, he added quickly, "You've never bothered your head to think of such things, I hope. You're fully convinced in your own mind that these Anabaptists are taking the wrong attitude, aren't you?"

Heinrich stopped, for there was a knock on the door.

"You go, Catri," Heinrich said with a sudden look of agitation. "That could mean anything."

Catri pulled herself up and went reluctantly to the door. In the dimness of the oil lamp she did not recognize him at first.

"Why, Peter," she cried, "it's you."

"Of course," answered Peter. At the sight of Regina his eyes grew bigger, his lips parted. "I hope I didn't frighten you." He removed his hat.

"Come in," said Catri. "But please, please don't say that Lord Englehard has to see Heinrich right now. We haven't had our supper yet." She closed the door.

"Well, good!" laughed Peter, "I came by special permission to eat with you."

"Did you really?" Catri gasped.

A look of disappointment crossed Peter's handsome face. "Or didn't you really mean it when you asked me?"

Across the room Peter's eyes met Regina's. The sweet, serious expression on her lovely face seemed almost to frighten him.

Catri laughed. "Of course, I meant it, Peter," she answered assuredly. "I meant every word of it. Take off your coat and make yourself at home."

"Make yourself at home," added Heinrich with a genial smile. "Draw up a chair and sit here beside me. These women have me occupied as you can see, and I must say I rather enjoy it for a change, too. I haven't done this often."

"Peter, you'll just have to excuse me this time. I'm sorry, but we weren't looking for you tonight."

"Well, I can go back if it doesn't suit, Aunt Catri. I suppose Lisette might have a bite of something she'd give me, if I asked her."

"No, you won't go back. You are as welcome as anyone ever could be; only you took us by surprise. I'm surprised the lord let you off at such a busy time; but it's quite all right. You see if we had known you were coming we would have had a real meal prepared. I've been busy all day working on a dress for Regina."

Peter bowed courteously. "Good evening, Regina," he said.

"Good evening," answered Regina.

"It's a lovely dress Aunt Catri is making. I'll say that."

"But we didn't intend for anyone to see it before it was all done. But I guess it doesn't matter now, does it, Regina?"

Regina shook her head. "I guess not," she admitted shyly.

"We'll have something ready to eat in a little while, Peter," declared Catri good-naturedly. "It might be only bread and soup, but we'll find something."

"Please don't go to any bother because I came. Fix what you were going to. After all, Aunt Catri, I'm only your nephew, and I don't want you to treat me like company."

Regina disappeared into her bedroom. She did not take time to light the candle. Carefully she put the new dress across the bed and felt for the hook where she knew her brown dress was hanging.

"Cut some bread and cheese," Catri told Regina. "I'll heat some milk for soup. I'm so sorry it had to happen this way."

"What do you mean, Catri?"

"I wanted your dress all finished before Peter came."

"The new dress? Why?"

"Then you don't care?" whispered Catri.

"Care? No, Catri. I don't care. I like the dress, of course, but I don't care that it's not—"

Peter came into the kitchen holding tiny Frieda in his strong arms.

"Remember," he said, "you ladies are not to go to any extra bother because I came."

"You're hungry, and I know it," laughed Catri. "And what we have to set out will be ready in a short time. How about giving Frieda back to Heinrich and going out after a pail of fresh water?"

"With the greatest of pleasure," answered Peter.

XV

Catri did remarkably well in keeping the table conversation centered around topics other than the contention started by Conrad Grebel and the increasing trouble with his followers. She started by mentioning interesting happenings in Peter's childhood when they all lived together in Grandfather Landwirt's spacious twelve-room farmhouse near Kollbrunn. There Peter and his two younger brothers had played blacksmith and shod the old sawhorse, and Catri pretended she was their mother.

"I'll explain, Regina," began Catri, passing Regina the soup bowl. "My oldest sister is Peter's mother, you know. She married Alfred Reimann, and they lived with us on the home place for ten years. So you see I know all about Peter's life from the day he was born."

"Wait a minute," laughed Peter; "you were only six months old when I was born."

"That's right, Peter," answered Catri. "Well, I can remember from four years on. Anyway, Regina, we grew up together and had lots of fun as children. I know all about the naughty things Peter has ever done as well as the nice and funny things, and he knows all about my naughty pranks, too. That's why Peter and I feel pretty close to each other. His two brothers have disobeyed authority by slipping off to fight for the King of France, and his parents are both dead; so I claim Peter as my own. By the way, Mother was here to see us the Sunday you were gone, Regina. She asked about you."

"She did?"

"Of course. I was glad to tell her you were doing fine."

"What did she say about the twins?"

"She practically went into a rapture over them. She wants us all to come over sometime and bring you along."

"Me?" asked Regina.

"Yes, of course. She likes you very much. But I doubt if we could go before spring since Heinrich is so busy here."

Before the supper was half over, Catri very tactfully had Regina helping in the conversation, too, telling about her childhood, her brothers, her parents, her appreciation of nature. She described the scenery in and around Weisslingen and the sunset on the Alps on very rare occasions. Regina was unconscious that her cheeks glowed, her eyes shone, her smile grew more radiant as the hour passed. Even in her brown faded dress she was beautiful. Peter watched her admiringly. Across the table his eyes met hers a number of times.

After supper Peter helped clear the table.

"This seems like old times again," beamed Catri. "I hope things will make a turn so you can come more often."

"I hope so, too, Aunt Catri."

Crash! As Regina was clearing the table she dropped the beautiful soup bowl. It broke in a dozen pieces right in front of Peter, splashing thickened milk on the floor and all over his shoes.

"Oh!" she cried. "I'm sorry, Catri. I'm sorry, Peter. Look at your shoes." She covered her face with her hands.

"Don't feel bad about that," Peter said comfortingly. "It will easily wash off."

"But the beautiful bowl," cried Regina, sadly. "Catri, how can I ever make this right with you? I'll try to replace it someday."

"Don't worry, Regina," said Catri. "It was only a soup bowl."

"But your very best one. I've often heard you say how you prized it. Didn't you tell me your favorite aunt gave it to you as a wedding present?"

Peter started gathering up the pieces.

"Yes, Dear," said Catri. "But please, we'll not let this spoil our evening. Accidents will happen with anyone."

"I know," Regina said, "but I'm sorry I was so awkward. But I didn't mean to, Catri."

"Of course you didn't mean to," Peter ventured. "We all know that. See, it's all gathered up now, and if you give me a damp cloth, I'll soon have my shoes and the floor cleaned, too."

"I will replace it if I possibly can, Catri," Regina insisted.

The crash frightened the twins. Both cried lustily. So while Catri helped Heinrich quiet them and put them to bed, Peter offered to help Regina in the kitchen.

He wiped several dishes, looking at her in silent admiration.

"I seldom do this in the castle kitchen," he began timidly. "Do you like to?"

"Yes, I do here. I never had to at home because I helped Father on the farm. It's something different for a change."

"My father always said it's a good thing for all of us to do something every day we don't like to do. Most boys don't like to wipe dishes. At least my brothers didn't."

"Then your father would say that it was good to do something they didn't like, I suppose?"

"Yes."

"Did it help?"

"I think perhaps a little. I'm not certain."

"I guess I'll have to try saying that, too, then."

"Do you have to do something every day you don't like to do?"

"Just about every day. Sometimes twice."

"Oh!" Regina looked up hopefully. "Is it what you had to do Monday morning?"

Peter's hand stopped wiping the cup he was holding. "Monday morning? I don't recall doing it Monday morning, but I had to do it twice this evening. Monday morning—" Peter swallowed hard. An awkward pause followed. He cleared his throat.

"You were washing Monday morning, weren't you?" he said softly.

"Yes, every Monday morning and other mornings besides. The twins, you know, make a lot of washing necessary."

"Yes, of course." Peter put the cup on the table and picked up another. "I went by when you were talking to Andreas," he continued.

"Yes."

"Then you did see me?"

"Yes."

"You didn't wave, did you?" Peter's voice was low and a bit unsteady now.

"Did you wave to me?" she asked. "I supposed you were waving at Andreas. Yes, I saw you."

"At Andreas?" Peter rubbed the dish towel over and over the cup in his hand. "I see Andreas many times a day," he said. "I waved to you, but I don't want to do anything improper, Regina. Yesterday I waved again and you did not answer. If I was out of place, I beg your pardon. Please tell me."

"You see," Regina said, "I was so taken back at what you were doing, I just didn't feel like waving. I couldn't, Peter."

"Oh, you mean—?" Peter's straight shoulders sagged for a moment. His face felt warm. "I don't quite understand you, Regina. I was obeying orders, you know. You wouldn't want me to be a coward, would you?"

"Indeed not," answered Regina. "I hate cowards. I mean when I saw what you were doing—sending that poor couple up to the castle—it made me feel—well—so awful. I had to think, What if they had been my own parents? They looked so harmless and—and—"

Peter stared at Regina in amazement.

"Regina, but your parents aren't Anabaptists!"

"No."

"And surely never will be."

"I don't suppose so." Regina looked at him beseechingly. "Doesn't it hurt your soul to have to take those people up to the prison?"

"Hurt my soul?" For a long moment Peter looked at Regina.

"Yes."

"Yes," he said softly. "I guess it does. At least, if you think it should, I'd say it does. But I can't be a coward now. Lord Englehard is really counting on me, you know. I've been with him for three years trying hard to work my way up. I can't give way to my feelings now, Regina."

Slowly he wiped another dish.

"There is one thing that would really hurt my soul," he said at length. "One thing."

"And what is that?" she said.

"If I really cared for a girl and she'd drive me away."

A delicate sad smile played around Regina's lips. "And lock you in prison?" she asked. "And bring you nothing but bread and water for days?"

Peter laughed very softly.

"If I didn't know better," he said, "I might be tempted to conclude you were an Anabaptist sympathizer. You surely are most extraordinary."

"Oh, no. I'm not," she answered quickly. "I'm very ordinary. I just never could stand to see anyone suffer—relative, friend, or stranger."

"And so that would include me, wouldn't it?" laughed Peter. "I'm not a relative or a stranger exactly, but I hope a friend."

When Catri came into the kitchen, Peter was wiping the last spoon and Regina was pouring the dishwater into the wooden pail near the door.

XVI

"Come here, Catri," called Regina one Sunday morning. "Frieman has a tooth. Did you know?"

"No. Then that's why he cried last night! Regina, our baby troubles are only beginning, I suppose. I'm glad Heinrich bought them each a bed, even though it does crowd our room. At least they can't kick each other now. Heinrich was awake all night. It wasn't the babies' fault, though. He can't seem to decide what to read in church. Did you hear him reading one Scripture and then another?"

"Yes."

"Sometimes I feel like going in there and taking that Bible and burning it."

"Why, Catri!" Regina gasped. "Why do you say that?"

"Because it always—" She hesitated. "Well, not always, but it usually gives him a headache. I pity him more every Sunday. There's so much in the Bible that is too deep for us to understand anyhow." Catri sighed. "So no wonder he has such a hard time finding what he wants to read to his congregation."

"But I can't understand," said Regina.

"Neither can I, Regina, but since all this trouble, nothing is like it used to be. Nothing."

"Do all the pastors feel the same way?" Regina asked. "Do they all have such a time on Sundays?"

"I wish I knew," sighed Catri, wearily. "Heinrich says the Anabaptists read the Bible because it makes them calm and happy and unafraid. Even unafraid of what anyone will do to them. But of course, that's just Anabaptist talk. Heinrich

99

says they're under some evil power or influence that makes them act the way they do. Heinrich says Satan has power. It's not the Bible that makes them act like this. For Heinrich's sake I actually dread to see Sundays come. Say, Regina," Catri pressed a forefinger against her cheek, "you've been here with us now for more than four months."

"Yes—yes, I know."

"And I've never heard you talk about the Anabaptist trouble. Heinrich and I are discussing it all the time. How can you keep so quiet?"

Regina's cheeks grew warm. "Well, you see," she faltered, "I know so little about it—I'd rather just listen."

"Then it's not that you aren't interested in Heinrich's work and all his troubles?"

"No." Regina patted Frieman and held his little head close to her cheek. "Oh, no."

Catri picked up her coat and walked slowly toward the front door. "I'll be going now, Regina. The service likely will not last long. I hope the babies sleep now. Look, Regina. Someone is coming. Who can that be?"

A tall, well-dressed young man was tying his horse near the gate when Regina looked out.

"It's my brother Michel! It is!"

"How lovely! Ask him to stay for dinner."

"I'll go lay Frieman down. You meet him, Catri. Tell him I'm coming."

Catri greeted Michel with a hearty handshake. "Just go in. Regina is happily surprised. She is putting the babies to bed. I'm going over to the church service, but I'll soon be back."

"Thank you." Michel smiled and bowed courteously.

"Michel!" Regina met him at the door. He kissed her on each cheek.

"So early. How did you manage it? I'm thrilled!" She led him into the house.

"I was lonesome to see you," Michel said. "I decided I'd

come and see you for a little while, then go over home. Bad weather might set in any day, you know."

"Do take a chair, here," she said. "I'll take your coat and hat. It's so good to see you, Michel."

"Have you been home lately, Regina?" Michel asked, pulling up a chair.

"No. I'm waiting for Hofmeiers to tell me I can take a day off. The babies are fussy now and I hate to ask. I want to go before it gets cold."

Michel looked through the house. "This is a nice place to work, Regina," Michel said.

"Yes, I like it here. It's a cheery little house, isn't it? And Hofmeiers have been kind. Tiptoe into that room there and take a look at the twins. Do. They are sleeping. You never saw two sweeter babies in your life."

Michel went quietly into the bedroom and back again.

"Aren't they dear, Michel?"

"Yes."

"Sit here beside me," whispered Regina. "And now while we're here alone for a little while, let's talk fast. Do you have any news from Hans?"

"Not a thing from him, but I've heard there's plenty of excitement over in the Emmental."

"What do you mean, Michel?"

"The Anabaptists have been holding secret meetings, and many have been taken to prison."

"Oh!"

"Friday I heard a man from Lucerne say that as many as fifteen at a time were forced to walk all the way to Bern to be tried. I have to wonder how Uncle Rudolf and Aunt Margrit are faring."

"Father never went over there, did he?"

"No. I begged him not to. Things in Zurich are pretty tense, too. You probably know all about it."

"What do you mean?"

"Felix Manz and George Blaurock were holding a secret meeting in a forest near Gruningen the other day and were seized. They're in the Wellenberg prison now."

"I heard the pastor telling Catri something about it, but I didn't hear it all."

"In March, Grebel, Manz, and Blaurock were in prison, sentenced to live on bread and water till they died. But somehow they all got out that time."

"I remember."

"A lot of people thought after Grebel died this trouble would die, too, but it's worse now than at any time. Manz and Blaurock have been going on teaching and preaching and baptizing in spite of threats and mandates. They act like they think civil law doesn't amount to anything. I think it is stupid of them. I can't understand their attitude. They profess to be spiritual leaders, but—well, I can't see it, Regina. This past week we've been printing a paper Zwingli is putting out in another effort to check this mad movement. He calls Grebel a satanic hypocrite and his doctrine a vice, a malicious, unchristian, offensive weed which must be destroyed before it spreads any farther."

Regina folded her hands and held them tightly clasped in her lap. She watched Michel intently.

"He says these Anabaptist leaders are to be feared more than a disease or wild beasts or enemies or war. I don't suppose the situation over here is any better."

Regina's glance never shifted. "Michel," she said, "the situation here is no better. And I think I can't stand to watch one more Anabaptist being taken up that hill to prison."

"Why do you say that, Regina? I should think you'd be used to it by this time."

"Used to it? No, Michel, I'll never get used to that! I wish they would take them up some other way, if they have to, so I wouldn't have to see it. Just yesterday I saw Peter—he's one of the lord's horsemen—taking two young couples up the hill and I could hear them singing while they went past, until they got to those two big weeping willow trees near the bridge. It sent an awful feeling through me, Michel. I doubt if I will ever forget it as long as I live. Wouldn't you hate to be Peter?"

Michel sat thinking. "He wasn't beating them, was he?"

"No. They didn't need to be beaten. They walked along singing just as though they were going to a wedding or church service, Peter following on his horse. Oh, I'd hate to be Peter or any one of those men who have to go out and bring them in," Regina shivered.

"Someone has to do it, Regina. We'd be in a worse mess if no one obeyed the government. Have you thought of that?"

Regina's serious eyes studied her brother.

"I guess maybe you're right," she whispered. "Do you think after all Zwingli is right?" she touched his arm.

Michel fumbled with his vest.

"I had to state my belief before Bartsche and a board of trustees yesterday or give up my job."

"Why?"

"Bartsche overheard me asking that man from Lucerne some questions or else the man told Bartsche what I asked him. I'm not sure which, but I do know I have to be more careful from now on. He may have been a spy sent in to draw me out. I have to wonder."

"But—but I thought you often said you were tight-mouthed in the shop, Michel."

"I thought I was, but I said things are getting more serious."

"Oh!"

"Regina, I came over to warn you, not to scare you. Do be careful what you say or ask."

"And—and what did you ask that was so out of place or so very wrong?"

"Regina, I haven't long to stay. I want to get home by noon, if possible. No use going into that. I came too near bringing

103

disgrace on the family and myself. Bartsche was angry with me. But it's all fixed up now. You can be thankful you live here where you can let the pastor do the worrying for you, Regina."

"Catri said I should invite you to stay for dinner," Regina said sadly, "and now you talk about leaving already."

"I can't stay, Regina. I must be going." Michel stood up, tall, handsome, broad-shouldered.

"Why, Michel," cried Regina. "You just came! I'm not nearly done talking to you. What belief did you state before all those men? Tell me. I've got to know that."

"I agreed that Zwingli is doing the best or better than any other reformer could do. And I promised that I will henceforth ask no foolish questions nor make any remarks to cause anyone to suspect where I stand. I promised not to say anything that would give anyone any reason to think I am an Anabaptist sympathizer or wavering in my loyalty to and support of the state church, and so on and so forth. I took my stand, Regina, that Conrad Grebel started a bad thing."

"Oh!"

"Good-by, Regina," Michel reached for his coat and hat. "I'd stay longer, but I must get home. It's been nice to see you this little while. I'm so glad you came here to work for the pastor. Here you are safe."

"And—and you're going to warn the folks, too?"

"Yes, yes!" He walked toward the door. "What shall I tell them about you?"

"Tell them I'm all right. Tell them I'll come home to see them as soon as I can. Tell them not to worry about me. Tell them I'm trying to be careful and that I pray for them and Hans every night." She held his arm. "Tell them I'm still searching."

"Searching for what?"

"The answers."

"Answers to what?"

"Our questions."

"What questions?"

"Michel," exclaimed Regina, "the same questions we've been searching the answers to for more than two years."

"I think we might as well quit searching, Regina." Despair was in Michel's voice. "We might as well quite asking ourselves those questions. If the preachers and theologians and doctors and lords can't find the answers, how can we? If men as smart as Ulrich Zwingli and the council can't stop this commotion by preaching or writing pamphlets, or by persecution, how can we figure it out? Let's stop trying. No one knows the answers. Does the pastor?" Michel pointed toward the stone church across the yard.

"No," answered Regina sadly. "He does not know the answers."

XVII

In the weeks following, the dark cloud which hung over all of northern Switzerland grew darker. Repeated threats of war between the Catholic and Protestant cantons furnished background for the growing unrest between the Anabaptists and the Zwinglians. Things in and around Kyburg were in constant stir. Heinrich Hofmeier made repeated calls to the castle and sat in long consultations with Lord Englehard and the board of trustees. Often he left home early in the morning and was gone most of the day. Sometimes he and Peter went away on horseback together and held private discussions in the yard on their return. Whenever he was home, he was tense and nervous and drank wine from the jug he kept in the kitchen cupboard. Once Heinrich did not come home until long past midnight. That night Catri cried.

Since the garden now needed no gardening, the gardener never came down to work. Regina often saw him, nevertheless, going up and down the castle hill on his brown horse. Several times he came over and talked with her when she was hanging up the wash.

"Regina," he remarked one morning, "the next time Peter comes down to take a meal with you, fix fresh bread and hash."

"Why that?" Regina wondered.

"I heard that's what he likes." Andreas' eyes twinkled.

"Go on, Andreas," said Regina reprovingly. "You don't have time to stop and tell me such foolishness and I'm not interested either. But since you're here, I want to ask you something. Do you know Zurich very well?"

"Zurich is a big city, Regina. Why?"

"Could you tell me where there's a store in Zurich that sells soup bowls?"

"Soup bowls? Well, now, I suppose there's more than one store that sells soup bowls, if I could just think." Andreas scratched his head. "I think there's a store that handles all kinds of pots and pans and bowls about a five or ten-minute walk south of the Great Münster Church. But I'm not positive. Want me to find out for you?"

"Don't bother, Andreas," answered Regina. "I just wondered."

"I might forget to ask anybody with all this hubbub going on. The lord is vexed because we haven't rounded up Johann, the monk, yet. He says he's almost certain he's hiding some place in this neighborhood."

"Why does he think that?" Regina asked, studying Andreas' plump face with her big serious eyes.

"Because so many Anabaptists from around here have been brought in. Someone is baptizing them; they won't tell who. There's going to be some excitement yet, unless I miss my guess. There comes Peter now. We're to try once more." Andreas crossed the yard and mounted his horse and the two were off.

* * *

"When will this end, Heinrich," sighed Catri a few mornings later. Her voice sounded depressed, sad, and even fretful.

Heinrich looked at Catri with tired, troubled eyes. "God only knows," he answered, pulling on his overcoat. "I wish someone was smart enough to give a solution. All the governments, all the lords and preachers, all the Catholics and Protestants together with all their committees and boards and delegates don't seem to be able to check this thing. It looks as though all of Zwingli's books and speeches have failed." Heinrich reached for his hat and walked to the kitchen door. "The only thing left now is to use more severe measures of persecu-

107

tion. Zwingli says this doctrine has got to be uprooted, and he is right."

Regina was bathing one of the babies on the kitchen table.

"Please go out the other door," she said. "He might take cold if you open this one."

"Of course. I didn't notice." Heinrich turned and kicked his shin on the rocking chair. He let out an oath.

"You're too tired to start out," Catri cried, following him to the door. "I'm sorry the chair was in your way. Where are you going today?"

"To Zurich again." He fastened his coat and tightened his belt.

"For what, Heinrich?"

"Some Anabaptists are to go before the council. The prison up there is so full they don't know what to do with them any more. Since some of them are my former church members, I've got to be there to hear what they have to say. I'd rather do almost anything else today."

"Must you go?" sighed Catri.

Heinrich drew a long, deep breath. "Of course. But Simon will be in that group. I can't understand why he's allowed himself to get under this satanic power. I must be off. Here they come already."

* * *

From the kitchen window, Regina caught a glimpse of the procession coming down the hill. She wrapped the baby snugly in his blanket, and hurried across the room. She stood watching.

Andreas and another man she did not know were leading the procession, each on horseback. They were carrying spears polished until they shone. Thirty calm-faced prisoners, seven of which were women, were following, walking at a rapid pace. Last of all came Peter on his horse, and he, too, carried a spear. Regina was paralyzed. The pastor mounted his horse and took his place at the rear beside Peter. She stood motionless until the procession was out of sight. Quickly she wiped her eyes with a corner of the baby's blanket.

Slowly Regina finished Frieman's bath. When she took him into the bedroom, she found Catri crying.

"What's the matter?" she asked tenderly.

"I'll be all right," answered Catri, trying to smile. "Things just aren't what I expected; that's all." She sat on the edge of the bed, looking down as she rubbed her hand over the woolen spread. "I guess I had too rosy a dream of being married to a pastor, Regina. I had no idea life would be so uncertain and mixed up and disappointing. I hardly have a husband these days. Gone all day and sometimes all night, and when he is at home we have no family life at all. You know how it's been. Heinrich's so tired and nervous he hardly takes time even to look at the twins." She wiped her eyes. "I shouldn't be telling my troubles to you. There's nothing you can do about it."

"I don't mind your telling me, Catri," said Regina. "I feel sorry for you. Really I do."

"And I feel sorry for Heinrich. I guess I shouldn't pity myself like this, but—I'm sure if he had it to do over, studying to become a priest would be about the last thing—oh, dear, what am I saying? I'm entirely too free in expressing myself to you. Forget it, Regina. I'm nervous and upset this morning. I wish I could run home for a while and unload to Mother."

"Well, why don't you?"

"You don't mean that. Leave you here alone with these two babies?"

"Why not? Heinrich will likely be gone all day. So there won't be any dinner to get. You could go and get back before dark and spend several hours with your mother. You haven't been anywhere since I came. And your mother has been here only once. Why don't you go?"

Catri sat thinking. "You don't think it's too cold?"

109

"It's not real cold outside. The sun is shining. You have a warm coat."

"And you wouldn't mind, if I'd leave you here alone?"

"Not a bit, Catri. The babies will keep me company."

"Then I'll turn about fair play. I'll let you have off one day next week if I go today."

"All right, that's fair enough. While you are getting yourself ready, I'll make you a cup of hot tea."

"Thank you, Regina. You are kind to me and thoughtful."

XVIII

The day was not long for Regina. After finishing Frieda's bath she played with the babies on her bed for almost an hour before tucking them into their own beds for their forenoon nap. It was soon noon, for there were ashes to be carried out, hearths to be cleaned, sweeping, dusting, and general straightening up that needed to be done throughout the house. After that Regina made a plum pudding, for she was certain that Catri and Heinrich would both come home hungry.

As for Regina, since witnessing the scene from the kitchen window that morning, she had no appetite. Placing a chair close to the fire in the living room, she decided to mend her stockings while the babies slept. The house was clean, warm, and quiet. With one stocking slipped over her left hand, her threaded needle in the other, she sat watching the smoldering embers before she put on another piece of wood. She was glad to be alone. Michel's last visit had confused her more than ever.

When the twins awoke, Regina was still sitting by the fire, the stocking still on her hand, unmended. She put it down and hurriedly prepared their midday porridge.

It was growing dusk when Catri returned. "I'm so glad you made it possible for me to go home today, Regina. Were the babies good?" Catri asked.

"Of course. They slept unusually long, and only the last hour has Frieda been fussy."

"I suppose it's her teeth. As soon as I warm myself I'll take her. I don't suppose Heinrich got back yet, did he?"

"I haven't seen him."

"Do you know what Mother told me, Regina?" Catri stood with her back to the fire, her hands behind her. "She told me I should be ashamed of myself for fretting and talking the way I did to you. She said I should be proud of Heinrich and help to put dignity into his office and responsibilities and help him be courageous. I ought to be glad to make a sacrifice for such a worthy cause. He's out trying to help save the church. I see it now, Regina. I'm sorry I talked the way I did. I'm ashamed. I'll admit I've been rather babyish. Mother reminded me, too, that I'm setting a poor example before you. Oh, I'm so ashamed, Regina.

"Mother said Peter stopped in and chatted with her a few minutes the other day when he was in the neighborhood, and he let the cat out of the bag. You know Peter's always been confidential with Mother. From what he told Mother, I guess he thinks you're someone pretty nice, Regina."

"Me?" Regina asked astonished, almost frightened.

"You mean you aren't thrilled?" asked Catri in a tone verging on disappointment.

"Well—I—why, Catri, he—he—hardly knows me—and anyway, Andreas said he might become a knight and I'm only a common, ordinary—"

"Peter become a knight?" laughed Catri. "You don't know Andreas. He was just talking. Lord Englehard has often told Heinrich he wished Peter were eligible. He's so strong and handsome and brave. If he could only find Johann Ferlinden and bring him in, then I do believe Lord Englehard—" Catri stopped short. "What's wrong, Regina? You look as if you were about to faint. Are you sick, Dear?"

Regina sat down. Catri took Frieda out of her arms.

"I'll be all right in a minute," Regina said. "I haven't felt just exactly well all day."

"Then why did you tell me to leave you? Go in and lie down a little while. I see you cleaned the house and set the table. I hope you didn't work hard all day long."

112

"No, Catri, I didn't work too hard. And I really don't want to lie down. If I don't eat any supper and go to bed early, I think I'll be all right in the morning."

*　*　*

Several days later while Lisette was polishing the railing on the stairway, she heard every word the lord and Peter were saying, for they were standing in the hall at the foot of the stairs.

"Before I forget it, Peter, the pastor asked me last evening if we had an extra horse he could borrow for tomorrow."

"An extra horse? What for?" asked Peter.

"He said they promised their maid she could have tomorrow off and she wants to borrow a horse so she can go home and come back by way of Zurich. I believe he said she wants to do some shopping. I told Heinrich I'd ask you. You know better than I do what you've got there."

Peter thought a moment. "We have two horses, Beth and Bel, that are gentle. I think she could handle either of them."

"Then you see to it that one of them is delivered to the pastor's gate not later than eight o'clock tomorrow. Heinrich has been very faithful in co-operating with me, and it's not often that he asks for a special favor. I know he can't spare his own horse."

"Of course not," agreed Peter.

Lisette rubbed the railing furiously; then hurrying to her room above the kitchen, she exchanged her shoes for an older pair and went directly to Lady Englehard's room and rapped gently.

"Come."

Lisette bowed. "Lady Englehard," she began, "it is ever and ever so long since I've gotten a new pair of shoes. Mine are badly worn and scuffed."

Lady Englehard glanced down at Lisette's shoes.

"If you could let me go to Zurich tomorrow, I could buy a new pair."

"Do you have the money?"

"Yes, I've been saving, Lady Englehard."

"It would take you all day, Lisette; we couldn't spare you that long."

"But, Lady Englehard," ventured Lisette, "Peter has two horses, Bel and Beth."

"But they aren't his horses, Lisette."

"No, Lady Englehard, I know. Only I heard the lord telling Peter he could loan one of them to the pastor's maid to go to Zurich tomorrow; so I thought perhaps I could borrow the other one."

"You mean you and the pastor's maid are friends?"

"No, Lady Englehard, I have never even spoken to the pastor's maid. I've seen her in the yard twice when I went down to Kyburg for you. I wouldn't be going with her, but if I could borrow a horse, I wouldn't need to be gone long." Lisette's hands behind her fumbled with her apron strings. She shifted from one foot to the other.

"I'll have to see what Lord Englehard says," answered Lady Englehard. "You do need new shoes. But nothing, positively nothing, dare interfere with the lord's plans, you understand that."

"Yes, Lady Englehard, I understand."

* * *

At eight o'clock the next morning, Peter was at the gate with Beth well curried and mane combed.

"Good-by, Regina," called Catri from the door. "We'll be looking for you this evening. Give your folks our best regards."

"I will."

Peter removed his hat and bowed and helped her on to the horse.

"You said one time you were fond of horses," reminded Peter, smiling and handing her the reins. "That was the first time we met out there by the garden fence. Do you remember?"

114

"Yes," she answered softly, "I remember."

"This is the first time I've had the privilege of helping you enjoy one," Peter's voice was low. "It makes me very happy to be the one to bring Beth down for you," he stroked Beth's neck.

"And I do thank you, Peter."

"Do your parents know you're coming today?"

"No. I had no way of telling them. They'll be greatly surprised, I'm thinking."

"I know they'll be happily surprised, too."

"This will be my second visit home since I came."

"Now take care of yourself," Peter said. "And don't get lost in Zurich."

"I won't," she laughed. "I've been there several times."

"When you get back tonight, I'll come down and get Beth, unless I'm out for Lord Englehard. You'll be back before dark, won't you?" Peter rubbed Beth's nose and straightened her mane.

"I must be," she answered.

XIX

Friedrich and Melka were sitting at the breakfast table talking when Regina walked in without knocking.

"Don't be frightened," she said quickly. "I knew I would surprise you, but," she put an arm across her mother's shoulder, "don't be alarmed. I haven't been dismissed, and nothing bad has happened to me."

She kissed her mother, then her father. "You're eating rather late, aren't you? Is there any warm milk left?"

"No, Dear, but I'll warm some. You must be cold. Take off your wraps. You'll be with us all day, I hope. Do tell us how this happened."

"I can't stay quite all day," Regina pulled off her woolen gloves and head scarf. "I broke Catri's best and cherished soup bowl. She doesn't know it, but I want to go back by way of Zurich and get one to replace it."

"Back by way of Zurich? You can't do it, Regina."

"Why not, Father? The pastor borrowed one of the lord's horses from the castle barn for me."

"That's different. Here, let me hang up your coat. I thought you walked. But even so, you can't stay long and get back to Kyburg before dark. Did you put the horse inside?"

"Yes."

"Strange neither Mother nor I heard you coming. We were so busy talking."

Regina sat down and drew the chair up to the table. "I came early because I want to leave by noon or before." She looked at the clock. "I ought to get back then before dark. My, it's good to be home!"

116

"I'm very glad you came, Regina. Mother don't wash the dishes. Let's talk while Regina's here."

"Here's the milk, Dear, and I brought you some bread, too. Regina, you look thin. Are you working too hard at Hofmeier's?"

"No, Mother, I don't have to work any harder than I expected to. I'd much rather be busy than not."

"And they're good to you?" asked Father.

"Good!" answered Regina. "I really don't know how they could be kinder to me. I'm all right. And I'm not much thinner than I was."

"Do you get enough to eat?" asked Mother.

"I get all I care for. It's you and Father who look thin. Are you getting enough to eat? Father, you seem tired and troubled."

"Mother and I have lost our appetites and hours of sleep in the past weeks, Regina, mostly over Hans, I guess."

"Over Hans?" Regina set the cup on the saucer. "Have you heard from him?"

"Nothing. Not one word. But Michel has been telling us how things are going over in the Emmental."

"Michel came to see me."

"He told us he did. He told us how he warned you, Regina. He says it is terrible for the Anabaptists to oppose the government. The more I think over all he's been telling us, the more I'm convinced he's right. And, Regina, Michel is in a position to know."

"What do you mean, Father?"

"I mean what I said, Regina. Michel must be right. He says the Anabaptists simply cannot be taking the right attitude. When I think how Uncle Rudolf allowed himself to be influenced, I—I just can't sleep, to think Hans is over there! We've both lost sleep over all this. Michel said the government is really going to take this situation in hand. I mean they are doing it right now."

117

"Don't look at me so shocked, Dear. Until recently, Michel urged and even begged me not to go to Langnau. I know he thought I was too uncertain about the Anabaptists, but listen, Regina, since Michel has had to take his stand, we're taking ours, too. Yes, God helping me, we're going to Langnau to plead with Hans to come home before he brings disgrace on the family." Father stood up and ran his hands deep into his trouser pockets.

"Disgrace?" whispered Regina. "You—you really mean you are going to Langnau?"

"If we're living by morning, we're starting out unless we leave today yet. We'll bring Hans along home with us, if possible."

"And you, Mother? You're going, too?"

"We've talked it over from every angle," answered Father. "It's settled. I'm going. And it's settled I can't leave Mother alone. If you were here, it would be different."

"And how will you go?" asked Regina.

"On horseback. I've already traded material for a horse for Mother."

"I wondered why there were two horses in the shed. But, Mother," cried Regina, "it's sixty-five miles to Langnau and it's winter. You know how cold it gets in January."

"We've talked it all over many times in the last week. That's why our breakfast was so late this morning. We talked until after midnight last night. The Anabaptists get out in all kinds of weather, and if they can, we can, too. I have good warm clothes."

"Regina," put in Father, "when Heinrich Hofmeier was here one time, he said it's not an easy job nor a pleasant one, but if we all work together, we'll get the Anabaptists conquered. It looks pretty much now like a hopeless task, but Michel said we've got to do our part. You should have heard him the last time he was home. He was really worked up. We've got to stand together as a family, Regina."

"But, Father," cried Regina.

"I should never have allowed Hans to go back to Langnau. It was a mistake. I see it now. Hans was too young."

"But you know how he felt, Father," declared Regina, feebly. "Michel even helped him go through Zurich."

"I know. But he disobeyed authority. If Michel isn't careful and if we don't support him, his whole future will be ruined." Father buried his face in his trembling hands. "I've got to go and bring Hans home and I've got to try to help Rudolf see the mistake he's made."

"But he's already been rebaptized," said Regina.

"But he can recant," cried Father. "Some others have."

"And—and you really think he might?"

"I'll do all in my power to make him see it." Friedrich Strahm got to his feet. He leaned against the wall and looked out the window, down across the garden lot. Regina got up and stood beside him.

"You didn't talk like this the last time I was here, Father." A tear fell on Regina's dress; then another.

"Yes," he answered softly. "I know. But I'm sure I am a little wiser now than I was even though I've never been able to get a Bible. Michel is smart, and he says if I did have one, it would confuse me more than ever. I'll just let him tell me what to believe from now on."

"Tell me, Father—" Regina wiped her eyes. She did not finish her sentence.

"Michel would have been relieved of his job in the print shop if he hadn't made his stand. Think of it, Regina, after he's worked so hard to learn the trade."

"Yes, he told me, but—"

"Michel is not stupid, Regina."

"I know." Regina looked at the floor.

"It would have been a disgrace, if he would have been taken before the Zurich Council to be questioned."

"You think so, Father?"

"Dear, Regina." Reproof and kindness were in his low voice. "Don't plague me with such questions now. By this time you surely know better. You've been at the pastor's home for five months now. And thank God you are there. I wouldn't have considered letting you go into any other home in the entire canton. You can see with your own eyes how hard the pastor is working to save the church. Surely you have learned the answers to your questions, Regina." He walked back and forth across the kitchen. "I sincerely hope you will never allow yourself to go through all the torments we've been through. It's been terrible."

"Tell me, Father," she whispered, looking up into his thin troubled face.

"I can't," he answered. "I can't. I want to forget." Friedrich Strahm placed his hands on his wife's shoulders. "You surely could tell we were both undecided about this whole situation when you were home the last time," he began, trying to calm himself.

"Yes, but I didn't blame you, Father. I thought we all were disturbed—even Michel."

"But I am convinced now that even if Zwingli may be wrong on a few points," Father put his hands behind him, "he's still a great man, Regina, and worthy of our respect and support. No one is perfect. Some good people like the Wittmers and Brohens have been hoodwinked into believing this doctrine. Some of the Anabaptist views might even seem right on the surface, but they can't be right, Regina. It's a deceptive doctrine. I wish I'd never seen Johann Ferlinden. I'm going to forget him. We must take Michel's advice and stand together as a family, Regina. We must be loyal to the church and the government. We must go to Langnau and bring Hans home. We must do what we can to help Uncle Rudolf see his mistake before it's too late." Friedrich Strahm was trembling.

"Father, you make me cold all over," Regina whispered. "And you are all ready to start out, Mother?" she asked sadly.

"We know it's an undertaking, but we've both been so worried about Hans, I'm willing to try anything. It can't be worse than what we've been going through, Regina. We'll take two days for the trip. We'll stay in a hotel some place the first night."

From where she was standing, Regina could see out over the cold Weisslingen Valley. How bleak it looked! How unlike the night she and her father had seen the gorgeous sun on the distant Alps!

"Michel said no one knows the solution," she said at length. "No one." Her voice sounded far away, dismal, and sad.

"That's right. No one knows, but the solution to our problem, Michel says, is to stand true to what we were taught all these years. We'll get nowhere if everyone opposes authority. Regina, give me a message to take to Hans."

"What do you mean, Father?"

"Something you say may go a long way in bringing him back."

Regina stood looking out the window. Once smoke curled out of every chimney in the valley. From where she stood she counted three lonesome, smokeless chimneys.

"Well, tell him I'm very eager to see him. And—and—Father—" her voice broke.

"Yes."

"Why don't we have prayer together before you start out and before I go back to Kyburg?"

Mr. Strahm studied Regina a long minute before he spoke. "Has the pastor taught you how to pray?"

"The pastor?" she asked through a mist of tears. "I have never heard him pray except the day he baptized the twins."

"What?"

"That's right, Father. We bow our heads at the table, but if he prays other times, he does it in secret. I thought perhaps he would teach me to read the Bible, but he says I'm better off not to know it."

"Well, perhaps—perhaps, after all, the secret prayers are the best anyway. That's the only way we know how to pray. Let us bow our heads now." And Father sat down.

Regina bowed her head, tears welled up in her eyes, and the next moment she was shaking with sobs.

XX

Mrs. Strahm broke the silence. "Why do you cry, Dear?"

Regina wiped her eyes and pushed back her hair. "Please, Mother, I could not explain, if I tried. I'll not cry any more, if I can help it. But—I—I hope you and Father," she picked at the corner of her handkerchief, "are doing the right thing." She paused to brush away a tear. "But now that you have really made up your minds to go, why not get ready and go with me as far as Zurich?"

Mr. Strahm looked at his wife.

"Shall we?" he asked presently.

"Tomorrow might be stormy. I'm ready any time you are."

"Then let's go with her. I'll lock up the shop and set things in order while you pack some lunch to take along."

"The whole thing shocks me," said Regina, leaning against the back of the chair. "It just doesn't—I mean nothing seems real or something is wrong."

Friedrich Strahm crossed the room and folded his daughter in his arms. He was struggling to keep back tears. "This whole thing has been very hard on us," he said. A tear fell on Regina's blond hair. "No one knows what we've gone through. I know you can't understand, but I'm trying to make a bright future for all my children." He held her out at arm's length and looked into her face. A tear trickled down his cheek. "Regina," he said in a husky voice, "I'm doing the best I know. I'm standing between a thousand fires and this way seems the best. Don't make it hard for us to go. Please have a little faith in me, for I'd risk my life to make you safe and happy." He dropped his arms.

123

"I do trust you, Father," whispered Regina. "You're the best father on earth. And I love Hans and Michel and I—" She could not finish.

"Regina, sometimes I've wished I could go to sleep and wake up and all this trouble would be ended," cried Mother. "This decision has not been an easy one to make."

"Many people have wished that, Mother. I suppose even Catri wishes that. She is tired of all this confusion, too. But if the trouble would be ended when we awake, that still would not keep us from wondering who really had been right after all."

Slowly Friedrich Strahm walked toward the door that led to his shop and turned the knob. "Life is strange," he said, "and very real."

It was one o'clock when the three on horseback neared Mathis Bartsche's print shop in Zurich.

"You go in, Father," suggested Mother, "and call him out. Regina and I will wait here."

But at that moment Michel himself stepped out of the shop and started walking in the opposite direction, coat collar turned up, hat pulled down.

"Michel," called Father.

Michel stopped abruptly and looked around, and began running toward them. "What does this mean?" he asked breathlessly.

"We're on our way to Langnau. We just stopped to say good-by to you."

"And you, Regina? Are you going, too?"

In a few sentences, Father explained everything to Michel.

"Then tie your horses," he suggested. "And come along to my boarding place and we'll eat together. I'm off now for dinner. That way you can warm yourselves before you go on."

"Thank you, Michel," said Mother, "but we want to get as far as possible before night. I'm not cold. And we have lunch with us."

124

"I do hate to see you two start out. Remember what I told you and be careful. I'll come home a week from Sunday to hear all about it. I expect to see Hans then. Tell him I said so. You're doing the right thing, I know. Good-by, Mother." He held her hand to his lips. "Good-by, Father," he said, shaking his hand. "Do you have any kind of weapon with you?"

"I have a hatchet in my sack here, but I hope I won't need to use it."

Regina and Michel watched their parents until they reached the corner.

"They really took your warning to heart, Michel," Regina said, trying desperately to keep back the tears.

"Yes," answered Michel. "But let's not talk about that here on the street. Remember what I told you. We've got to be careful. Someone might be watching or listening."

"Oh, that's right. Then tell me, Michel, where can I find a store that sells dishes and bowls? I want to get a bowl for the pastor's wife; then I'll be on my way."

"I'd go with you, if I had time—and be glad to."

Carefully Regina followed Michel's directions. First she tied her horse in the square not far from the Great Münster Church. With very little difficulty she located the store from that point and purchased the bowl. Although it was not exactly like the one she had broken, it was as large and almost as pretty. And the price was only a little more than half the amount she had anticipated paying. Twice she counted her money before leaving the store. Slowly she walked along the street, stopping occasionally to look at the merchandise displayed in the shop windows. She lingered in front of a shoe store, then walked on to the next corner. Returning, she entered the store and priced a pair of shoes hanging in the window.

"Wouldn't you like to try them on?" asked the merchant.

"If it's not too much trouble."

"Trouble?" smiled the merchant. "It would be no trouble whatever. That's what I'm here for. Take a seat."

The shoes were too large, but the merchant tied on others until he found a pair that fitted her perfectly.

"Exactly what you want, isn't it?"

"Yes," nodded Regina. "And if you please, I'd like to ask you to wrap them together with this bowl someway so I can carry them on horseback without too much difficulty. I have to go to Kyburg with them."

"I'll see what I can do. I'll make a bundle out of heavy twine so you can hook it onto your saddle. How's that?"

"Fine," smiled Regina.

"So you live over at Kyburg?"

"I work for Pastor Hofmeier and his wife."

"I used to live at Kyburg myself. Lovely spot, beautiful country, nice people. But that was before the Hofmeiers were there. I've heard he and Lord Englehard are quite active in rounding up the Anabaptists. I suppose you get in on lots of excitement over there around the castle these days, don't you?"

"Yes," she said. "More than—" she bit her tongue.

"Well," said the merchant, walking over to the counter, "the way things are shaping up, we'll get in on some excitement right here in Zurich and maybe very soon at that. I know you've heard through the pastor about Felix Manz and George Blaurock, those bold Anabaptist leaders."

"I—well, I've heard their names."

"They're in the Wellenberg prison, you know, and Manz, at least, won't get out of this canton alive again. But you know all that, I'm sure."

Regina walked toward the door. She looked down the street. "I must be on my way," she said. "If you'll do up the bundle, I'll thank you, for I must get back before dark."

"Certainly," the old man answered genially, but it took him a long time to fix the bag handle. His hands shook and he did it over the third time before it suited him.

"Here you are, lady," he said at last. "I hope it will be all right."

"Thank you. It will be."

Regina hurried. It would take her three hours to ride to Kyburg and the sun was well past midday. It was dark in Kyburg by five-thirty.

She had gone not more than a five-minute walk when in the distance in front of her, she heard shouting. Along the river, across from the fish market, she noticed a crowd of people, gathering from every direction. They seemed to be watching something on the other side of the river. She walked still faster until she was at the very edge of the crowd. Across the river, she could see men coming from the direction of the courthouse, one leading another and a man on each side of the man being held. They were talking earnestly to him in vehement tones with dramatic gestures.

"Don't recant now, Felix," shouted someone from the crowd.

Regina stood on tiptoe. A woman in black was leaning against the iron railing along the river bank, hands outstretched toward the group on the other side. Regina pressed her way through the crowd until she could see the woman's face. It was earnest and tear-stained.

XXI

"God help you, my son," shouted the woman.

A strange hush fell on the crowd. In the woman's clear voice there was love instead of terror, only love and submission.

"He will help you be true to the end, Felix," she called. "Go fearlessly to your death, Son, for you will soon be in glory with God forever."

Regina clutched her twine handle. The fingers of her free hand were clenched deep within her coat pocket.

She saw the four men coming close to the river's edge.

"Save your life. You can," shouted one of the men, grabbing the prisoner by the shoulder.

"It's not too late yet," shouted the other. "All you need to do is recant. Do it now, Manz!"

"Those men are preachers," someone in the crowd remarked. "He is a fool for not listening to them."

"No! No, Son!" shouted the woman in black. "Be true to the end. The end, Felix, is only the beginning of eternal life. God has saved you, and you know it. Don't give up now, Felix, no matter what they tell you. Don't give up."

Beside the woman stood a young man. "Don't deny Christ now, Felix," he called. "It wouldn't pay, not if you'd gain all the world. I'll soon be with you in heaven."

As the four men across the river passed the fish market, the prisoner raised his arms toward heaven and shouted, "God has opened my eyes. He showed me the truth. It is God who has given me knowledge and wisdom that I might know how to escape eternal and never-ending death. Why should I recant now? Never! Never! Praise God, my Lord and Christ in heaven, for my sorrows and sadness are already turned into eternal rejoicing."

"His face is like Johann Ferlinden's," Regina gasped. "He has peace and happiness." Her heart pounded as the crowd pressed around her. What if someone had heard her!

"Look at the water," shouted one of the preachers. "That means certain death unless you recant. Say the word now. Stop this folly and face reality. Say the word."

"Hurry!" shouted the other minister. "Before we get there. Say you'll give up this silly doctrine and your life will be spared."

"No!" shouted his mother and brother in unison.

"Don't turn back now," added his mother. "It's the end of life that counts most, Felix, my son."

Tears streamed down her face. Her simple black dress accented the look on her face. Through tears her dark eyes shone with triumph. Regina watched her spellbound, trembling.

"You know you are right, Son," she shouted.

Her voice sent something quivering through Regina's body. There seemed to be no trace of doubt or fear in her eyes, only admiration and faith. "You know the perfect love that casts out fear of death, Felix," she called.

Across the river the prisoner was led to a boat. The crowd watched breathless while the boat moved slowly toward the center of the river to the little fishing hut, a mere platform with open sides and a roof.

Blinding tears welled up in Regina's eyes. She could see one man hand the other a rope as the three stepped from the boat to the hut.

"Who is it?" whispered someone behind her.

"Felix Manz, the heretic," whispered another.

The executioner tied the prisoner's hands. But his peaceful face was lifted heavenward. Regina's glance shifted to his mother's face, and she saw there the same peace.

129

"Praise God for the light," he shouted in a strong voice that did not falter. "Praise God who has called me into His kingdom. Oh, how could I betray Him now who has given me peace, joy, and love unspeakable and full of glory? Praises to God forever!"

Regina stood watching, listening, with a strange profound reverence that bordered on worship. She could not move. She could not even swallow.

The prisoner made no resistance. He cast no unkind or condemning glances at his executioner. The silent awe-struck crowd remained almost motionless. It seemed that suddenly the whole world stood still.

His mother lifted her arms once more as though she wanted to tell all the world something of eternal importance and her very life depended on the telling of it.

"Let neither life nor death nor men nor angels, nor principalities nor powers, separate you from the love of God, Felix." She smiled through her tears. "Soon I will see you in glory where we will never be parted. They can destroy your body, but not your soul, Son. You have lived the life you can die by, thank God. Give your body a living sacrifice. He gave His life for us. Be true, Felix." Her arms relaxed.

The two men held the prisoner at the edge of the platform as if to give him one last opportunity to recant. Then they slipped his tied hands over his flexed knees and thrust a stick through his legs behind his knees.

As if beholding a heavenly vision, Manz lifted his eyes and began to chant in Latin. His clear voice reverberated. The Anabaptist leader was thrust into the icy waters of the Limmat River.

Men moaned softly.

Women came near fainting.

The crowd waited for his mother to scream, but she did not. When all signs of life were gone the men lifted his body back into the boat.

"Thanks be to God," cried his mother. "Thanks be to Christ for helping my son give his life for the sake of the Gospel. He loved the truth and taught it."

Manz's brother put his arm around his mother. On his face was no regret or retaliation, not even dismay.

Tears streamed down Regina's cheeks, and as the crowd dispersed she made her way toward Manz's mother. She hesitated. Her legs trembled. With one hand outstretched, she gently touched the woman's arm. "Tell me," she cried, "was he your own son?"

The woman looked up, glad surprise on her face. "Yes, my own son, Felix."

"And—and he was killed because he—?" Regina's words choked in her throat.

"For preaching the truth, my child," she answered, her dark trusting eyes shining. "Thank God, he baptized those who came repenting and confessing and believing. He gave his life because he was a true disciple. But his work will not die. I believe as long as the world stands, the teachings God had Conrad Grebel bring to light will be preached and followed. Many may yet have to give their lives, but others will carry it on. I know they will."

"Then," stammered Regina, "infant baptism isn't enough, is it?"

The woman caught Regina's wrist and held it tenderly. "My dear child," she said with compassion, "it cannot be. He that believeth and is baptized shall be saved. I may be executed, too, very soon, but thank God, He has forgiven my sins. I'm ready to go. I've confessed Him before men."

"And—and—" Regina could not speak for crying. The crowd was pressing around them.

"Just seek with all your heart, child," whispered the woman, bending forward for someone nearly knocked Regina over. "God will help you find the answer," she said softly. "We must hurry, for we want to follow the body to the cemetery."

131

Regina clutched the twine handle of her bundle and stood for a minute to get her bearings.

Somehow she reached the square where she had tied the horse. Somehow she found her way out of the city and on the road to Kyburg—back to the pastor's cozy house.

XXII

"She hasn't come yet?" Peter queried Catri.

"Peter, I don't want to worry," answered Catri, "but it's getting dark, isn't it?"

"And cold," answered Peter.

"If you had time, I wouldn't care. No, I'd better not suggest it. She'll surely be here soon."

"Lisette borrowed a horse to go to Zurich and she isn't back either. Lady Englehard is almost angry. I just came from the castle."

Without another word, Peter went out of the house, dashed across the yard, and mounted his horse. When Catri looked out the window, she heard Peter's horse going around the bend on the trot.

He had not gone far when he met her.

"Good evening, Regina," Peter exclaimed. "Catri has been anxious about you." He turned his horse around.

"I'm sorry," said Regina. "I should have been home sooner."

"Did you lose the way?" he asked, riding beside her.

"No."

"It's not safe for you to be out on the road alone after dark," suggested Peter. "And I hear someone coming. It could be a rough character."

"It's a young girl," Regina replied. "She's been following all the way from Zurich."

"A young girl? Maybe it's Lisette. She borrowed a horse to go to Zurich today."

"I wouldn't know. I've never met Lisette," answered Regina.

"Lady Englehard will scold her, I fear," said Peter confidingly, "for she was to be back in time to start supper at four-thirty."

"I hope Catri won't be angry with me," said Regina. "I promised to be back before dark, too."

"Angry with you?" laughed Peter softly. "You had the whole day off and you had a long way to go. Don't worry, Regina, Catri won't get angry and even if she did, she couldn't stay that way long with you."

"Peter," said Regina reprovingly. "You must not."

"Must not what?"

"You must not talk to me like that," she answered softly.

Peter chuckled. "What if I can't help it? Regina, you are sweet. I've been wanting to tell you for weeks."

"But you—you must help it. You don't know me, Peter. I'm not sweet. I'm—I'm sinful," she whispered, "and wicked." She bit her lip. Quickly she brushed away a tear.

"Indeed," remarked Peter in a horrified tone. "Where have you been and who has been filling you with such crude notions? Please tell me you're not serious."

Regina made no answer. They were nearing the bend in the road and they would soon be at the foot of the long, steep castle hill. The horse behind them quickened its pace after a slap and from the bend it followed immediately behind Peter and Regina, until they reached the pastor's gate, then went on up the hill.

"It's Lisette, all right," said Peter. "And very likely she will think up some excuse to have me draw three pails of water when I get there."

Peter helped Regina dismount.

"My bag," she said, "hanging there on the saddle, Peter."

"Certainly," he unhooked it. "I'll carry it into the house for you."

"Thank you, Peter, but it's not necessary." Regina reached for it. Reluctantly he gave it to her.

"Sometime," he said, looking down at her, "as soon as I have

134

a chance and the weather is agreeable, may I have the pleasure of your company for a longer ride? We could go together some place, for I am almost certain I can get permission from the lord to use Beth again sometime."

Regina waited a moment before she answered. "Tonight I could not promise that, Peter."

"I hope I am not intruding," suggested Peter. "I never did ask. Perhaps you already have a special friend."

"Oh, no. It's not that."

"Good," said Peter, a little relieved and much delighted. "Then there may be a chance to work my way up to your approval."

"I must be going in," she said. "Catri will be quite displeased with me, I'm afraid. You see, Peter, I—"

He waited, but the sentence hung unfinished. "Remember the night I wiped dishes for you, Regina," his voice was rich and low. He stood outside the gate. "You said you couldn't stand to see anyone suffer; how did you say it—relative, stranger, or friend?"

"Something like that, I believe."

"And I told you that night it would hurt my soul, if I really liked a girl and she'd drive me away. You won't send me away tonight without an explanation, will you, Regina?"

Regina opened the gate.

"You—you—wouldn't understand, Peter, if I tried to tell you," she said sadly. "Let me go now and think it over, won't you?"

Peter stood speechless.

"You may go," he said at length. "And good night, Regina."

"Good night," she answered, and hurried to the door.

"Regina," exclaimed Catri. "Peter has been here twice to get the horse."

"He has it now," answered Regina. "He came to meet me."

"How lovely!" said Catri with satisfaction. "But did you have some difficulty in finding the way?"

"No," answered Regina. "I'm very sorry it got so late. I stopped in Zurich and," she unwrapped the package, "I got this for you."

"Because you accidentally broke mine?"

"Of course, it was awkward of me. I should have been more careful."

"But you didn't need to do this, Regina. It's lovely though."

"I know I didn't need to do this, but I wanted to. And I got these new shoes. It took longer than I thought it would."

"They're nice. But your eyes, Regina, you look as though you've been crying."

Regina took off her wraps and stood by the fireplace. "My parents left for Langnau in the Emmental today," she said. "It was hard to see them go. It did make me cry."

"Why did they go to Langnau?"

"To see my brother Hans."

"Are they going to stay long?"

"No. They're coming back soon."

"Isn't Hans the one—" The door opened and Heinrich stepped in.

"Well, I see you got back, Regina. I know Catri is glad, if no one else is."

"Yes, I was just telling him this evening, Regina, that if the day was as long and lonesome for you when I was gone as it's been for me today without you, I pity you, even if it is late to do it."

"I got along all right that day," answered Regina. She took her wraps into her bedroom.

"Heinrich," said Catri, "Regina said her parents left today for Langnau to see her brother Hans."

"To see Hans?" inquired Heinrich. "I hate to learn of them going over there now. Hans had better be coming home instead. Things over there are pretty uncertain."

"That's why they went—to bring him home," explained Regina.

"Fine," remarked Heinrich. "But that's what they should have done months ago. The thing that took place in Zurich today should make all sane-thinking parents more conscientious about doing all they can to protect their children. While you were in Zurich this afternoon, Regina, you might even have gotten in on that public execution."

Regina felt weak.

"Please don't mention that any more tonight," begged Catri. "I've heard all I can stand for one day, Heinrich. And I'm sure," went on Catri, "Regina would have gone out of the way to avoid seeing that—as tenderhearted as she is. Someday while the sun is shining I'll discuss it, but let's not do it now. I have too many bad dreams over all this as it is."

Catri continued, "That's right, Regina, Frieda has been begging for you the last hour. See, she wants you to pick her up. I know they both missed you today as much as I did."

"Were they fussy?" Regina held Frieda out at arm's length even though her arms were still trembling. The baby laughed out loud.

"I think they fussed just because they missed you, Regina," Catri laughed. "See how delighted she acts."

"When do we eat?" asked Heinrich.

"Very shortly," answered Catri. "What I have for supper is ready as soon as you and Regina are."

Regina ate but little.

"Aren't you hungry?" asked Catri, passing Regina the platter of cold meat.

"Don't think a thing of it," said Regina. "I get streaks like this sometimes when I'm not hungry."

Regina drew water from the well and filled the teakettles before retiring.

The night was dark, but she knew where the well was without a lantern.

"Regina."

137

She jumped. Her heart stopped.

"Regina," came a louder whisper. From behind the pine tree emerged a dark figure! Regina was too frightened to scream or run.

"Regina, it's me. It's Hans. Don't be sacred. Sh-h. Don't run." He clutched her arm. "I've been here waiting and praying for almost an hour."

"Why—why, Hans!" gasped Regina. "You scared me stiff. How did you get here? The folks left just today—today noon for Langnau to bring you home."

"What!"

"Yes. Oh, Hans! I'm only dreaming. It can't be you."

"But it is. Listen, Regina," he whispered. "You do what I tell you. Will you?"

"What?"

"After every one in the house is sound asleep, slip out quietly. See. Dress warm. I'll be waiting here for you. Right here."

"You'll freeze."

"No, I won't. I'll wait here until you come."

"But—but how did you know I was here, Hans?"

"Go back now. You'll find out. Remember, don't tell a soul. Slip out quietly. It's important," and Hans disappeared in the darkness out of which he had come.

Regina stumbled toward the house.

Fortunately no one was in the kitchen when she entered. She filled the teakettles as usual, but her hands and legs shook. She stood in the kitchen pinching her arms to calm herself.

"Regina," called Catri, from the living room. "What's taking you so long in the kitchen? Come now. You're tired. What you don't get done tonight you can do tomorrow."

"I was just filling the teakettles," answered Regina, "and putting away a few things," she tried to steady her voice. She cleared her throat. "That's one thing Mother taught me. She said it's always a satisfaction to get up in the morning when the house is in order."

"Were they surprised to see you?" asked Catri when Regina came into the living room.

"Yes, and glad. Shall I rock the babies to sleep?"

"Mother said she's afraid I'm letting you spoil them," laughed Catri. "But don't take Mother seriously. She was only teasing." Catri looked into the bedroom. "It looks as though Frieman is expecting it. He's waving his arms frantically. Frieda is practically asleep already. You can rock Frieman if you want to. Really, I'm more tired than I've been for weeks, and just as soon as he's asleep, I'm going to bed myself."

"For some reason I'm tired, too," said Heinrich, who had been nodding by the fire. "This was a hard day for me."

Regina knelt beside her bed and remained there for a long time. The house was dark and still.

Fully dressed, boots on, coat fastened, scarf tied, gloves in her hands, she stood at her open door listening. Carefully she tiptoed across the room, feeling her way along the table edge.

Once more she listened, standing at the door. Slowly and carefully, she lifted the latch and slipped out into the night. Before she reached the well, Hans caught her hand, and without a word led her out through the garden and helped her over the fence.

XXIII

All the way up the long castle hill, Lisette muttered. As she rehearsed her intentions, her black eyes became slits. That pale-faced, sobbing thing from Weisslingen crying in public! What a disgrace to the pastor and lord, and Peter stooping to escorting her!

He wouldn't be so proud when the lord found out!

Lisette tied Bel near the archway for Peter to take care of when he came. And with every step across the paved courtyard her story grew. She listened for the sound of Peter's horse. He had not yet started up the hill.

As soon as she saw Lady Englehard's stern countenance, her intentions wavered. The lady's lips were drawn thin and there was unmistakable displeasure written on her plump face. She stiffened her shoulders and lifted her head before she spoke.

"You will not get a horse to go to Zurich soon again, Lisette," she declared emphatically.

"But, Lady Englehard, let me explain," began Lisette, clutching her shoe package.

"Not now," objected Lady Englehard, pointing with her forefinger to the stove. "Your work is waiting. The men are hungry. The lord will not stand for such as this again. His work must not be detained. When you say you'll be back, you are to be depended on or we'll find another cook."

"But, Lady Englehard," began Lisette the second time—this time with less boldness, "there's a special reason."

"Let the reason drop," interrupted Lady Englehard, placing a hand on each hip and frowning. "It is unthinkable that a servant in this castle would dare talk back to me. Get busy

140

now before the lord becomes enraged. I'm thankful indeed we have our own personal cook who can be depended on. You will not be advanced at this rate, Lisette."

Lisette removed her wraps with trembling hands as Lady Englehard walked out of the kitchen, her silk dress rustling.

Half an hour later when Andreas came in, Lisette was making low and unhappy sounds. Peter followed Andreas. They took their places at the table as several other servants entered.

Andreas tapped his fat knuckles on the table top.

"Did the stove break or the fuel run out tonight?" he asked, looking at Lisette tormentingly.

She ignored the question, but continued stirring the soup in the iron kettle, frowning worse with each round of the long-handled, wooden spoon.

"Come on Lisette," called one of the servants impatiently. "Cold or hot, cooked or raw, we've got to eat now."

Lisette dipped the lukewarm soup from the kettle into a large bowl and without a word set it down before the hungry men, beside the bread and apple spread. She gave Peter one significant glance. He did not notice; he was looking at nothing, wrapped in meditation.

"How many prisoners do we have tonight?" asked Andreas between bites. "I'm talking to you, Peter," Andreas nudged Peter's arm.

"You asked me what?"

"I said, how many prisoners do we have tonight?"

"Six. All men. And six too many," answered Peter.

"It's my turn to watch tonight," Andreas said, tapping his fingers on the table.

"Is it? You're right, it is, and I'll make no objections. I'm going to report to the lord and at ten sharp you be on hand, for I want to crawl in—I hope, for the rest of the night. The pastor seems a little more optimistic this evening. He thinks things may quiet down since what took place in Zurich today."

141

"What do you think?" asked Andreas.

"I'm tired thinking," said Peter. "Bring Andreas and these other fellows some more bread, Lisette," he called.

Lisette jumped and proceeded to slice bread.

"I sorta wish I could have seen it," said Andreas.

"I can't exactly say that," answered Peter, thoughtfully. "I came too near drowning myself one time when the ice broke. I still remember how it felt."

Andreas gave Peter a quick, lingering glance. "You must be tired tonight."

Long after Peter went to his room above the stable, he sat on the side of his bed, elbows on his knees, face in his hands, his eyes open, seeing nothing, for the room was dark.

* * *

Not until they were near the bottom of the long hill beyond the garden did either speak a word.

"Hans," whispered Regina, "where are you taking me? It's dark."

"Thank God it is." Hans whispered, still holding her arm. He stopped abruptly and faced her. "Now," he whispered, "before we go any farther"—he listened, first turning his head in every direction—"I'll tell you what's happened." He drew a deep breath. "Do you want to hear it?"

"Of course. Must we whisper even down here?"

"Better. Uncle Rudolf, Aunt Margrit, and I all went to a secret meeting in a barn over near Langnau."

"An Anabaptist meeting?"

"Yes."

"When?"

"A week ago last Sunday night. About twenty people were there and Johann Ferlinden was preaching and baptizing."

"Johann Ferlinden!"

"Yes."

"But, Hans, they're hunting him. He was up in the castle prison and got away."

"I know. He told me."

"And where is he now?"

"I'll tell you later."

"You know, Hans?"

"I knew where he was this afternoon."

"But, Hans! They're hunting him all over these parts! They've offered a reward to anyone who can tell where he is."

"They have? Say, listen, Regina, you won't turn me in if I tell you something now, will you?"

"Turn you in? What do you mean?"

"I've got to know before we go on. I knew I was running a risk to do this, but the last time I saw you, I felt you were sympathetic with Uncle Rudolf and you thought it was all right for me to go back to Langnau, didn't you?"

"Yes, I tried to understand you both."

"What is your attitude now since you've been living with the pastor at Kyburg?"

"But how did you know I was over here?"

"Johann Ferlinden told me."

"Johann Ferlinden! How did he know?"

"He said when he was put into solitary confinement, he overheard two castle watchmen talking outside the door."

"About me, Hans? What did they say?"

"I'll tell you later. We've got to be going. It's a long way. I mean if you want to go."

"To where?"

"But you haven't answered my question. Where do you stand now? Do you really want to know the truth?"

"Truth about what?"

"About God. About life. About what's right," he shook her arm. "You know, Regina."

" And about the Anabaptists?"

"Yes. About everything we've got to know."

"Oh, Hans!" cried Regina. "I've been praying for months, for months, Hans. Only God knows how I've been troubled."

143

"Then come," whispered Hans, taking her hand. "I know the way."

"But, Hans," Regina held back. "When will I get back? You said it's a long way. You really know what you're doing?"

"Come. I know exactly. If you want to know as bad as I do, you'll risk anything."

"But I've got to be back before daylight."

"If we hurry I'll get you back."

Hans led Regina down the hill as fast as her feet would take her.

"Thank God, the ground is frozen and there's no snow on it. This way. I think we can get there in three hours, if we hurry."

"Three hours!"

"Can you?" he waited for the answer.

"I—I hope so. But it's after ten now."

"We'll make it, if we keep going. Just trust me, Regina." Facing the cold wind, they walked fast until they reached a wooded section which made a welcome windbreak. The dark pine trees painted the blackness of the night even blacker. Hans held Regina's arm tightly. They stumbled over unexpected rocks, miniature gulleys, and dips in the road.

"Tell me now," whispered Regina. "You say you're willing to risk anything. Hans, what's happened?"

"I shouldn't tell it all tonight," answered Hans. "Much has happened. I don't want to make you afraid to go on with me. Sometime I'll tell you everything. But you said Mother and Father left today for Langnau?"

"Yes. They wanted to bring you along home with them."

"Why?"

"Michel's been talking to them. He's afraid Uncle Rudolf has been influencing you. Michel is against the Anabaptists now."

"Michel is?"

"Yes. The folks have been undecided, baffled like I've been.

144

Whenever Father talked about going to see you, Michel objected. But now he wanted them to go, for he convinced them Uncle Rudolf did wrong. Michel has been influenced in the shop. But what will they do when they find you're not there?"

"God only knows, for I'm almost certain Uncle Rudolf and Aunt Margrit won't be there either."

"Why not?"

"Because they've very likely had to flee persecution, too."

XXIV

The open valley winding around the mountain was dotted with farms, but in the night only a few were faintly outlined. Now and then a dog howled. Steadily, Hans and Regina hurried past the woods, down another slope, then up a long grade. A large flat rock beside a big tree at the top of the hill offered an ideal resting place, but they had no time to rest. The naked tree branches scraped each other in the cold wind.

"I'm surprised at Michel," began Hans after a prolonged silence, "but I can't really blame him too much. He may have been sincere in what he told the folks."

"I think he was. Michel has tried to be honest. Sometimes I thought he must be right."

"I'm anxious to hear what you will say after you've heard Ferlinden."

"You mean we might? Oh, Hans!"

"We'll see. Then I must decide what to do."

"You mean you still don't know? After living all this time with Uncle Rudolf?"

"I'm desperate, Regina. I know Uncle Rudolf is genuine. There's no doubt about that. But—I've been going with a girl."

"A girl?"

"Yes, and she is against the Anabaptists. I've got to have you help me get this settled."

"Me help you? I thought you came to help me."

"I did. But I don't want to do something to disgrace the family. She thinks it's shameful for families to be separated over this. And now you say Michel has taken his stand?"

"Yes. But does this girl know how undecided you've been?"

"I've tried to keep it from her. She has no idea, I'm sure, how it's been troubling me. And she doesn't know I heard Johann Ferlinden."

"Do you love her?"

"I thought I did, even though we don't agree. She's wonderful, pretty, very pretty, and comes from a nice family. And she loves me."

"But, Hans—"

Horses' hoofs; "Regina; come," whispered Hans, and he pulled her down beside him into the shallow ditch along the edge of the road.

The horses galloped past, and Regina clutched Hans's hand. Not until the sound of their hoofs had died away in the distance did Hans whisper, "Shall we go on?"

"Do you know where to go? I'm turned around now."

"Yes. I came this way this evening."

"Then tell me what you started to tell me 'way back there about the meeting in the barn. It's not so windy now."

"I went with Uncle Rudolf. He's been trying to help me understand why the Anabaptists believe as they do. I told you Johann Ferlinden was there?"

"Yes."

"I have always tried to protect Uncle Rudolf. He is sincere. So is Aunt Margrit. It was a wonderful meeting. Ferlinden was about ready to baptize a man when two officers broke in and people scattered in every direction. Some ran outside and some hid under the hay, and several were seized. The owner of the farm grabbed Johann Ferlinden in one hand and me in the other, because we happened to be right there beside him. He reached down, pushed back a wide board under the hay and dropped both of us into a hole, and came in after us."

"Oh, Hans!"

"Wait till I tell you. Don't get excited. It was a space between the house and the barn about the width of my shoulders.

He pushed the board back in place and we were in there for three days. I still can't figure out how he did it so skillfully and we weren't caught."

"Why did you stay in there for three days?"

"Because it wasn't safe to come out. The man's wife slipped us food twice a day. The officers came back several times and searched everywhere. We could hear them talking and going through the hay with pitchforks, and searching all through the house."

"But didn't they question the wife?"

"Yes, but she would only say, 'I haven't seen them.' "

"But you said she brought food to you."

"She did. But she slipped it to us from a crack in the kitchen wall down by the floor, under the cupboard. She did not lie. She did not see us. After the third day they thought we weren't anywhere on the place, and that is when Johann Ferlinden and I started for Kyburg. While we were in that hole together those three days, I really learned to respect him. I was telling him about my family, and he remembered being in Father's shop. He remembered seeing you that day."

"I remember him and what he said that day about not being afraid."

"He's not afraid."

·"Not even afraid to come back here where he knows they're hunting for him?"

"No. He's trying to locate his wife."

"His wife?"

"He was married only a month when he was picked up. When he escaped, he couldn't find her. He thought she might have gone to friends in the Emmental, but he didn't find her there either. He wonders now if she might be in prison. We had quite a time getting over here. It took us five nights and, Regina, we had one narrow escape after another."

"Please don't tell it now, Hans."

"No, I don't want to now."

148

"But you haven't told me yet what Johann Ferlinden heard the watchmen talking about. Just tell me that much."

"He said he heard them talking about Regina Strahm from Weisslingen working for the pastor. He knew at once it was you. They said you were an attractive young lady and he gathered from what the younger of the two said that he was going to try to see you every chance he got. What does that mean, Regina?"

"It doesn't mean anything more than just that."

"Has he been seeing you often?"

"Not often."

"Then you do know who I'm talking about?"

"Yes."

"I told you something confidential. Aren't you going to do the same? You're keeping something from me."

"Hans, I have nothing to tell except that it will never—"

"Never what?"

"Never amount to anything. Hans, it can't. He even helps to take prisoners into Zurich to be tried! Oh, Hans, today I saw Felix Manz being drowned."

"What!"

"I did, Hans."

"Where?"

"In Zurich. In the Limmat River. I was there. I saw it with my own eyes."

"Johann Ferlinden doesn't know that."

"I talked to his mother. After watching that, I could never be interested in someone who helps round up Anabaptists and puts them in prison, even though he's handsome and kind. Kind to me, and related to the pastor and in good standing with Lord Englehard at the castle. I wish sometimes I'd never met Peter. I've wished sometimes the pastor from Kyburg had never seen me."

"It must be after midnight," whispered Hans as they left the road, crossed a frozen stream, and ascended a gentle slope

149

toward a small, one-roomed wooden hut. Without hesitation, Hans knocked gently three times, waited a moment, then repeated the sign. The door opened slowly. Faintly Regina saw the face of a slender, white-bearded man.

"It's Hans," whispered Hans.

"Come," said a low kind voice.

Hans led Regina inside. The soft glow from the low quaint stove was the only bit of light in the small room. It felt wonderfully warm and comforting.

"Sit here," said the old man, pushing a homemade stool over to Regina. "God bless you." He shook her cold hand with his warm one. "You made it. How I've prayed the whole evening! And now you're here."

"My sister," said Hans, dropping on the floor beside the stove. "Excuse me, Regina; this is Moses, Johann Ferlinden's good friend."

"Here is milk for you to drink before we start out. Weary pilgrims must be refreshed," he said softly.

"I never knew milk could taste so good," Regina smiled.

"Nor I," added Hans. "Did anyone stop here tonight?"

"No one. Why?"

"About an hour or so ago someone passed us on horseback. We hid in the ditch."

"I heard horses going past twice tonight, but strange as it may seem, no one has ever stopped here. No one has ever questioned me. I guess they figure I'm just a harmless old man who knows nothing of what's going on in the world. It's God. That's what it is, just the hand of God. Shall we go now?"

Hans, though tired, got up immediately.

"We have no time to lose, Moses," he said, "for my sister must get back to Kyburg before daylight."

"Her name? You told me."

"Regina."

"Yes. Here, Regina," said Moses. "Take this homemade cane. You will need it. Here's one for you, Hans."

He led the way. The hill a quarter of a mile distant was steep and Regina was indeed grateful for the cane. As they trudged steadily upward, her heart pounded, and she had to stop several times long enough to get her breath. At the top, they stopped to rest a little. "From here you must be very careful," whispered Moses. "Keep always to the left. I will go first."

Bending now, they walked under low-hanging pine tree branches. Between steep cliffs and at the bosom of the mountain a great cavity appeared which from the road far below was entirely hidden by the heavy evergreen foliages, tangled bushes, and overhanging shrubberies on the hill in front.

Moses found the narrow rocky path; Regina and Hans followed close at his heels. Occasionally furry bushes and bare twigs swept their faces. Regina caught hold of the branches to steady herself. To the right dipped a deep gorge.

"Be careful of the log," whispered Moses. "It must have fallen today."

Hans caught Regina's hand and helped her over it.

"And careful here," whispered Moses. "Use your stick. There's a broken place in the rock."

From there the path went downgrade. In some places it was slippery.

"Hans," whispered Regina.

"Yes?"

"I hear water trickling."

"It falls into the ravine from an overhanging rock. We're almost there."

"Will we have to go under the water, Hans?"

"No."

As they approached the dark opening, Moses tapped his stick on the rock three times. He waited a moment, then repeated the sign.

From the cavity came a man's low voice.

"Moses?"

"Moses and my two friends," answered Moses.

"Come," said the voice and from far back in the opening a man appeared, carrying in one hand a lighted candle and in the other a Bible.

Regina knew at a glance it was none other than Johann Ferlinden.

XXV

As Regina, Hans, and their guide, Moses, came near to the cave entrance, Johann Ferlinden greeted them with a gentle smile.

"Peace be unto you," he said in a whispered prayer. "Welcome to this beautiful God-made cathedral." And, turning to Regina, he added, "Perhaps you don't remember me, but I stopped in your father's shop one morning."

"I remember you well," answered Regina. "You are Johann Ferlinden, the converted monk. The things you told my father that day have made me do a great deal of wondering and praying. I have been troubled ever since."

"Come. Let us go in where its warmer." Johann led the way deeper into the cave. "To me," he said, "nothing just happens. Our lives are planned by God. I did not know why, but I knew I was supposed to stop in the shop that day. And you were supposed to be there to hear what I said. Your brother, Hans, was supposed to be rammed into that hole along with me. God helped us make this trip over here in safety. He planned it, otherwise we never would have made it. God has prepared the wonderful cave in this rock where we can hide tonight from our enemies. God prepared the heart of my friend, Moses, and told him to befriend you and lead you here. Moses has also brought me food and this candle. You see, Regina, God leads those who will allow themselves to be led. He does this by His Holy Spirit who speaks to us and makes us certain what we feel we should do is right. He also leads us by the Bible and through the help of His servants. You say you have been troubled and distressed?"

"Very much," answered Regina, "for months. You could tell that morning you talked to Father that he was badly distressed, couldn't you?"

"Yes, and I felt very sorry for him. I have often prayed for him. Is he still so confused?"

"More than ever. He has definitely taken his stand against the Anabaptists. Today he and Mother left for Langnau to bring Hans back before he disgraces the family and becomes an Anabaptist."

"But you see, Regina, that God planned that Hans wouldn't be there! Hans has been open and frank with me. He has told me about his spiritual struggles and almost he was persuaded to be a disciple of Christ, but he insisted he must first find you. I told him he must make his own decisions, that this Christian experience is a personal matter and he shouldn't wait to see what you or anyone else would say. He agreed, but still insisted he must find you first. And now you are here. How merciful God has been to spare his life and yours to this present moment. I am here to help you in any way I can. Tomorrow I may not be here. I know I'm being hunted. I realize God has been exceedingly kind in saving my life this long and it's for a purpose."

"Did you know Felix Manz was drowned today?" asked Hans.

"No."

"Regina was in Zurich and saw it happen."

"Yes," said Regina. "And since I saw his face and heard his dying testimony, I must know how to find what he had. If you could only tell me, I would be very happy. Some say it's impossible for anyone to know whether one is saved, but he was confident to the end."

"Manz was a great soul," Ferlinden said. "I know he was ready to go. Regina, God has the answer to your soul's need and it is no secret. He has given us His word that we may not be troubled or hindered or walk in darkness but know

154

the truth and walk in the light. For God is truth and light and life. Hans, will you hold the candle please, so I can read from the Bible?" Bowing his head, Ferlinden prayed, "Let now Thy servant speak through Thy Word, for Thy Word is truth and forever settled in heaven. Bless these two young hearers and give them peace with understanding. Amen."

Turning to Regina, he said, "Now tell me what you already know about the Bible."

"I know very little," she said. "Father has wanted to get a Bible for two years. Hard times came when many left the neighborhood; so he never could afford to buy one. All I know about the Bible is what I've heard read in church and what I've overheard Heinrich Hofmeier read, but it's been only enough to make me dissatisfied. I wish you would tell me everything the Anabaptists believe."

"To tell you everything in one evening would be quite impossible, Regina," he answered, "but I will tell you what we have time for. How long will you stay?"

Regina looked at Hans for the answer. "She has to be back before daylight. She slipped out, you know, and I promised to get her back."

"Then I must talk fast," said Ferlinden. "Listen to the words of Jesus. He said, 'I am the way, the truth, and the life: no man cometh unto the Father, but by me.' The way of salvation is found by faith in Christ and not alone through the state church as many believe. No one will be lost by obeying Jesus Christ. We must know and receive the plain teachings of the Bible in order to be saved. Whenever there is a difference between the teachings of the Bible and the church, the church is always wrong, because God's Word is true and forever settled in heaven. The Bible is the highest authority and the final authority. Those who accept and believe and obey the Bible find peace, joy, and assurance that they're willing to suffer and even die for. This is salvation.

"But I must show you first the way to accept this salvation as the Bible teaches. We've all been born sinners. The Bible says there is none perfect and that we have all sinned and come short of the glory God planned for us. Christ died on the cross that we might have salvation, not by working for it, not by joining the church because the government demands it, but by faith, by believing that that is our only means of salvation. Then we become children of God.

"The Apostle John says in his Gospel that, 'God so loved the world, that he gave his only begotten Son, that whosoever believeth in him should not perish, but have everlasting life. For God sent not his Son into the world to condemn the world; but that the world through him might be saved. He that believeth on him is not condemned: but he that believeth not is condemned already, because he hath not believed in the name of the only begotten Son of God.'

"Regina, we could never pay for our salvation. Your soul is worth more than all the world. God gave His Son, Jesùs Christ, to die so that all who accept Him as their salvation may be saved. Anyone who believes Jesus is God's Son and follows Him may be saved. God is no respecter of persons.

"You have been wondering. You've been troubled and distressed. That's the kind of person Christ died for. He came not to call those who think they are righteous but sinners like you and me! He asked those who labor and are heavy laden, troubled and worried and confused to come to Him for rest, peace of mind, and peace of heart.

"Christ says, 'Hans and Regina, give me your hearts and let your eyes observe my ways. If any man or woman thirst for the truth, let him come to me and drink of salvation and eternal life.'

"When we draw near to God, seeking answers to our problems, God's Spirit draws near to us. When we call upon Him in the day of trouble, He promises to deliver us and asks only praise and thanks in return. A psalmist of Old Testament times said, 'I sought the Lord, and he heard me, and delivered me from all my fears.' God does the same for us today."

Regina listened spellbound.

"Do you understand that, Regina?" Ferlinden asked.

"Yes; please tell me more."

"There is no other possible way for any of us to be saved than by Christ's death. After He died on the cross, He was in the tomb three days. But He rose from the dead. You've heard about that, haven't you, Regina?"

"Yes."

"And because He rose from the dead, we too can be raised up out of our sins by the power of God. If we confess our sins, He is faithful and just to forgive us our sins and to cleanse us from all unrighteousness. The Apostle Paul describes the experience of the Christian in these words found in the sixth chapter of his letter to Christians in the city of Rome. 'Know ye not, that so many of us as were baptized into Jesus Christ were baptized into his death? Therefore we are buried with him by baptism into death: that like as Christ was raised up from the dead by the glory of the Father, even so we also should walk in newness of life. For if we have been planted together in the likeness of his death, we shall be also in the likeness of his resurrection.' Isn't that wonderful?

"If you confess with your mouth Jesus Christ as Lord and believe in your heart that God raised Him from the dead, you are saved."

"And infants can't confess," said Regina.

"That's right, Regina, nor can they believe in their hearts. Nowhere in the Scriptures does Christ or His disciples teach anything that would support infant baptism."

"Then infant baptism can't save me?"

"What do you think, Regina?"

"I'm almost sure it can't. I'm not at all satisfied."

"The Bible says that he that believeth and is baptized shall be saved and that we should humble ourselves in the sight of

157

the Lord. An infant doesn't know anything about sin, or believing, or humbling himself. But this teaching on baptism, Regina, is only part of the Gospel. Christ says that if we love Him, we will keep His commandments. That means that nothing in His Word will be hard for us to obey. We will obey because we love Him.

"The Bible teaches us we are to be separated from the world unto God. The Apostle John wrote many centuries ago that we must 'Love not the world, neither the things that are in the world. If any man love the world, the love of the Father is not in him.' When we love Him, the things of this world lose their attraction. God is a jealous God. He wants us to love Him above any other person or thing.

"Who then could decide for us? Our parents, our pastor, the government, the church? No, Regina. We are all saved upon our own individual confession. No one can confess your sins but you yourself. No one can pledge your love to God for you. Do you understand that, Regina?"

"I think I do."

"A person who loves the Lord with all his heart and accepts Jesus as his Saviour becomes a son of God. He is a new creature. He is born again. Not as a child is born, but he is born of the Spirit of God. As soon as we're born again, all things become new. Old things pass away, our old desires and ambitions, evil habits and selfishness—everything. Regina, it's wonderful. The only way you can know how it is, is to experience it.

"With this new life comes the same peace Felix Manz and Conrad Grebel had. It surpasses all understanding. God says that He remembers our sins against us no more forever. He casts them away as far as the east is from the west. That's wonderful, Regina. Those who die in their sins will have to answer to God for them on the judgment day, but those who die saved need have no fears.

"The Lord is our salvation, and we need have no fear. He

158

is the strength of our lives, and we need not be afraid. When God is for us, it matters not who is against us.

"The Bible also teaches true discipleship which means that our entire way of life must be patterned after Christ. That means we can't hide our identity, for everything we say and think and do will be an outward expression of our inner experience with Christ. 'Whosoever will come after me,' Jesus said, 'let him deny himself, and take up his cross, and follow me.' It's not attending church every Sunday. It's far more than that. It's living with Christ and for Christ every moment of every day. We are no longer our own, but Christ's, for He has purchased us with His own precious blood, and put His Spirit within us to guide us and make us want to follow Him. Do you understand that, Regina?"

"Yes," she said. "Tell me more."

"Regina, you must also know that God does not promise an easy life to those who follow Him. He promises His children misunderstandings, suffering, trials, hardships, but He tells them to count it all joy when they fall into many kinds of temptations, knowing that the trying of faith worketh patience.

"When our minds are stayed on Christ, we can have perfect peace. And even though you may have to stand against your parents, Regina, you can know Christ stands with you. The Bible asks children to obey their parents, but when parents ask their children to do something contrary to God's will, God's higher law that we should obey Him rather than man must be our guide. 'He that loveth father or mother more than me,' Jesus said, 'is not worthy of me.' "

"And that would mean a friend, too?" asked Regina.

"It would mean any person or anything that could keep us from serving God with all our hearts. Unless we love Him above everything else, we do not really love Him. God gives us love in our hearts for everyone, but when that love is greater than our love for God, it becomes an idol. We will love all men—even those who despise us and seek to destroy us. Jesus said that he that hateth his brother is a murderer, and we know that no murderer has eternal life.

"I can't get done thanking God for bringing me to the light of the whole Gospel. My heart was heavy, my soul restless and disturbed, when one day on the road I saw a little booklet written by Zwingli against the Anabaptists. In that booklet, Conrad Grebel was mentioned. I began to seek and search and pray as you have been doing, Regina. As time went on I learned little by little what Grebel and the other Swiss brethren believed. I met Felix Manz one day and he instructed me and gave me a burning desire to learn what the Bible really teaches. Now he is gone, you tell me. He did not live in vain, if before he died he gave you this desire to know the truth. It is up to me to help lost troubled souls find Christ."

Regina's face glowed and her blue eyes shone.

"I wish," she whispered, "I wish I could be baptized tonight before we go back. Yesterday when I saw Felix Manz die I knew he had what I wanted."

"You believe Jesus is the Christ the Son of God, who died for your sins, and that by believing you can be saved from eternal punishment, Regina?"

"Yes.'

'And you confess you've been a lost sinner and away from God?"

"Yes, I do."

"And you're willing to forsake the world tonight and give yourself wholly unto God for as long as you will live?"

"Yes, I am. Hans," said Regina, looking up into his face, "you said you were waiting to see what I was going to do. I am taking this step, whether you do or not."

"I'm waiting for him to ask me the same questions," said Hans.

"Oh, Hans!" cried Regina, "I wish we could be baptized together."

"God bles, you, Hans," cried Johann Ferlinden. "God bless you both. Moses, over there is the jar of mountain water you caught for me tonight. Will you bring it over? God provides all our needs, you see. At the entrance of His cathedral He provided the water with which to baptize you. Will you kneel?"

Together Hans and Regina knelt on the bare earth floor of the cave. Johann Ferlinden baptized Regina. Then he asked Hans the same questions and baptized him. With a hand resting on each bowed head, he prayed, "God, grant these souls peace in greater measure than they have had distress. And as Thou hast promised, supply their needs; especially courage and strength in place of fear. But, above all, we pray that as they have heeded Thy invitation to come unto Thee for forgiveness, they may hear and obey Thy voice throughout their lives. In Jesus' name, Amen."

Hans helped Regina to her feet. "Thank you, Hans," she whispered, "for bringing me here. Sometimes I thought God would never answer my prayer, but I was never so ready to receive His answer as today. I want to love Him the rest of my life because He saved me."

"Yes, Regina, we will love Him forever, and it does not matter whether we live here long or short. Knowing Him means more than life."

"And God will help you be faithful to your promise to Him," said Ferlinden. "He will help you let your lights shine. What do you expect to do now, Regina?"

"I don't know. If I tell Hofmeiers, they will be horrified or angry. If we tell Michel, he will say we've disgraced the family. What shall I do?"

"That is not for me to say, Regina," answered Ferlinden. "God will lead you day by day. You will meet opposition, but God will help you through it all. Trust Him completely. What are you going to do, Hans?"

"I'm going to go home and wait until the folks come back.

By God's help, I intend to tell them everything. If they turn me out, then I don't know what I'll do. I will try to convince them what I have is real. If Regina can get back to the Hofmeier home and keep this from the pastor and his wife for several days at least, maybe God will show us what to do."

"Trust Him," said Ferlinden. "God has your lives planned."

"We must go, Hans."

"God bless you both," said Ferlinden. "And pray with me that if it's His will, I will locate my wife. If I go out, I will very likely be picked up. I will stay here until God sends me word to leave."

"I will pray," said Regina.

"So will I," added Hans.

"Thank you. And if we never meet again on this earth, I expect to meet you both in heaven," Ferlinden added softly, following them to the entrance of the cave. "Depart in peace."

Hans helped Regina over the garden fence at the Hofmeier home. "Thank God, we made it," he whispered. "And God help you get safely into the house. I'm going home now and crawl into bed and sleep for two days. After the folks come back, I'll slip over here some night to let you know how things are. Be on the watch when you come out to the pump."

"I'll be watching," she answered. "Good-by and God bless you."

XXVI

Regina awoke with a start. Catri was standing beside her bed.

"Are you sick, Regina?"

Regina sat up straight and rubbed her eyes. "Did you call me?"

"I called you twice. Are you sick, Dear?"

"No." Regina threw back the covers. "You called me twice? I'm sorry. Why, Catri, you mean it's—?"

"Yes, the sun is up." Catri laughed. "Don't you hear the twins? Heinrich said being outside all day yesterday must have made you sleepy." Catri walked to the door. "I told him I'd just let you sleep but I couldn't wait any longer to find out if you were all right. I'm glad you're not sick. Heinrich had to leave; so I ate with him."

"And I didn't hear you?"

Catri laughed. "I just told you, Regina, so you won't need to hurry to get our breakfast." Catri closed the door. Regina dropped to her knees beside the bed.

* * *

All day Lisette wore a look of determination as she dashed about the castle kitchen, baking, scrubbing, cleaning, and scouring. Not for months had the kitchen been cleaned so thoroughly. That task finished, she made her way to Lady Englehard's chamber.

"Come."

Lisette bowed politely. "Lady Englehard, what will you be pleased to have me do for you now? The kitchen work is all done."

"You may polish all the brass, all the copper, and all the silver in all the rooms on this floor. You know what I mean. That will keep you busy all day. But for coming home late yesterday, you may do exactly that. You are to do this besides your regular work, you understand."

Lisette's countenance fell. She had often been told to do polishing in the various rooms, when she wasn't occupied in the kitchen, but never had she been assigned such a job for one day. Frowning and mumbling, she descended the stairs with less speed than she had ascended.

"It's not fair," she muttered, pulling one rag after another out of the bag behind the storeroom door. "If I would have done what she did—" She tore one rag in two and slammed the door.

* * *

Although her legs ached, Regina was surprised she felt so well after she had washed and dressed. She drank a cup of tea, ate two slices of bread, then bathed the twins as usual. Several times she hummed softly as she went about her work.

"I'm glad you're happy today," said Catri. "The way you looked last evening, I was afraid you'd be sad all day."

* * *

Supper was over and the washed dishes were stacked when Lisette entered the lord's office, rag and cup in hand.

Lord Englehard was sitting at his highly polished table, one hand resting on the silver inkwell, his gaze fixed on a paper before him.

"What are you up to now?" he asked frowning.

"Your honor, I knocked and you said, 'Come.' "

"But what are you up to with that cup and rag?"

"Your honor, Lady Englehard told me to polish your silver inkwell and the brass candlesticks, and the—"

"What?" came the lord's agitated voice. "This time of the day? I mean night? You're mistaken. It's time for you to be going to bed, Lisette."

"I know it is, Lord Englehard, but—but—she told me I had to do it today yet."

"But you've been polishing in almost every room I've been in today. Every time I turn around there you are with that rag and cup. She knows how that annoys me."

"But you see, Lord Englehard," began Lisette cautiously, trembling, "she told me to polish in all the rooms today for my punishment."

"What punishment?"

"Your honor, for coming home so late from Zurich."

"And just why were you so late? The lady was much displeased."

"Lord Englehard," ventured Lisette, wetting her lips and stepping closer to the table, "I was all ready to start home when I saw the crowd gathering along the Limmat River."

The lord scowled, "You mean you loitered to see Manz drowned? I wouldn't even have allowed Peter to go to see that, if he would have asked. Is that the reason you wanted a horse to go to Zurich?"

Lisette shifted from one foot to the other. "No, I knew nothing about that until I got there. No, Lord Englehard, it wasn't the drowning I stayed to see, but something else that shocked me and that you should know."

"What's that?"

Lisette bent forward. "The pastor's maid was in the crowd and she acted very shameful."

"Shameful?" asked the lord, pushing his chair away from the table. "Explain." He started to get up, but didn't.

"Oh," Lisette began, "you would have thought Manz was her own brother the way she cried and carried on."

"Cried?"

"And that is not all," added Lisette, trying not to smile. "She even went over to talk to his mother and brother."

"Whose mother and brother?"

"Felix Manz's. I know that's who they were."

"She talked to them!" Lord Englehard got up.

"I saw it with my own eyes, Lord Englehard."

"And you're sure it was the pastor's maid?"

"I know it was. I watched her every second. That's why I stayed there. And I followed her all the way home. I know it was Regina; that is her name, Lord Englehard. Regina, from Weisslingen."

Lord Englehard clasped and unclasped his hands. He ran his fingers through his hair.

"And that's why you came in late?"

"Yes, Lord Englehard. I wanted to tell you last night, but I didn't have a chance."

"But as many times as I saw you today, why didn't you tell me before now? Don't you realize how serious this could be?"

"Oh," said Lisette, shuddering. "That's why I could hardly make myself tell you, Lord Englehard."

"And what did she say to the woman?"

"I couldn't hear, Lord Englehard."

"You may be sure of this one thing, Lisette," said the lord, shaking his finger, "that if you haven't told me the truth tonight, you will be punished and you will have to do something far worse than polishing copper and silver. But," he added with a gesture of his open hand, "if you are telling me the truth, you will not go without your reward. You may be excused now. No matter what Lady Englehard has told you, you let this room go for tonight." He followed her to the door and out into the hall. He stood at the window looking down into the courtyard below.

"Lisette," he called, "if that's Peter coming there, tell him to come up to see me before he puts his horse away."

"Yes, Lord Englehard."

Smiling, Lisette ran across the courtyard. "The lord wants to see you at once, Peter. Oh, it's you, Andreas. I thought it was Peter. Where is Peter?"

"I think he's in the stable."

166

"You tell him Lord Englehard wants to see him at once and before he puts his horse away. It's important."

Lord Englehard was standing with his hands behind him when Peter entered.

"Your honor," Peter said, "you called for me?"

"I did, Peter," he said, drawing a breath. "There's nothing in the world as unpredictable as a woman, is there?"

"I guess not, Lord Englehard. Andreas said Lisette told him you had to see me. What has she done?"

"It's the pastor's maid."

"Who?"

"Pastor Hofmeier's maid."

Peter stared. "What has she done?"

"That's exactly what I'm going to find out and tonight yet."

"What do you want me to do, Lord Englehard?"

"I want you to go get her at once."

"And—and then what?"

"Bring her up here to me. Go and do as I tell you. I want to see her at once. If what I heard is not true, then the one who lied about her will be most severely punished. If it is true, she certainly must be questioned."

Peter's feet seemed leaden as he walked out of the room.

Peter hesitated before he knocked. Through the window he could see Regina on the rocker holding both babies in her lap. Frieda had a little hand up to Regina's face, trying to pull a strand of blond hair which hung loose at her temple. Catri was sitting nearby, smiling at the three.

Peter knocked so softly no one heard. Lifting the latch, he opened the door gently. "I hate to intrude on such a happy scene," he announced, stepping inside.

"Why, Peter," smiled Catri. "Come in. Did you knock?"

"I did, but you didn't hear; so I just made myself at home and walked in."

"That's what you're supposed to do all the time," said

Catri. "Come on over and sit down. Isn't that a picture on the chair there?"

"A very pretty picture."

"Sit down," invited Catri.

"I can't," he said; "I came by special command." Peter cleared his throat.

"But Heinrich's not in yet," said Catri.

"It's not Heinrich I came after," said Peter in a low serious voice. "It's—it's Regina this time."

"Oh," said Catri. "Regina never mentioned it. You say by special command? That sounds important."

Peter's hand shook and his tongue seemed paralyzed. He could not look at Regina.

"Lord Englehard," he said, looking at Catri, "sent me down to bring Regina up to the castle."

"Regina? Why does he want her up there?"

"I couldn't tell you, Aunt Catri. He just sent me down to get her. He said he wanted to have a talk with her."

"Peter, you're joking. It's bedtime."

"I'm not joking," said Peter. "And I don't want to scare either of you, but someone has put out an evil report about Regina, and the lord must ask her about it."

"What!" cried Catri. "An evil report! Not about Regina!"

XXVII

Regina looked into Catri's frightened face. "I guess you'll have to take the twins," she said, "so I can get ready."

"You mean you're really going to go?" cried Catri.

"Shouldn't I? If the lord told Peter to come and get me, I'll have to, won't I?"

"But you don't even act excited, and I'm all worked up."

"I'd better go, Catri, and have it over."

Catri took Frieman and handed him to Peter. "Here," she said, "hold him for me a minute."

"Regina," Catri said, taking Frieda, "do you have any idea who's responsible for this?"

"I have no idea," answered Regina. "I'll be ready in a minute, Peter," she said, going into her bedroom.

"If only Heinrich were here," exclaimed Catri. "I don't understand what's keeping him. He's got to come, Peter. This is outrageous."

Regina was not long in getting ready, for she did not take time to change her dress. When she came from her room, Catri's eyes filled with tears. "Don't let anyone get by with lies about you," she cried.

"I'll just tell the truth, Catri," answered Regina.

"But what a sad ending to our happy day," cried Catri. "Peter, you bring her home, will you?"

"I certainly will not let her come down the hill alone," answered Peter. "What am I to do with this baby? Take him along?"

"Lay him in on my bed," said Catri. "If only Heinrich were here to go along."

"Please don't cry, Catri." Regina hugged her as she went out the door.

"In my excitement I forgot to bring a horse along for you, Regina," said Peter, before they reached the gate.

"I can walk," said Regina.

"You walk? Indeed, you will not. You ride my horse and I will walk. Do you know who has been tattling on you, Regina?"

"No, I don't, Peter."

He helped her up onto his horse.

"I hope you're not afraid," said Peter softly.

"Why should I be?"

"If it's something bad, it can't be a true report. I'm glad you're not afraid."

Just before they reached the weeping willow trees, Peter stopped. "Regina," he said, "I've taken quite a few Anabaptists up this hill in the past few months."

"Yes. And I've often wondered how they felt and how you felt doing it, Peter."

"But I was going to tell you I'm glad this is different," he said gently. "You're riding on my horse and I'm ready to defend you. If I can be of any assistance, please let me know. Regina, all you need to do is speak the word."

"Thank you, Peter."

"You know I would do anything in the world for you."

"Thank you."

All the way up the long hill, Peter walked with head bowed. Not until he helped her dismount at the castle entrance did he speak again, and when he did, his voice was a little unsteady. "Regina," he said, "whatever this report is, I will never believe anything bad about you. You're not afraid now?"

"No. But you'll have to show me where to go. I've never been in the castle."

He opened the door. "Step inside until I tie the horse. I'll be right in."

Peter led Regina up the stairs to the room where he had taken many others.

At the sight of Regina, the lord's stern lines softened a little. "Sit down here," he said, pointing to a chair near his own at the table. "You may be excused, Peter, but wait in the vestibule until I call."

"Yes, Lord Englehard. I'll be waiting."

"You may take off your wraps, if you like," said the lord to Regina.

Regina removed her coat and head scarf, and draped them over the back of the chair.

"Your name?"

"Regina Strahm."

"And you've been working for Pastor Hofmeier, I understand."

"About five months."

"How do you like your work there?"

"I've enjoyed it very much."

"Who is your father?"

"Friedrich Strahm, the weaver at Weisslingen."

"Were you home recently?"

"Yesterday."

"In the afternoon?"

"In the forenoon."

"When did you get back to Kyburg?"

"Last evening."

"What time did you get back?"

"I'm not sure of the hour, but soon after dark."

"What time did you leave Weisslingen?"

"Before noon."

"Where did you go from there?"

"To Zurich."

"What did you do in Zurich?"

"I purchased a bowl and a pair of shoes."

"Did you stop any place else in Zurich?"

"I stopped to see my brother Michel."

"Where?"

"He works at Mathis Bartsche's print shop."

"I see. And how long were you there?"

"Not very long."

"Then why did you get home so late? You must have been detained somewhere."

Regina waited a moment. "I stopped to watch what was going on along the river."

Lord Englehard leaned forward. "And what was going on along the river?"

"A prisoner was being drowned."

"And what kind of prisoner?"

"An Anabaptist prisoner."

"Do you know his name?"

"Felix Manz."

"And what do you have to say about the drowning?"

"What do you mean?"

"Do you think the authorities did right in having him drowned?"

Regina thought a moment. "I have no right to criticize authority," she answered. "But I believe it's wrong to kill anyone."

"Then you mean to say that that Anabaptist, as wicked as he was, had your sympathies and you condemn authority for drowning him?"

Regina hesitated. "I was very much touched," she answered. "It made me sad because his life was taken, but it also made me glad because—" She hesitated again.

"Finish what you started to say," commanded the lord.

"Because he had no fear of death."

Lord Englehard toyed with his silver inkwell, opening and closing the lid.

"You don't think under any circumstances it's right to get rid of a man who persists in his evil work of going against the

172

church and the government, spreading damnable heresy like Manz did?"

Regina's cheeks flushed. "The Bible says only those who believe and are baptized shall be saved."

Lord Englehard frowned.

"You shock me," he said. "You seem to know something of Anabaptist gibber. Have you ever talked to Pastor Hofmeier like this?"

"He has never asked me these questions."

Lord Englehard shook his head. "Never has? Does he know you were in Zurich yesterday?"

"Yes."

"And does he know you stopped to watch the drowning of Manz?"

"I did not tell him I did. He began to say something about it, but his wife told him not to talk about it."

"Why?"

"She said something about having bad dreams."

"Bad dreams, indeed! But at the drowning, is it true that you cried?"

"I believe I did. Yes, I remember I did."

"Did you know Manz?"

"I never saw him before that day."

"Then why did you cry?"

"I couldn't help it. He was so brave and true to the last, and his face shone with a strange light. I will never forget."

Lord Englehard opened and closed the lid of the inkwell. Suddenly he gripped the edge of the table. "You have talked with Anabaptists, haven't you?" he asked.

"I spoke a few words to his mother."

"Right there in public?"

"I just asked her if that was her son, and why he had to be drowned. Was it wrong for me to ask her that?"

"It was wrong for you to get near her or any other Anabaptist," came the lord's emphatic voice. "They are to be feared

173

as much as deadly serpents! You did very wrong," he added. "It was a disgrace to your father as well as to the pastor. As long as you are working for him you should be very careful of your conduct. He carries a very important responsibility in this canton. How many other Anabaptists have you talked with?"

Regina hesitated. "Just a few," she answered.

"When?"

Regina's fingers picked at the folds of her skirt. "Last night," she answered.

"Last night? In Zurich?"

"No."

"Where?"

"I cannot tell you."

"You cannot?" demanded the lord. "And why not?"

"I—I mean I choose not to," she answered softly.

"You mean you refuse to tell me!"

Regina's cheeks got red. "It would not be fair to tell you, Lord Englehard."

"Fair to whom?" he demanded.

"Fair to the ones I talked to."

"Of course, you refuse to tell me because like all the other Anabaptist sympathizers, you don't want to expose anyone. That's it, isn't it?"

"That is it," answered Regina. "I will expose myself, but no one else, Lord Englehard. I have to have my own faith. I will have to die my own death."

"You mean—" Lord Englehard leaned forward. "You certainly can't mean you have already decided to accept this wicked, deceptive doctrine of devils?"

"If you mean the Anabaptist faith," Regina answered calmly, "I have."

Lord Englehard leaned back in his chair. The tenseness of his face relaxed.

"You most certainly have been deceived, Child," he said at

length. "You have no idea what you have said. Listen to me now. If I let you go back, will you promise to behave yourself and never, never talk to another Anabaptist and do only what the pastor tells you?"

Regina sat up straight. She looked at the lord with serious eyes.

"Will you?" he repeated.

"But I did not start out to turn back, Lord Englehard," began Regina. "The peace I now have in my heart is worth more than life. I waited and prayed long months for it. I cannot promise you that, for I have no more intentions of turning back than Felix Manz had."

The lord arose. "You mean—" he cleared his throat. "You mean Pastor Hofmeier's maid is willing to go to prison?"

"If it must be, I am willing to go to prison," Regina answered. "I know God will not let me go there unless it's His will."

"But," declared the lord, "the prision is not like this room, Child. The prison is dark. And it's bare, and cold."

"But God will be there to help me bear it."

"You are only talking, Child," cried the lord, waving both arms. "How old are you?"

"Nineteen."

"And you talk like this? Nineteen! You can't realize what you're saying. You have not thought this through. You've acted on the spur of the moment." He cleared his throat again. "You haven't been baptized, I hope."

"Yes," answered Regina. "I've been baptized, because I believe with my own heart."

"Do you realize what this will mean?"

"I knew what it would mean before I made the decision."

"What does it mean? Tell me, if you think you know."

Regina bowed her head for a moment. "It means misunderstanding," she answered, lifting her head, "and separation from my family, and imprisonment."

"Go on," said the lord. "And what else could it mean?"

"It might mean cold and hunger and solitary confinement before my death."

"And you are not afraid of all of that?" he asked.

"No," answered Regina, "for with all that there is also peace and joy and everlasting life."

The lord hesitated a moment, then walked slowly to the door. Stepping to the top of the stairway, he rang a bell.

Peter came instantly.

Regina stood waiting in the doorway, her coat and scarf hanging over her left arm. In the light of the hanging lamp in the hall, Peter noticed at once that she was still undisturbed. He breathed a quick sigh of relief.

"Ready to go back now?" he asked.

Lord Englehard cleared his throat. "Put this young lady up in the third cell in the tower," he said, and before Peter could ask any questions, he retreated into his room and closed the door.

Peter's face turned ashen as he grabbed the railing and stared at the door Lord Englehard had just closed.

"In the tower!" he gasped. "Not you, Regina!"

"Yes," she answered softly, "he meant me."

XXVIII

For a moment, Regina stood clasping and unclasping her trembling hands. She bit her cheek to keep back the tears. "I—I guess it's necessary now, Peter," she said feebly.

With hands that shook, Peter took Regina's coat and scarf and hung them across his arm. "What awful thing has someone told that you deserve treatment like this?" Gently he took her by the hand.

She trembled. "I'm going to fight for you," he said.

"No, Peter," answered Regina, "you will not fight for me. I have—I have done what the others have done that you brought up the hill. This is not different."

"What!" gasped Peter, dropping her hand. He looked down at her.

Regina took a deep breath. "I have taken my stand with them, Peter. You put them in prison and I deserve the same treatment, don't I?"

"But—but, Regina. I—I can't bear to do this! I can't!"

"Do it, Peter," she said. "Do it quickly, and go back and tell Catri where I am."

Peter led Regina up another flight of stairs. The hall above was dark.

"Stand here, Regina, until—" he groped with both hands—"until I find the door. The light is out."

He groaned and at the same time Regina heard him turn the lock. She shivered. "You'll get cold up here, Regina."

"Peter," she said softly, "it will not be colder for me than it was for the others, will it?"

"Regina," Peter found her trembling arm and led her toward the opened door, "it is always dark and lonesome up here! I can't bear this!" His voice sounded desparate.

"But I won't mind," she answered. Quickly she brushed away a tear. "I'll close my eyes and see the picture I have of those peaceful, happy faces I saw yesterday. And I don't think I'll mind the stillness so much either, Peter. I'll—I'll forget everything and think about the wonderful things I heard them say."

"Yesterday?" whispered Peter. "What are you talking about, Regina?"

"Yesterday when I was in Zurich."

"In Zurich?"

"Yes, Peter. Someone reported to the lord something they saw me do there."

"Was it Lisette?" Peter grabbed the casing of the prison door. "I wondered if—if she was up to something. What is this, Regina? Tell me quickly."

"Whoever it was," she answered, "told the truth. Go ask her, if you want to know. But do not condemn her, Peter. I did cry," and Regina's voice trembled, "and I did talk to his mother."

"Whose mother? I don't understand."

"Felix Manz's mother. And I am not sorry. As long as I live, I'll thank God I was there to see it all and speak to her."

There were hurried steps on the stairway now, and voices.

"Good night, Regina," said Peter and he closed the door and locked it.

"Peter," called the lord impatiently.

"Yes, Lord Englehard. I'm here."

"Why isn't there a light?"

"I don't know. It was dark when we came up."

"Have you put her in yet?"

"Yes, your honor."

"Go get a light," ordered the lord. "The pastor wants to talk with her."

But Heinrich did not wait for a light. "Where is that door?" he demanded, groping ahead of the lord. He stumbled.

"Go straight ahead," said the lord. "To the right now."

"Ah, here it is." Heinrich beat on the door with his fist. "Are you in here, Regina?" he said as he gasped for breath.

"Yes."

"I must talk to you at once."

"Why is Peter so slow with that light?" he demanded, beating on the door again.

"Can't you talk to her in the dark?" asked the lord.

"No!" shouted the pastor impatiently. "I want to see her face while I'm talking."

Peter was soon back carrying a lighted lantern.

"Open," commanded the lord.

Peter obeyed. Regina was sitting on the prison bed, a wide wooden ledge built against the stone wall. Her hands were folded in her lap.

"Peter, you come inside the door there and hold up the light," said the lord, standing near by.

Heinrich staggered across the cell floor and sank on the ledge beside Regina. He breathed hard. Regina could tell at once he had been drinking. He pulled out his handkerchief and wiped his flushed face. "I—I came to take you back home with me," he panted. "There's a terrible mistake somewhere, Regina."

Regina did not answer. Lord Englehard watched her, his forehead deeply furrowed.

"I—I simply refuse to believe you're guilty, Regina," continued Heinrich, wiping his face again. "I came home expecting to find you all in bed and instead Catri is frantic and both babies crying. You simply can't stay here overnight."

"But Lord Englehard told Peter to put me here. Peter only did his duty."

"Maybe so," panted Heinrich. "And no doubt Lord Englehard feels he has done his duty, too. But it's my duty to get you out of this place. This is unthinkable, Regina! My maid in prison! It dare not be!"

"Did the lord tell you?" she asked.

"But I can't, I won't believe it. You, after living under my roof these months! Haven't we been good to you, Regina?"

"You have been very kind to me, Heinrich."

"And Catri?"

"She's been wonderful to me, too. It's not that. I have nothing but love in my heart for all of you. I couldn't have worked for anyone who would have treated me any nicer."

"Then why did you leave the lord under the impression you've become an Anabaptist?"

"What the lord has told you is true," answered Regina. "Unless I love God more than I do Catri or the twins or my parents or anyone on earth, I'm not fit to be His disciple. I have enjoyed being in your home. But for a long time I have been searching for the answers to my questions."

"What questions?"

"Just why the Anabaptists are willing to leave their homes and why they believe as they do. Everyone of them I ever met had something I wanted. I have prayed for months for God to show me in some way if they were all wrong and you who oppose them are right."

Peter shifted the lantern. Lord Englehard fumbled with something in his pocket and worked his lower jaw back and forth, grinding his teeth.

"We had no Bible at home to read for ourselves. But I was convinced yesterday when I watched Felix Manz being drowned that he knew the answer and had something real. I could feel it. I could see it on his face. I could see it on his mother's face."

Heinrich groaned and the lord shook his head.

Regina continued. "I prayed all the way home for God to help me find the kind of peace Manz had. I knew I wanted it more than anything in all the world."

"And—and you actually think now you've found that peace?" asked Heinrich weakly.

"I do not only think it, I know it," answered Regina, and in the light of the lantern her deep blue eyes shone.

Heinrich leaned forward. "And when did you say you got this?" he whispered.

"Last night."

"When last night?" Heinrich's eyes bulged.

"I could not tell you the hour," answered Regina. "It was sometime between midnight and dawn."

"She's beside herself," whispered Heinrich. "Come outside. I want to talk to you. Bring the light, Peter, and close the door."

Heinrich's thick voice was tinged with new dread. "Something has happened to her," he said. "That is evident. Catri said she was upset over her parents' leaving for Langnau. I remember. She ate hardly any supper last night. She likely cried herself to sleep, too. Watching Manz must have given her bad dreams. She wasn't herself this morning, because she overslept—and that's not like Regina. This idea that she found some sort of peace between midnight and dawn proves it's just an illusion. I don't like to see her up here alone like this, but—" Heinrich wiped his face. "Maybe if she is alone overnight, she'll snap out of it. But—"

"But," interrupted the lord, tapping Heinrich on the arm, "wait a minute. Illusion or no illusion, she must be dealt with. You may try to excuse her, but the fact remains she's been talking to Anabaptists somewhere. Her speech betrays her. It's a pitiful situation and I feel sorry about the whole thing, but she's got to stay in this prison until she clears herself before the board."

Heinrich Hofmeier's eyes snapped. His face twitched. His chest rose and fell with laborious breathing. "Right away the first thing in the morning," he said, "you must have the board of trustees meet to take care of this."

181

Lord Englehard frowned. "After all, Heinrich, who's running this castle? Lord Englehard or Heinrich Hofmeier?"

"But Regina Strahm is my maid," cried Heinrich. "And she's been a victim of circumstances. Her parents are over there in Langnau. She needs love and protection and it's my duty to see that she gets justice. Let me talk to Lisette."

"She'll get justice, Heinrich," said Lord Englehard. "Don't worry about that. I'm no more anxious to put her in this prison than you are. But she's staying right in there tonight."

"Then will you let me bring her a bowl of warm soup?"

Lord Englehard shook his head. "You've seen her enough tonight. Let her alone to think this through. One night in there will be all she'll want."

"But if she can't sleep, she won't be able to answer the questions when she comes before the board," insisted Heinrich.

"Heinrich," the lord put an unsteady hand on the pastor's shoulder, "you'd better go on home and try to get some sleep yourself. You'd better drink a little more wine, too. Peter. Where's Peter? That's strange! Peter! I thought he was standing there holding this lantern. Peter."

But Peter did not answer. The lantern was hanging on a nail on the wall above the lord's head.

* * *

Catri's eyes were red from crying when Peter came in. He sank on a chair and covered his face with his hands.

"Didn't you see Heinrich?" asked Catri.

"Yes. He's up there now talking to Lord Englehard."

"Isn't he going to bring Regina home soon?"

Peter shook his head. "I don't think so."

"Why not?"

Peter jumped and hurried toward the door. "Because he had me put her in cell number three in the tower!"

"What! Heinrich! Never, Peter! You're beside yourself!"

"No. No. Lord Englehard! Catri, I've got to run back."

"Peter! He can't! He can't! Not Regina, in prison!"

182

XXIX

Andreas was standing guard in front of cell number one when Peter returned from the Hofmeier home to relieve him.

"About time you're coming," Andreas said. "It's way past ten. What's going on out there?"

"Out where?" asked Peter.

"Why, the pastor tore up the steps awhile ago, and he must have been discussing something important with the lord. When he came down a bit ago, he looked stern and upset, and he grabbed my arm and said, 'Andreas, this is the most awful thing that's ever happened in Kyburg,' and before I had a chance to ask him a thing, he tore out the door."

"You mean you haven't heard?" asked Peter.

"Nothing except what Lisette said to me this morning. Peter! You look upset yourself."

"What was it?"

"She said, 'Just wait till the lord and his lady find out what I know and Peter won't want permission to run off down the hill for supper soon again.' I couldn't figure it out to save me."

Peter grabbed Andreas by the shoulder and shook him. "It adds up to something just as cruel and impossible as Lisette is herself. I know, for Lord Englehard told me just now."

"What is that?"

Peter's voice was sad, husky, tired. "You'd never guess," he said, "who Lisette is responsible for sending to cell number three above us."

"Who?"

Peter put a trembling hand on Andreas' shoulder again. "Regina Strahm, the pastor's maid."

"Not Regina! How could Lisette do such a dastardly thing?"

"By the use of her tattling tongue," answered Peter. "Whether it's right or whether it's wrong, she did it. What makes it bad is that Regina says she told the truth."

"You say all this took place in here tonight? And I knew nothing of it? And you say she's up in number three?"

"Yes," said Peter.

"But it's cold up there and dark as pitch," cried Andreas.

"I know it," answered Peter. "But she's not afraid, or else she's putting on an awfully brave front. She walked in as calmly as if she would have been going into her own bedroom at home."

"No, Peter!" Andreas' eyes glared. "You wait till I see Lisette, and there's going to be some fuzz flying! What is this horrible thing Regina is supposed to have done?"

Peter ran his hand over his hair. "I want to stay out of it as much as possible, Andreas," he answered. "I'd rather you'd hear it straight from Regina's own lips. You may go now. I came to take over. There are five men in the cell?"

"No. Seven tonight."

"Peter."

Peter turned. "That's Lord Englehard. What could he want now? I'll run and be right back."

"You called me, Lord Englehard?"

The lord was standing in the hall, a cup in his hands. "Here," he said, holding out the cup. "Take this to the young lady. The pastor is frenzied. This might help her get a night's sleep. The lantern is hanging where you left it. Why did you sneak off like that, Peter?"

"Lord Englehard," answered Peter, "I had to run down and tell Catri."

"Catri?"

"The pastor's wife, your honor."

"But you are not to leave without permission. You know that, Peter. She knew she was up here."

184

"Yes, your honor. I will not do it again. But you see, Catri is my aunt and she expected her back. She knew nothing whatever of any of this, and it's a terrible blow, Lord Englehard."

"Terrible blow is right. This is uncanny." The lord frowned. "Go now," he said, "before the milk gets cold."

Peter reached for the lantern. He was trembling when he tiptoed toward the prison cell door. He stood motionless, listening. Regina was talking to herself. "Oh, my heavenly Father, Thy will—"

Peter pressed his ear against the door. The voice within faded into incomprehensible phrases and presently he heard her begin to sing. He waited before he rapped.

"Yes."

Peter unbolted and swung open the door. "Regina," he whispered, "here." He walked over to her, lantern in his left hand, holding out the cup in the other. "The lord sent you this. Please drink it while it's warm."

"What is it, Peter?"

"I'm not sure, but it looks to me like warm milk. Don't you like milk?"

"Yes, very much. But," she did not take it, "are you sure there's nothing else in it?"

"Shall I taste it?"

"Please."

"I'm positive it's only sweetened milk, Regina."

She took it from his outstretched hand. "Thank you, Peter, for bringing it. And thank the lord. It was very kind of him. But I can't understand this. I expected nothing but bread and water in prison and now you bring me this."

Peter's sad face brightened. "I am very sure Lord Englehard never did such as this for any other prisoner," he said.

"Then he should not do it for me," cried Regina, "for I am no better than any of them. But I will drink it since you were kind enough to bring it."

"Regina," Peter said, "I think it simply can't be true that I had to put you in here."

She handed him the empty cup. "And, Peter," she answered, gently, "I thought it could not be true that you had to take all those other Anabaptists up the hill. And I had to see you doing it, not once, but again and again, and then even took them down the hill and on into Zurich to be tried."

Peter stood dazed.

"That couldn't possibly have hurt you like this does me," he said softly.

"But it did, Peter," she said quietly.

"But you didn't know any of those people, did you?"

"Not personally, Peter. But I felt a strange nearness to them. I couldn't explain it at the time. But now I know."

"Why?"

"Because my soul was searching for that same Spirit they had." Her face became more radiant with each word. "And now that I have it, too, and I'm born of that same Spirit, we are all brothers and sisters in the family of God. Every true Anabaptist is my brother and sister. We are closer to each other than to our own brothers and fathers and mothers. We all share and suffer and rejoice together. Do not pity me, Peter," she said, smiling. "I never was so happy in my life."

Slowly Peter backed to the door. "Good night, Regina," he said softly as he closed the door. But he opened it again. "Is there anything more I can do for you before I leave?" he asked.

"Nothing, Peter."

* * *

"What did he want?" asked Andreas impatiently.

"He wanted me to take a cup of milk up to Regina."

"Milk? To a prisoner? This time of night? Then she won't be held long, for whoever heard of Lord Englehard doing that? Cell number three? Reckon I could slip up and see her tonight yet?"

186

Peter drew a long, long breath. "Andreas," he said, "you're a watchman. You know where the key is. Lord Englehard sent her milk so she can sleep. But, do as you like. But listen, if you do, you do it at your own risk. See? Don't tell her I sent you up and don't you tell Lord Englehard or anyone else I said you could."

Andreas scratched his head. "Maybe I'd better wait until morning. But I doubt if I'll sleep a wink all night."

* * *

Catri was sitting by the fire crying when Heinrich came in, red-faced and frustrated.

"I just now got Frieman quieted," Catri sobbed. "Heinrich, I'm sick. And I'm worn to a frazzle. Peter came down and told me she's in prison! Heinrich, I'm nearly beside myself!"

"Not only you, Catri," Heinrich panted. "I told Lord Englehard he must call her before the board of trustees to-morrow morning. And may God help her to tell this thing straight. I'm convinced she's bewildered over something that's happened. Listen to this," and Heinrich repeated everything he could remember that Regina had said.

"Oh, Heinrich," cried Catri. "My head aches. I ache all over—"

"Let's go to bed and try to sleep a little while the twins are quiet. If we talk like this, they'll wake up. All our fussing won't help the situation tonight."

Early the next morning Catri climbed the long castle hill, leaving the twins in Heinrich's care.

"What will I do if they cry all the time you're gone?" asked Heinrich, bewildered.

"You said you would keep them. Shouldn't I go after all?"

"Of course. Go. I want you to. I'll manage somehow."

Catri rapped on Lord Englehard's office door. She rapped the second time. Her eyes shimmering with tears, she stood at the top of the stairs waiting. She started down the stairs. then waited. Someone was coming from above.

187

"It's you, Andreas. Where is the lord this morning?"

"I couldn't say. He seldom shows himself this early."

"I wanted to see Regina. I have to see her."

"I just came from there. She's up in number three in the tower."

"I know. But won't I have to get special permission from the lord?"

"Come with me," motioned Andreas. "I will unlock the door."

"You say you saw her this morning? How is she?" Catri grabbed Andreas' sleeve.

"I'll let you decide that when you see her."

Catri held back. "Oh, Andreas, don't tell me it's that bad," she whispered. "How can I stand it?"

"Come," said Andreas, leading the way.

Catri was sobbing before Andreas got the door open. Regina rose to meet her.

"Regina," cried Catri, throwing her arms around Regina's neck, and smoothing back her beautiful black hair.

"Don't cry for me, Catri," she said. "I'm all right. I'm only sorry I can't help you with the twins today. Kiss them for me."

"But, Regina," sobbed Catri, "tell me it's not true that you are joining that awful sect."

"Yes, Catri," answered Regina softly. "I know now that I've wanted to be one with them for months. I mean I wanted something that would completely satisfy and give me peace of mind. I wasn't sure what it was, but I knew when I watched Felix Manz going to his death that he had what I wanted."

Catri jumped up. "And—and you mean you made up your mind then and there on watching a man die? Regina!"

"It was his—his spirit," answered Regina, softly, "his dying testimony that convinced me. That and his mother's love and faith. Something whispered to me then in my heart. I can't explain it, but it was like a voice calling me to confess all my sins and hold nothing back."

"Oh, my dear Regina!" cried Catri, sadly. "I'm so sorry, so sorry now Heinrich ever borrowed that horse for you. I had no idea you would run into something like that. If you only hadn't gone to Zurich. I'll think of you every time I look at that soup bowl. After all, we've told you about this evil doctrine! Regina, it simply horrifies me! You, Regina! I can't believe this. Won't you please swear and tell the board of trustees today you'll forget it all and come back to us and start over?"

"Catri," answered Regina, "I could never do that. I would be giving up my joy, my everlasting life. I would sooner spend the rest of my life in prison than do that. If you could only understand how happy I am."

"Poor Regina," cried Catri. "Heinrich told me you were confused, but I had no idea it was this bad. We were so hoping by morning you would be all straightened out. Regina, Regina!"

"Don't cry for me, Catri," pleaded Regina. "I am straightened out at last. I was confused and disturbed for a long time. I wish I could make you understand how I feel."

Catri shook her head. "You will surely see your mistake yet," she sobbed, "and come back to us. I'm lost without you. The twins are lost. The house is empty. Nothing seems right."

"If I came back, Catri, I could never be the same."

Catri looked up sharply.

"I love you dearly," continued Regina. "And I love the darling twins. They have become such a part of me. But I had to give up you and all my family for my new love for Christ. Nothing dare stand between me and my loyalty to Him. Do you understand, Catri?"

"No, Regina, I do not understand," sobbed Catri. "It sounds so awful, so mysterious—that I can't help believing you've been hoodwinked into this. It's another example of how deceptive—" Tears streamed down her cheeks. "Andreas," she sobbed, "go along home with me—and bring back Regina's blue dress, and her comb. I want her to look her best when she goes before the trustees." Blinded with tears, Catri stumbled down the stairs.

"What more can we do, Andreas?"

Andreas shook his head. "I talked to her before you came until I saw it was no use. She's picked up Anabaptist talk some place."

"Andreas, I wish the lord would let you go to Zurich and tell Michel to come out. He could do something with her, if anyone could."

XXX

The sun was shining in the east windows of the large court-room when Peter brought Regina in. A strange silence like the stealthy stillness before a storm fell over the group. The six solemn-faced trustees were seated around the long table. To the lord's immediate left sat Heinrich, dismal and haggard. On his right sat Lisette, determined and bold. Her lips twitched as though trying to hold back a grin. The lord pointed to Regina.

"Stand here at the end of the table," Lord Englehard said to Regina.

"You may remain at the door, Peter," he added, giving Peter a glance. "This will likely not take long."

Regina stood waiting. Her fine features, and soft, blond hair were accented by her blue dress which fell around her slender ankles in graceful folds. Her dark eyes shone as though some new understanding had been given her. She did not wince under the nine pair of eyes before her.

"The purpose of this session is fully understood," began the lord. "And now that we are all here, we will have Lisette tell the trustees what she saw in Zurich day before yesterday."

Peter stood motionless, scarcely breathing. From his position at the closed door, he could see only Regina's profile.

Lisette stood. She looked at Lord Englehard's neck while she spoke.

"After I bought my shoes," she began, "I intended to come straight home. But I met a friend who told me to hang around the river for a while if I wanted to be in on some excitement. That's how I came to see the pastor's maid."

"Explain," said the lord.

Lisette swallowed. "She went over and talked to Felix Manz's mother a long time and hung around and watched. That's why I got home late."

"Did you hear what they talked about?"

"No. I wasn't close enough. But it looked as if they were having secrets. And she," Lisette nodded toward Regina without turning her head, "was crying as if it were her own son or brother."

"Did the woman go to Regina or did Regina go to Manz's mother?"

"She went to her. I mean Regina went to the woman."

"And you're sure it was Manz's mother?"

"I'm positive, because I heard her hollering to her son."

"What did she say, the woman, when she hollered?"

"She begged him not to give up."

Lord Englehard gave his men a significant nod. "What happened after that?"

"I came on to Kyburg."

"Did Regina come on home at the same time?"

"I couldn't say."

Peter's eyes widened.

"Didn't you tell me you came home together?"

"Yes. I followed her all the way."

"Did you see her stop any place after you left Zurich?"

"No, not after we left Zurich."

"Did you see her stop any place in Zurich after she left the scene of the drowning?"

"I couldn't say. She got lost in the crowd for a while."

"That will be all for now, Lisette. Regina," said the lord, looking at her with piercing eyes, "you heard what Lisette just told these trustees. Did she tell the truth?"

Peter held his breath.

"Most of it was true," answered Regina.

"Most of it? What part wasn't true?"

192

"I did not talk to Felix Manz's mother a long time."

"But you did talk with her?"

"Yes."

"Why did you talk to that woman?"

For only a moment Regina hesitated. "I wanted to get near her," she answered, "and I wanted to talk to her because I knew she had something within her that made me love her and I wanted her to speak to me."

The lord's voice was dry and husky and a trifle unsteady. "And what do you think that something within her was?"

Slowly the color crept into Regina's pale cheeks. Her happy eyes gleamed. "I know now it was Christian love."

"Christian love," the lord echoed feebly. "You do not know that she and all the rest of the Anabaptists are full of evil, satanic witchcraft? It was the biggest mistake you ever made in your life, young lady, when you gave way to such an emotional landslide." Turning now to the trustees he added, "You see now," he repeated, "the treacherous, deceiving manner in which these Anabaptists display their doctrine."

The trustees all nodded. Heinrich squirmed.

"Tell us now," continued Lord Englehard, turning again to Regina, "What is your attitude this morning after a night in prison? Have you changed your mind?"

"I did not start out to give up so easily," she answered. "I am determined to remain faithful to the end."

Humiliated, the lord's glance swept the line of trustees. Heinrich looked wretched, wounded.

"And when did you decide to believe this false doctrine?" asked the lord. "Just on the spur of the moment?"

"Oh, no," Regina readily answered. "For a long time I wondered why some of our best neighbors and friends were willing to leave their homes. I couldn't understand. My father couldn't give me a satisfactory answer. I often fretted over this. I knew one thing, they were not satisfied with their infant baptism, and—and so I wondered if my own baptism

193

was enough. I know now it was not, for I had to confess with my own mouth and be baptized upon my own faith. My parents couldn't do that for me, nor the church."

Lord Englehard shook his head despairingly.

Heinrich's face grew red. "All of Zwingli's teachings ignored," he said sadly. "All of my—" he stopped short and covered his face.

"You have not only shocked the pastor," commented the lord, "but you have mortified him, dishonored and disgraced him shamefully, as well as the Holy Christian Church. Do you admit to this group here that you have also been rebaptized?"

"I—I do not mean to disgrace the pastor," said Regina. "He has been very good to me. He will not have to answer for my sins or for my baptism. Yes, I have been baptized."

"When?" shouted the lord.

"Recently."

"How recently?"

"Since the drowning of Manz."

"And where?"

"In God's cathedral."

The trustees looked at each other.

"Where did you say?" repeated the lord.

"In God's cathedral."

Peter stepped forward.

"And where is this cathedral?" asked Lord Englehard.

"Where it has always been."

"Locate it geographically."

Regina thought for a moment. "I'd better not try," she answered. "I might tell you wrong."

"Well, is it in this canton?" Lord Englehard tapped his fingers on the table.

"As far as I know, I have never been out of the canton."

"And you were baptized with water?"

"With water and the Spirit."

"And who baptized you?"

194

"One of God's servants."

Lord Englehard leaned forward. "What is his name?"

"Christian."

"Christian?" shouted the lord.

"Yes."

"Does he have any other name?" asked the lord impatiently. "What is it, Regina?"

"I would rather not tell."

Lord Englehard turned to the trustees. "You see now what we have on our hands, another full-fledged Anabaptist. Do any of you have any suggestions? Lisette, you may go to your work."

"Ask her about her parents," suggested the oldest of the trustees.

"Regina, the pastor told me your parents went over to Langnau to bring home one of your brothers to save him from Anabaptist influence. Is that correct?"

"Yes, it is."

"A very noble and commendable act. When did they leave?"

"Day before yesterday."

"When will they be back?"

"I do not know. Soon, I believe."

"And you are certain your action will greatly displease them, aren't you?"

"I fear it might."

"Might?" gasped Lord Englehard. "You know it will. It will almost kill them. Any young lady as attractive as you are surely must be the hope and pride of any parents. Doesn't the Bible teach that children are to love and respect and obey their parents?"

"Yes, it does," answered Regina. "I have always loved and respected my parents, and I do now. I know J disobeyed my father when I talked to Felix Manz's mother, for he often warned me to be careful about asking any questions, but my Father in heaven told me I should. He is above my father—my

195

earthly father. Oh, I know it was God who told me to speak to her."

The lord cleared his throat. "What do you suppose your parents will do when they return and find you here in prison?"

Regina's eyes filled with sudden tears.

Peter's lips parted as he watched her face.

"They will listen to my story and when they find out how happy and settled I am at last, well, I hope they will accept the faith, too."

The lord clenched his fist. Heinrich Hofmeier reached over and touched his arm. "Give her three days to come out of this," he whispered. "Three days will bring a change."

"Shall we send this Anabaptist back to prison?" asked the lord, glancing at the trustees.

"Yes," came the unanimous answer.

"Take her back, Peter," ordered the lord. "And nothing but bread and water."

Regina gave him one fleeting glance when she passed him as he held open the door. Without a word he led her back up the stairs to cell number three.

"Good-by," he said softly, closing the door. "You'll get thin on bread and water."

"Good-by and God bless you," answered Regina.

From the single narrow barred opening, Regina could look far down the road below, the road on which she had come to Kyburg less than six months before. The tower window, no wider than her upper arm, admitted enough light during the day so that Regina could see quite distinctly the only object in the cell, a piece of a log. Regina was kneeling beside the log seat when Andreas brought her the bread and water at noon.

"Thank you, Andreas," said Regina, smiling.

He went through strange motions with both hands on his lips and chest, shaking his head in distress and frustration.

196

"What's wrong, Andreas?" asked Regina.

Again Andreas went through the same strange motions.

"You mean you would like to say something and can't?"

Andreas nodded repeatedly.

"You mean you were told not to talk to me?"

Andreas nodded. He blew his nose.

"That's all right, Andreas," whispered Regina. "I understand. We're friends anyway, aren't we?"

Andreas looked frightened. He made one quick nod of his head and immediately closed the door.

* * *

It had long been dark in the prison cell when Peter met the pastor and a young man at the door of the castle.

"This is Michel, Regina's brother, Peter," said Heinrich.

"You mean you want to see her?"

"Yes. Of course."

"The lord, you know, said no one is to speak a word to her."

"This is different," retorted Heinrich. "He came all the way from Zurich to see her, and he must see her tonight. Come!

"By the lord's permission, I'll unlock," answered Peter.

"He knew Andreas went over to tell him," argued Heinrich. "We can't waste any time. Take us up and be quick about it."

"You wouldn't ask me to disobey the lord, would you, Heinrich, not now?"

Lord Englehard appeared in the hall above, agitation written on his face. Heinrich flew up the steps. "Michel is here, her brother. He wants to talk to her."

The lord nodded. "Let him do all the talking, Heinrich."

"Get that light," Heinrich said to Peter. Peter swung open the door. Regina was sitting on the wooden ledge when Peter stepped in. The two men followed. "Michel!" exclaimed Regina. She threw her arms around his neck and kissed him. Taking him by the hand she pulled him to the bunk beside her. Heinrich stared, flushed, breathing heavily. Peter held the lantern.

Michel sat studying Regina's face. He did not speak. Reaching over, he took hold of her wrist and held it. Minutes passed and Michel said nothing, just looked at Regina with an anxious confused expression.

"Did they tell you also not to talk to me?" asked Regina, at length.

"No," said Michel, sadly, taking a deep breath. "I'm just trying to figure this all out."

Regina smiled. "Do not try any longer," she said softly. "I am not sick and I am not disturbed. I have found peace and Christian love. I know now it is the answer, Michel. When we love Jesus, our Saviour, we are unafraid. We have no fear."

Michel's lips moved. "Christian love?" he repeated.

The prolonged silence made Heinrich uneasy. He coughed nervously.

"Since I am here," said Michel at length, "I am at a complete loss to know what to say to you, Regina." A tear ran down his cheek, then another.

"There is nothing to say, Michel," she said. "You would not scold me, for that would not be like you. You must not pity me, for I don't want that. You must not argue with me, because it would only make you unhappy and me stronger, unless, of course, I could convince you I've taken the right way."

"Convince me!" cried Michel, his face turning pale. "All Heinrich has told me, all Catri has told me must be true. I was hoping they were mistaken or that by this time you had changed your mind." Slowly he got to his feet and backed to the door.

"I'm not angry with you," he said. "But I am terribly disappointed and hurt. Good-by, Regina. I'll come back again some evening and I hope you'll be ready to let me help you." Struggling to keep back the tears, Michel hurried down the steps and out into the courtyard.

XXXI

Catri hugged her babies close and cried over their soft little heads. Her haggard, tired eyes searched Heinrich's face for the answer every time he opened the door.

"No change?"

Disappointed, Heinrich shook his head each time.

"But this is the third day," cried Catri.

"I know. But she is as immovable as ever."

"If I would go up and talk to her once more, Heinrich, maybe I could say something."

Heinrich shook his head despairingly.

Catri fretted. "Just once more, Heinrich. There's nothing like trying. Maybe today she'd reason with me. If I'd tell her how the twins cry for her day and night, wouldn't that touch her, Heinrich? She did love these babies and I know she wasn't pretending."

"But you know what she says. She's transferred her love now."

"Oh, it's so impossible; it's so unbelievable; it's stupid, yes, stupid and I always thought Regina was an intelligent girl."

Heinrich shook his head.

Catri continued, half crying, "We should have taken her into our confidence more, Heinrich. I never did try to find out what she was feeling so badly about that morning. Sometimes she was so quiet. I often wondered what she was thinking about, but I didn't like to pry. If I could only do it all over again. If only we would have insisted she go to church every other Sunday, at least," Catri bit her lips nervously. "If only we would not have taken so much for granted, Heinrich."

"What do you mean?"

"Well, we just supposed she understood how awful this false doctrine is. You should have told her, Heinrich. You should have instructed her and warned her every day of your life."

"I know," he said. "But why bemoan that fact now? We'll know better when we get the next maid."

"The next maid!" cried Catri. "Oh, Heinrich, how I hate to think of someone else taking Regina's place! But God knows how badly I need one. I never realized until now how much Regina did for me. I can't get over this, Heinrich, and I never will as long as I live." Catri sank into a chair and dug her finger tips into her hot cheeks. "Even though she has disappointed and deceived us, I'll never forget the nice times we had together. Did you talk to her today?"

"Yes, the lord and I both talked to her."

"What did she have to say?"

"She has an Anabaptist answer for every question."

"And will she say yet who baptized her?"

Heinrich shook his head. "One of God's servants called Christian. That's all we know."

"And she won't tell where it happened or when?"

"Same old answer. Sometime between midnight and dawn in God's cathedral. When she says that," said Heinrich, "I think it's all in her imagination. I still have hopes that a few more days will bring her out of it. Unless she manifests a change of heart by nine o'clock tonight, she'll be transferred to the torture chamber."

"No!" Catri screamed. "Not Regina! In that horrible place!" Her hands pressed her cheek bones.

Heinrich started pacing.

"There is nothing else to do," he reasoned. "It wasn't my decision."

"But, Heinrich! It's damp in there! And ten times worse than the cell in the tower. You mean—?" She clutched Heinrich's arm.

"No, no. They won't torture her. Just let her look at the wheel and the—" Heinrich dropped his head on his arm, leaning against the mantel shelf. "It makes me sick," he said. "Why did I ever get tangled up with her? Every time I go up there she gets me so tied up in knots inside, I can't think straight. Peter is disappointed, too."

"Of course, he is. He'll probably never trust another girl."

"He told me this morning he was glad he can't talk to her. He doesn't want to."

"And Michel's trip 'way over here?"

"All for nothing. I never was so disappointed in my life. He had permission to talk to her, but he only sat there and would say hardly a word. After we got outside I asked him why, and he said he didn't know."

"Didn't know?"

"Catri, I've told you how it went. He just sat there and looked at her dumfounded, said he had his speech all made out, went over and over it all the way from Zurich, but when he saw her, his tongue felt paralyzed and he got a big lump in his throat because she acted and looked so happy. I'm going to Zurich to talk to Michel. He's got to come back tonight. If I can see Zwingli, maybe he can tell us what more to do. We've got to get her straightened out before her folks come back."

"Oh, yes, Heinrich, by all means or we'll get the blame."

"Don't you hear the twins?"

"Hear them? Of course, I hear them," cried Catri. "I need a maid."

* * *

With coat and scarf on, Regina stood shivering at the small cell opening. The long purple rays of night were slowly fading into black. The road far below had completely disappeared. Regina struck her feet together in an effort to keep warm.

The lock in the door clicked.

It was Peter with her second meal of the day, bread and water. Placing the lantern on the floor, he motioned to Regina.

"Thank you, Peter."

He looked around. He reached in his pocket and drew out something wrapped in a clean white handkerchief. Unfolding the corners, he held out in his trembling hand a slice of cooked meat.

"For me?" whispered Regina.

Peter nodded. He held it closer. When she did not take it, his eyes glistened with tears. He held it toward her beseechingly.

"How can I refuse it?" she whispered. "But is it right for me to eat stolen food?"

He nodded his head emphatically, at the same time slowly closing the door.

She followed him. "It's not?" she whispered.

He shook his head, pointing to himself.

She put her face to the opening. "You mean you did without and—" but before she had finished, the door was locked and she heard Peter running down the stairs.

* * *

At seven o'clock Lord Englehard, the pastor, and the board of trustees gathered in the council room.

"This case is taking entirely too much of our time," concluded the lord, leaning forward impatiently in his high-backed chair. "While we are working on this, we're neglecting other cases. Is her brother coming, Heinrich?"

"He said he would."

"It's three days now," continued the lord, frowning, "and no change except for the worse. This is my suggestion. Let's call her down to the judgment room and have her face each of us individually. Have your questions ready. If she will not recant after eight of us have interviewed her, she goes to the torture chamber. What do you say?"

"Agreed," came the unanimous reply.

Pale, but smiling and lovely, Regina followed Peter to the judgment room on second floor. Peter waited in the hall to open and close the door. One by one the trustees filed in, closed the door, and held their private interviews. One by one they came out, shaking their heads.

After the sixth trustee reported no success, Lord Englehard, in desperation, entered the room. He faced Regina across the slate-topped table, "You certainly realize," he began, "that even though you have impressed the trustees that without a doubt you are confused about part of your story, we must deal with you as a woman of nineteen."

Regina nodded.

"We as a board have been very lenient with you. But you have told all six trustees you will not recant. We are giving you one more chance."

"The pastor begs to be excused tonight. He is too broken-hearted and disgraced to try to reason with you again. Regina, I will ask you for the last time tonight, will you recant?"

"Not tonight," Regina answered, "or ever, if I keep my right mind."

The lord's face hardened. "Your brother Michel is coming to see you tonight yet. Did you know that?"

"No."

"Would you like to see him when he comes?"

"Very much."

"But you shall not see him," came the lord's emphatic reply. "You are going to be taken directly to the torture chamber from this room. You will be there in solitary confinement for as long as we deem necessary. This will be all." Lord Englehard stepped toward the door. "Only this yet," he said. "You realize, I suppose, that there's a dungeon under this castle, don't you?"

"Yes," answered Regina.

"Peter," called the lord.

"Your honor," Peter stepped to the door.

"Take this prisoner to the torture chamber. You are to watch with extra care. Remember, Johann Ferlinden escaped

203

from that place; so stand guard all night. If her brother from Zurich comes, he is not to see her. Trust no one. Understand?"

"Yes, Lord Englehard." Peter took Regina's arm and led her away.

It was not a great distance to the torture chamber. At the far end of the courtyard beyond the wagon and toolrooms, it stood away from the main part of the castle. But before the two were halfway across the courtyard, Andreas appeared.

"Where now?" he said.

"Can't you guess?" answered Peter.

"Not there!" Andreas pointed. "Regina," he cried, "please recant!"

"You would not say that, Andreas," she answered, "if you realized what that would mean to me, and anyway you forget you're not to be speaking to me."

Then Michel came running. "Wait," he called, "is that you, Regina?"

"Yes, Michel."

He reached her, panting. "They told me I can't see you tonight." Peter walked on with Regina. "Wait," called Michel. "I must see her. Wait, I must talk to her! Regina!"

Peter led Regina on. "I'm only obeying orders," he said with a calm, firm voice. "You go back and talk to Lord Englehard, and if he says you can get in to talk with her, I'll let you in."

Michel ran back to Lord Englehard's office.

"Your honor, why can't I see my own sister tonight?" Michel's face was red; his eyes, desperate.

"Six trustees couldn't do anything with her. What could you do? Every time she states her belief, she only makes herself feel that much stronger. You know how it was when you were a boy running in the dark because you were scared. The faster you ran, the more scared you made yourself. The same principle holds with these Anabaptists. She's wound up tonight. Seven of us just got through grilling her thoroughly. She's anxious to see you and tell you her decisions and fanciful notions, too. Every time they get a little bigger. Don't you see? I'm trying to help the poor girl. What she needs is absolute solitude. She's repeated her story until she actually believes it now. She'll get tired of that place over there, don't you worry. The very fact that I deprive her of talking to you tonight may mean her giving up."

Michel studied. "I hope you're right, Lord Englehard," he said. "I hope you're right."

* * *

Regina curled up into a ball in the corner of the cold cell and drew her legs tightly under her coat. The cell in the tower with its wooden floor and ledge bed, though cold, had been considerably warmer than this torture chamber with its damp ground floor. She rested her head on her knees and prayed. Outside she could hear Peter walking back and forth on the stones. She tried to sleep, but she had to shiver.

The night wore on.

"Regina."

Regina lifted her head.

"Regina," someone whispered.

She looked all around. "Did someone call me?" she answered into the darkness.

"Come to the door."

"Who's there?"

"Peter."

Groping, she tripped and almost fell. "Where is the door, Peter?"

"Here. Come this way. Are you there?"

"Yes."

"I'm going to disobey orders tonight and speak to you," he whispered.

"Won't you be punished, Peter?"

"I will take the punishment. But I can't go on this way any longer, Regina."

"What do you mean?"

"I've got to talk with you. I've got to tell you I'd give anything in the world, if I could only exchange places with you."

Regina hesitated. "That's kind of you, Peter, but I would not want to exchange places with you for everything in all the world. I mean that."

Peter sighed. "Oh, Regina! Can't I say something to show you how much I care? I can't live the night through without telling you I'm willing to be punished. I'm willing to die for you," Peter swung the door open. "Here is the open door. I'll set you free and take whatever comes."

Regina stood speechless. She held out both hands. The door was open.

"Peter," she cried. "You can't mean that. You're beside yourself."

"True. I'm wretched and unhappy. I don't know what to do. But you. You seem so happy, Regina."

"I am happy."

"I'd do anything to have what you've got."

"Peter," whispered Regina. "You mean that?"

"I do," whispered Peter. "I mean it with all my heart and soul. I'd go to the end of the world just to be worthy to tell you I love you. Here is the door. You are set free. Go, Dear One, quickly before they torture you more."

Regina stepped close. She felt for Peter's hand and clasped it with her slender one. "Then come with me," she whispered. "If you really mean that, you won't need to go to the end of the world. Come. Come quickly. Once we find the pastor's garden fence, I think I can remember the way from there."

"Regina," whispered Peter, placing his free hand on her shoulder. "Do you know what you are saying?"

"Let's go, Peter," she whispered, pulling his hand. "We'll have to hurry to make it before dawn."

XXXII

For an instant Regina tightened her clasp on Peter's hand, then trembling, she dropped it.

"What?" whispered Peter. "Are you afraid of me? Don't be."

"Peter, Peter," Regina repeated softly, "would you—I mean —are you ready to go to the end of the world to find peace of heart, regardless—"

"What do you mean, Regina?"

"Regardless of—of me, Peter? You can't run this risk just because of me. Is it peace with God you want?"

Peter grasped Regina's shoulder. "Whether I could ever be—" he hesitated. "I—I—yes, truly, Regina, to be sure, it's peace with God I want—the peace of heart you have, regardless if I ever see you again as long as—" he stopped short.

"As long as what, Peter?"

"As long as I live. God helping me, Regina, I want to set you free tonight. Please go quickly now before someone hears us. You have taught me many things I never knew before; I'll never be the same now. I would go to the ends of all the worlds to have the peace and faith you have, Regina."

"Come with me then," she whispered taking his hand; "I know where to go and someone who can help you."

The night was crisp. The distant glaciered mountaintops which had flamed in red splendor that afternoon were now a deep bluish-gray under the star-dotted sky. All was quiet. The stillness hung low in the cold air. Regina tightened her grip on Peter's hand. Swiftly, silently they ran across the castle courtyard, through the stone-arched entrance, and down the long, steep hill past the pastor's house. Cautiously they

207

tiptoed past the gate, following the drive on the outside of the fence, until they reached the rear garden entrance.

Regina stopped, breathless. "Did you hear something, Peter?"

"I wasn't sure."

"We've got to go through the garden now. We've got to. Come!"

"Why through the garden?"

"That's the only way I know to go. I must try to keep my bearings. If it wasn't quite dark— We must hurry, Peter."

"Listen now!" whispered Peter. "Did you hear that?"

"Oh! It's one of the twins crying. That means Catri will be getting up. Come! Hurry!"

They climbed the garden fence and ran down the frost-coated hill to the road below. On the road she stopped abruptly.

"What do we do now?" whispered Peter, bending to speak so that she could hear.

"Peter, I can't go another step unless I pray. Is this just a dream? Am I really free, Peter?" She searched his face in the shadowy darkness.

"Didn't I set you free myself?" he whispered.

"Yes, Peter, I'm sure you did, but I still can hardly believe it's actually true. Are you really going to go on with me now?"

"Go with you? Why do you ask me that? Didn't you invite me to come with you?"

"Yes," she whispered, "but tell me, Peter, tell me you are not fooling me tonight. I've got to know before we go farther."

"Fooling you!" gasped Peter. "Regina! What do you mean?"

Trembling, she clutched at his coat.

"Then you aren't going with me just—to come back and tell Lord Engle—"

"Regina!" choked Peter. "Since I've been working at the castle I've helped capture Anabaptists, but if I'm not sincere tonight, Regina, I hope the worst of tortures is put upon me. Regina, why do you mistrust me now? Please, please believe me."

"I must be sure, be absolutely certain, Peter."

"I know there's much deception these days," ventured Peter, "and it pays to be cautious. You've hated the things I've been doing for Lord Englehard, haven't you?"

"Some things," she nodded.

"And you can't imagine me being sincere, in taking this sudden turn? Is that it, Regina?"

"Well, Peter, I just want to be sure."

"And you must be. You have a right to be, Regina. But how can I tell you how I've hated myself for imprisoning harmless people? Ever since we talked at the Hofmeier home I haven't quit thinking about my job and I've hated it. Regina, believe me, I'm not fooling you tonight."

Regina bowed her head. "Dear God," she whispered, "thank you. Thank you for everything. You know all I mean. Thank you for Peter, who set me free. And, dear God, thank you now for his troubled heart, for I know you can give him the same peace you gave me. Help me now not to make a single misturn on our journey to find that peace and perfect love that casts out fear. Lead us through the darkness to the place we must find before morning. And, oh, dear God, give me strength. Amen."

Regina looked in every direction. "I know now, Peter," she whispered, taking his hand, "we follow the road leading north, and we have no time to lose."

They walked fast, speaking little. At times, when footing was sure, they almost ran.

"Regina, you haven't told me where you're taking me."

"But you trust me, don't you, Peter?"

"It has never once entered my mind to mistrust you, Regina. I told you I'd go to the end of the world, didn't I?"

"Yes."

209

"I'm ready for anything then. It's you I am anxious about. You haven't eaten much the past days."

"But I prayed for strength, Peter. God will give it to me. He has never failed me since I've learned to trust Him."

"And how far must we go yet?"

"I don't know, but it's quite a distance. We've got to keep going. It will take hours."

"Hours?"

"Yes."

"And then what?"

Regina shivered. "I don't know, Peter. God leads one step at a time. And if He is worth trusting at all, He's worth trusting tonight. Just think, only an hour ago—"

Peter pressed Regina's hand.

They began to walk.

"I knew it would mean death," Regina added, still thinking about the torture chamber where she'd been so shortly before.

"And you weren't afraid?"

"God takes away all our fears when we trust Him, Peter. God does that. I had all kinds of ideas what they might do to me next, but one thing I knew and I know now, I am determined by God's help to remain steadfast to the end, no matter what it might mean. I wasn't afraid.

"I was determined to keep the peace I'd found at any cost. I love my family, but regardless of what they have decided to do and believe about the Bible and the Anabaptist teaching, I had to make my own decision. No one else can be my conscience. That's something I must live with and answer for before God."

"But not every Anabaptist has remained steadfast," objected Peter. "I heard several swear off so they could be released. I saw two men turn white and shake like leaves when the torture chamber was mentioned. They recanted."

"The pastor told me that, too, so I would recant. But I had decided fully before taking my stand that if God could keep Felix Manz to the end, He could keep me, too, even if they'd drown me, and even though I wouldn't have a mother and brother on the river bank to cheer me and beg me to remain true to the end.

"Peter, you've got to come to the place like I did. You've got to want peace in your own soul. You've got to want the true satisfying answers to all the questions about right and wrong that torment you day and night. You've got to want that more than your position with the lord up in Kyburg Castle, more than your family, more than any other thing in all— Peter!" she whispered. "Listen!"

He clutched her arm. They both had heard it—a strange stir in the woods.

"Shall we go on?" whispered Regina.

"Let's keep going," Peter answered. "It might be only an animal. I wish I could pick you up and run now."

"I'll rest after we get there. My! I do hope it was only an animal, Peter. Peter, that piece of meat you gave me helps me more than you will know."

"I wish now I had slipped you two pieces. If I had only known— Never under God's heaven was there a girl quite like you, Regina. I love you." He saw her put a hand over her heart. "You are weak, Dear. Rest a little. This has been a hard day for you, I know, for it was hard enough on me."

Regina smiled, "Yes, but we've got to go on. God will help me. See," she whispered, "He's helping me right this moment."

XXXIII

Regina and Peter traveled steadily down one hill, up another, and on around the mountain. Fatigue and weariness gnawed at their bones. Evergreen boughs above them waved ominously like giant black plumes in the cold air. Regina pulled her scarf tighter. Finally she heard, to her joy, the ripple of a stream, one of those fed by a glacier miles in the distance, which gave her assurance once more that they were on the right road. Soon they would cross the wooden bridge, for which she was watching, and beyond that was the Alpine tableland and its mountain cave.

Suddenly Regina jumped.

"Don't be afraid, Regina," whispered Peter. "See, it's only one of those long-horned goats."

"Yes, I see now. I wish I wouldn't frighten so easily tonight. It's only that—"

"You're really not afraid of anything, I know," Peter said comfortingly. "It's just that you're tired and worn, and extremely alert. You were always the first to hear the twins whimper at night, weren't you?"

"How do you know?"

"Catri told me."

"She did?"

"She told me about you, Regina. She said you did your job very well, seeing what was to be done and doing it. She's missing you terribly. Poor Aunt Catri! I really do pity her."

"I love her, Peter. I loved it there, too, helping her with the twins; but nothing dare come between me and my love for Christ now. Absolutely nothing in all the world."

"Tell me more," begged Peter.

"About what, Peter?"

"The things I ought to know, but don't. The things about this faith you are so determined to be true to. I'm ashamed I'm so ignorant, but I was afraid to ask anyone anything."

"But you really did wonder?"

"Many times, Regina," Peter confessed softly, "especially since that night in the kitchen when you dropped the soup bowl and—"

"And you wiped the dishes?"

"Yes," answered Peter. "I knew that night that you had something that made me wonder and made me—" Peter bit his lip. They hurried on in silence. "I can't exactly explain, Regina," he continued at length, "but you did something to me that night. I began living to see you again, to talk to you. And as I was helping to round up Anabaptists, I wished I didn't have to because you hated to see the prisoners led up the hill to the castle."

"Peter," smiled Regina, "everything will be different from this night on, won't it?"

"I am more than ready," smiled Peter, "for you to help me make it be different. You will help me, won't you?"

"I am ready to help any honest soul find the light, Peter."

"And you're not afraid of me any more?"

"Perfect love casts out fear."

"You mean—" Peter's heart pounded. "Regina, you mean—"

"Greater love has no one than this, Peter," answered Regina, 'that he lay down his very life for a friend. And you're my friend, Peter. It's my love for Christ that has made you my friend, isn't it?"

"Why—why, yes, of course."

"And since He loves me so, I love Him in return. I have love in my heart for everyone. Nothing I can think of right now would make me happier than to be the one to help you find that same love, that perfect love that casts out fear."

Peter was silent. When he spoke again, his voice was hardly above a whisper, yet firm.

"I would rather have the peace and understanding you have, Regina, than have any other honor bestowed upon me."

"Peter," cried Regina, "you've made me happy tonight. Listen carefully to me and I will try to repeat the things Christian told me in God's cathedral the night I accepted this faith."

For a full hour, Regina talked, hesitating momentarily to rest her voice. Peter was an eager, attentive listener, a ready pupil. Step by step she explained to him her own feelings of unrest, her fears, her torments, her struggles of soul. She explained as best she could her own conviction of sin, and how she had prayed daily for the answers to the questions that haunted her. She explained how she finally found satisfaction of soul, and peace of mind when she heard the Scriptures explained, and took the Bible as truth to be obeyed instead of the teachings of the state church.

"Do you understand now, Peter?" she asked eagerly.

"I am beginning to, Regina. It's all so new to me."

"But you asked with an open heart."

"Everything you have told me sounds reasonable. You must know."

"I know what I've told you is true. But there's much more to know yet. Someday I do hope I can have a Bible of my own and know how to read it. If Michel would only be willing to teach me, but he says, like the pastor, that I'm better off if I can't read it. So you say what I've told you sounds reasonable and right, Peter?"

Not only admiration, but also conviction was in Peter's voice when he spoke, "The greatest reason why I'm convinced you are right, Regina," he said confidingly, "is because of you, yourself."

Regina looked up with a start. "Then I hope and pray that I will never, never be a stumbling block to you, Peter. It almost makes me tremble to hear you say that."

"Why tremble? I said it to make you happy."

"It does make me glad if I've had a part in this, Peter. But after all I'm only a new disciple in this faith, and remember I'm far from being perfect. You must rely on the Scriptures rather than on me, Peter. What if I would unthinkingly do or say something to cause you to doubt or stumble?"

"You won't."

"I don't intend to, Peter. I hope I won't, but I'm human. I feel very weak of myself."

"But as surely as Felix Manz convinced you he had something satisfying and real, so you have convinced me, and I just wanted you to know it."

"Thank you, Peter. I hope I can convince my parents, and my dear brother Michel, and many others who are as confused and distressed and undecided as he was."

Peter was very serious again. "I hope I can get to the place where I can—"

"Can what?"

Peter's voice was strange and a little unsteady when he spoke. "Can help you convince others," he said. "That would make me very, very happy."

Regina pondered. "My life is in God's hands, Peter," she said. "He has a plan for your life, too."

Regina hesitated, looking searchingly ahead. She pressed one hand over her thumping heart.

"What frightened you?" whispered Peter. "Do you see something?"

"Yes," whispered Regina. "I'm not exactly frightened. I'm only excited. See, we are nearing the place I've been watching for."

"What place is it?"

"See," she pointed. "Isn't that a little one-room wooden hut ahead?"

"I believe it is."

"Is this the right place, Peter?"

"How can I know, Dear?" whispered Peter. "Remember, you are bringing me to an unknown place. Doesn't it seem right to you?"

"What if it isn't after all?"

"Then I would say we're in a serious situation, for dawn's not far away."

Regina turned slowly, looking in every direction. "Yes," she whispered, "I'm quite sure this is the place. I was here but once, you know, but, Peter—"

"Yes?"

"Do pray with me before I knock on the door."

"And who lives there?" asked Peter.

"You will soon see. Just trust me, Peter; I mean, trust God as never before in your life."

"All right. I do, Regina."

Trembling, the two bowed their heads in a moment of silent prayer, then walked slowly, carefully toward the fast-closed hut door.

Regina lifted her right hand, hesitated only a tense, fearful moment, then, as she remembered Hans doing, gave three gentle raps, waited, and then repeated the sign.

Presently they heard a few padded footsteps within, the latch clicked, and the heavy door was carefully opened.

XXXIV

"Moses?" Regina spoke with a feeling of apprehensiveness.

But the moment Regina said his name, she recognized the old man's beautiful white beard. "Moses," she repeated with relief.

"Yes," came the man's low-toned answer. "Who comes here this time of night?"

"It's Regina, Moses. Hans Strahm's sister. Remember me?"

"Ah! Yes, of course, I remember," replied Moses.

"I have come back with a friend from Kyburg."

Moses held out his hands. "Welcome. Come inside. If you have come all the way from Kyburg, I know you are tired, and cold, and hungry."

"Yes," Regina said simply, dropping to the little homemade stool beside the stove. "This fire feels good."

Then for a moment she thought she was going to faint. She unfastened her coat and bit her lips. "Moses," she said, "this friend is Peter Reimann, one of the lord's watchmen at the castle."

"What?" gasped Moses, stepping back. "You say watchman! At Kyburg Castle!"

"Don't be frightened, Moses. It's quite all right. Let me explain."

"Well—well—take a seat, Peter."

"Thank you, Moses." Peter seated himself on another homemade stool in the corner of the room.

"Draw it up to the stove, if you like," motioned the old man.

"Is Johann Ferlinden still in the cave?" asked Regina.

Peter's hat dropped to the floor.

The gentle eyes in the old man's spare face took on a strange glassy sheen, and they looked at the young man on the stool as if they would pierce through him.

"It is nothing to cause you to be afraid," Regina assured him, getting quickly to her feet and stepping closer to Moses. "He has come with me for help. Believe me, Moses. I tell you the truth. You know I would not lie."

The old man's face relaxed. "Well," he began, "he was up there several hours ago."

"The Lord is good," said Regina. "I prayed that he was still there."

"I was up there, and talked with him since dark. I had to come home to get a little rest. I can't stand what I once could," continued Moses. "If it's Johann Ferlinden you want to see again, you'll have to start right now without delay. It won't be long now till morning breaks."

"I know," agreed Regina.

"But listen," added Moses. "Officers went past here twice today. I still don't know that I understand all this. I'm responsible for Ferlinden, you know," the old man's voice shook.

"Friend Moses," said Peter, "I give you my word of highest honor, that neither you nor your good friend, Ferlinden, will be harmed or trapped tonight, not any more than you were the night Regina came here with her brother. I do not blame you for wondering. I cannot blame you for mistrusting me, but I assure you I am honest about this. I came for help, not to harm you."

"Please believe him," cried Regina.

"Very well," agreed Moses. "I'll give you warm milk to drink, for I'm sure you're hungry. Then we must go."

"But you need your rest, Moses," Regina said as she watched the old man's unsteady hand pour the milk into two large cups. "Don't you think we could find the way ourselves?"

"I'd better go with you. This time of morning the grass is wet, and very slick. The rocks are slippery and treacherous

218

too." He handed them each a cup. "Besides, it's darkest just before dawn, you know. I'd feel better about it if I'd lead the way. Unless you're used to the place, it is dangerous climbing along that ledge. Here," he said, "I'll give you each a cane. You say you came all the way from the castle tonight?"

"We escaped," Regina said after drinking several swallows of milk. "I've been in prison there for three days on bread and water. Moses, this milk is wonderful—wonderful."

"You? In prison?" Moses asked.

"Yes. And Peter here set me free."

"And it's Ferlinden you want? Tonight?" Peter nodded.

"Then as soon as you've finished the milk, we must go."

"Regina," whispered Peter as the three walked under the low-hanging pine tree branches, "Andreas and I rode up and down that road past that little hut more than a few times recently in our hunt for Johann Ferlinden. I know we did. That very road. And I'm also sure it's this same old man with the white beard that we saw outside that hut one afternoon."

"And did you stop to talk to him?"

"No. We figured he wouldn't know anything we wanted to know."

"God didn't let you ask him, Peter."

"And you say there's a cave back here somewhere?" whispered Peter.

"You'll soon find out, Peter."

"But I never knew there was such a place in these parts. I'm positive Andreas didn't either."

"You weren't supposed to know, Peter. God has a way of protecting those He wants to protect."

"What?"

"God has prepared this place to hide His servants from you. You're only beginning to find out how wonderful God is."

Peter groaned. "I will not try to deny it."

The hill was steep and the grass slick. Slowly, steadily, Moses led the way. Regina was grateful for Peter's strong hand.

219

"Be especially careful now," warned Moses; "follow close behind me and keep to your left. The path is narrow and rocky. I'll be praying."

Carefully they edged their way along the semicircle of the gorge. At last as they neared the end of the treacherous tramp, Moses stopped a moment to rest. And then along the side of the mountain, the bushes and thickly matted foliage on the face of the gorge to their right slowly came into view. Dawn was breaking. Just ahead the slender silvery thread of mountain snow-water dripped from high above the cave entrance and splashed on the rocks below.

Peter followed silently at Regina's heels. Moses in the lead stopped just below the waterfall and tapped on the rock three times with the tip of his cane, waited a moment, then repeated the sign.

"Watch," whispered Regina, looking back at Peter.

Slowly they saw Ferlinden move out from the circle of the dark cave entrance. With outstretched arms he welcomed the trio.

"I'm back again with two weary pilgrims," announced Moses.

Ferlinden smiled. In the early dawning his eyes met Regina's and he knew her at once. But at sight of Peter his countenance changed abruptly. His arms dropped. He stood fixed.

"You helped me to peace and happiness," began Regina, smiling through a mist of tears. He caught her extended hand and shook it warmly. "And now," she whispered, "I've brought another. This is Peter Reimann from Kyburg Castle.

"He has come as your friend," Regina said with earnestness. "Do not fear him. Peter needs the help you can give him."

Johann Ferlinden stepped forward and caught Peter's hand. "Bless the Lord!" he exclaimed, "we've seen each other before, haven't we?"

For a moment Peter could not speak. He swallowed hard.

"Ferlinden," he faltered.

"Yes, Peter."

"I'm—truly—very—sorry," he faltered brokenly. "I—"

"Come on inside the cave," Ferlinden whispered. "It's not safe to stand here any longer. Morning is on us." He led the way, and they all followed. "We must keep ourselves hid. And inside there is a surprise for Regina."

XXXV

As they walked back into the cave Ferlinden made a beckoning motion.

"What! Not Regina! My child!" Friedrich Strahm ran to his daughter and clasped her in his trembling arms.

"Father!" sobbed Regina, "and Mother!" Regina tore herself from her father's embrace and threw her arms around her mother's neck and kissed her. "And Hans!" she exclaimed softly. "Tell me! What does all this mean?"

Friedrich Strahm tried desperately to control his emotions. "It means much." He wiped his eyes. "Maybe Johann Ferlinden will tell it for us," he said.

"Hans went all the way to Kyburg tonight," began Ferlinden, "hoping to meet you by the pump again, Regina. He wanted to bring you along back with him."

"Tonight?" gasped Regina.

"I mean it was last night. This is today already. He got back here only about an hour ago."

"We were heartbroken," Regina's mother cried. "Oh, Regina, you can't imagine how we felt when he came without you."

"We asked the Lord to tell us what next to do," continued Ferlinden. "Hans said you had to be located. He said he waited by the pump until he knew he didn't dare wait any longer. He knew he had to get back before daylight."

"But I wasn't at the pastor's house. I've been up in the castle prison for the past three days."

"You? In prison?"

"That's right," Regina answered.

"Because you were baptized?" asked Ferlinden.

"Yes."

"And you—you—?"

"No," replied Regina. "I did not tell who baptized me nor where it was done. They tried to get me to tell."

"What did you say?" asked Hans.

"I said Christian did it in God's cathedral. Oh, I have so much to tell, but not now. It's all been so exciting, so wonderful. But last night this prison guard," she pointed to Peter, "set me free. I had been transferred from the prison to the torture chamber."

"What?" cried Father. "Not you in the torture chamber!"

"Don't pity me," said Regina. "Please listen. This is Peter, Father, Peter Reimann. Father, Mother, Hans, this is Lord Englehard's right-hand horseman and watchman at Kyburg Castle."

"You mean I used to be all that," objected Peter modestly.

"That's right," agreed Regina, "but he did it. He set me free and came along with me, and all the way over I prayed that you, Johann Ferlinden, would be here yet, for he wants you to tell him all you told me the night I decided to accept Christ. I explained all I could on the way, but he wants to hear it again from you."

"I'll be more than glad to do that. And you were in Kyburg prison? No wonder Hans waited in vain by the pump. Oh, how we ought to trust God," smiled Ferlinden. "And, Regina," he whispered, "after you've heard your parents' story, you'll never question the leading of the Lord. Have you had peace, Regina, since the night you were here?"

"Yes, yes. Tell me about my parents."

"Your parents' trip to Langnau," began Ferlinden, "seemed to be all for nothing. But God in His great unspeakable love and wisdom had a plan in that, too, for now we can see how it's worked out for your good and we're—"

"Oh," cried Regina, clasping her hands, "go on."

"Last night after dark Hans brought your mother and father over here to see me."

She smiled.

The group stood close together.

"After I explained the Scriptures and answered their questions, they both accepted Christ. They were baptized here in this cathedral where you and Hans were."

"Mother! Father!" Regina kissed them both. "It seems almost too good to be true. But now what are we all going to do? We can't stay here. Will we go back home or go back to the castle and give ourselves up?"

Friedrich Strahm buried his face in his hands. "My child," he said, "we just thought we couldn't start out without you. We felt as if it would nearly kill us."

"Start out for where, Father? What do you mean?"

"The Lord willing, we're all going to start for Austria as early as it's safe to step outside the cave tonight."

"Tonight!" gasped Regina. "Tonight? Start for Austria?"

"You could never go back home now," explained Ferlinden. "I mean you couldn't go back and escape persecution or death. It's best, the only safe thing left to try, Regina. Your parents brought me the glad news that my wife fled to Austria last week, hoping to find me there. Think of it! I must go find her. And now that God has so marvelously answered our prayers and brought you here, we'll spend the day sleeping and praying in preparation for our long journey. It will not be easy."

Regina's eyes widened. "How wonderful! Oh, it's all so— so wonderful. I prayed many times that you and your wife would be united."

"If it's God's will, we will be. I have never doubted that for one single moment since the day I was taken from her."

"But what about Michel?" whispered Regina. "Mother, Father, how about him?"

Mother shook her head sadly. She put her arms around Father's neck; she felt his hot face against her forehead.

"It's sad, Regina," said Ferlinden sympathetically. "I know it's hard to leave a loved one behind, but we cannot stay here any longer.

"We'll have to leave Michel in the hands of a merciful God who has very miraculously spared my life and yours until this day. We dare not stay here another day, Regina. When we heard footsteps a while ago, we were afraid that someone was on my trail. But Moses' three knocks relieved my mind. Only by the love and providence of God have I escaped being caught on several occasions. Then when I saw you," Ferlinden put one hand on Peter's arm, "I thought for a moment my time had come." Johann Ferlinden shook his head. "Peter— Peter—" He pressed Peter's arm.

"I never knew before there was such a place as this. If I had— Tonight someone was on your trail, Ferlinden, but not to capture you. I came," Peter hesitated, his voice a bit unsteady, "as Regina has already suggested, because I want what all these have." Peter's eyes scanned the little group. "I want peace and salvation. Above all, I want to be able to face what is ahead."

"Peter!" Ferlinden said with deep feeling, "you can have peace and salvation."

"But you understand," began Peter seriously, "I'm a great sinner. I realize that as I never did before. I had a horrible job at the castle. I never want to capture an Anabaptist again."

"Praise God, Peter."

"Regina proved to me that this faith of yours is what I need. I must have it at any cost, Ferlinden." Peter's eyes glistened with tears.

A holy hush fell over the group, and they drew closer together.

"Bless God," whispered Ferlinden, pressing Peter's hand in his own. "You mean, Peter—"

Peter looked up. "I mean that I want you to explain how

I can be forgiven and—and—" Peter bowed his head. He could say no more.

Johann Ferlinden took his worn Bible from under his coat on a rock close by. He began to teach Peter as he had taught the others how all have sinned, how Christ died for all, and that those who accept His death as a substitution for them are saved from everlasting punishment and death.

Carefully Peter listened. An hour slipped by. Then through the thickly matted latticework of leaves outside the cave peeked the first rays of the rising sun.

"Let's move back farther into the cave," suggested Ferlinden. "We must take every precaution and keep our voices to a whisper. See, the morning light is breaking, and this will be an important day. And now, Peter," he concluded, closing his Bible, "what are you going to do about what the Bible teaches? Are you ready to accept Christ as your personal Saviour?"

Peter's answer was firm and unmistakable. "Yes, I am. And if you are willing now and you believe I'm sincere, I want you to baptize me. You have convinced me that infant baptism is not enough. I want adult baptism. I want to be one of you."

"Once you were blind, Peter, and now you see?"

Peter nodded.

"It will be with a sense of profound thanks to God, Peter, and—" he hesitated a moment, "and also a very deep personal gratitude to you that I baptize you today."

Peter stared. "Why gratitude to me?"

"You do not know?" whispered Ferlinden.

"I'm sorry," said Peter, "but I just don't understand what you are referring to."

"You mean," whispered Ferlinden, "you do not know that it was you who let me escape from the torture chamber?"

"Me?" said Peter.

"Yes, you, Peter. You mean you never knew that you didn't lock the door the night you guarded the torture chamber?"

"I—" said Peter excitedly— "I failed to lock the door! You mean—"

Ferlinden's voice was rich and tender when he spoke. "God's ways are higher than the thoughts of men, Peter. Little did I dream that I would ever have the privilege of telling you this myself. Much less did I suppose that you would follow me to this place to ask me to baptize you. You, Peter, of all men in Switzerland!"

"Nor I, Ferlinden."

"Peter, the night you failed to lock the door, I well remember how you and the other watchman were standing just outside discussing the pastor's beautiful maid. Remember that?"

"Go on," he whispered. "It could possibly have been."

"You unlocked the door to take my empty water cup. Thanks again for the bread and water, Peter. Remember?"

"Yes."

"Well, you forgot to relock the door." Ferlinden took Peter by the arm and shook it a little. "Only a watchman in love," he said with a twinkle in his eyes, "would have overlooked such an important task."

Peter wanted to glance at Regina, but he did not.

"But I thank God to this day," quickly added Ferlinden. "It was forgotten by divine planning, I'm positive. You didn't aim to overlook that, I know."

"No," whispered Peter, "to be sure. If Lord Englehard had known that."

Regina looked up into Peter's startled, troubled face. She touched his coat sleeve. "Peter," she whispered, "don't worry now about what Lord Englehard would have said or done. You can't undo it. Who would want to? Don't you see it, Peter? Don't you see now what I was trying to tell you on the way tonight—I mean last night, how God has led, and is leading us each step by step? Don't you see now that God used your forgetting to help Ferlinden? And He allowed me to be put into the torture chamber. Don't let this trouble you now."

Peter gazed into Regina's shining eyes, then turning to Ferlinden, he said, "I'm ready now, and I'd like to kneel on the same spot where these others did when you baptized them, if you don't mind."

"Gladly, Peter. Right over here on this smooth flat stone is the place." The group moved over.

Quietly Johann Ferlinden questioned Peter about his past life and his new confession of Christ. Peter answered each question and pledged his allegiance to God.

"And so," said Ferlinden, dipping mountain water from a can which Moses held, "God has provided the water with which to baptize you, Peter. Moses caught it for me last night. I now baptize you upon your own confession of Christ and upon your request. Baptism does not save you, Peter, as I explained, but is an outward sign of your inward cleansing which the blood of Christ has already done for you that moment you received Him by your own faith."

The cold mountain water ran down over Peter's head and shoulders and splashed on the ground.

"I do this in the presence of Almighty God and these witnesses here, in the name of the eternal Father, the only begotten Son, and the blessed Holy Spirit. Amen."

"Rise to your feet, Peter." Peter obeyed. "You are now a new creature in Christ Jesus. Old things have passed away from you. God has forgiven you. He will remember your sins against you no more forever. All things have already become new. Live always at peace with God and He will make your life a rich blessing to many. Remember, Peter, you are new in this faith. The devil will try you, tempt you in every conceivable manner, and will try to trip you and get you to turn back, but remember this also, that God will with each new trial and temptation make you able to overcome. I will pray for you. I am deeply concerned about you now. Peter, I will never, never forget you. I only wish I could be near to help you learn the Word."

"I wish so, too, Ferlinden. Thank you for all you've done for me. Thank you for helping me understand. Thanks for —everything."

"Peter," Regina said, clasping his hand in her slender trembling ones, "I've often prayed that you'd let God change your life."

"I'm glad you prayed for me," he whispered. "I'm glad you're happy."

"And isn't it just as wonderful—this peace—as I told you it would be?"

Peter nodded. "Yes," he whispered, "it is wonderful. Thank you for bringing me here."

XXXVI

"Ever since that night," Peter whispered, "when you broke Catri's soup bowl—"

Regina nodded.

"Well, I've loved you, Regina," he said. "You've known, haven't you, Dear?"

"I've tried very hard not to."

"Not to?"

"Yes."

Peter caught Regina's hands. "Why? Tell me, Dear."

"Well, Peter—how shall I say it—but—you see," she whispered, "until I knew you wanted to know the truth regardless of me, I—I—was determined not to—well, I mean I knew I just could not allow myself even to guess you cared. It just didn't dare to be true, Peter. The things you had to do, and you, just didn't seem to fit together and so—"

"But now," exclaimed Peter, "tell me that now you know I care, Regina. Will you, Dear?"

Regina blushed. She hesitated as Peter looked into her uplifted smiling face.

"Regina! You will believe me now without a doubt that I really love you, love you with all my heart?"

"I do, Peter."

"And I assure you I did not decide to be baptized just to win your love, Regina. It's deeper than that. I love you for what you are, Regina, but if we part today and I never see you again, I'm determined to be true to the vows I just made."

"I believe you now, Peter. I know you risked your life like this for only one reason. I know—"

"Say it, Regina," Peter urged.

She looked into his eyes. "Because—you love me."

"It's true, Regina, I love you with all my heart. I would gladly have given my life to set you free. I made up my mind you would go free regardless of what happened to me."

"I believe you, Peter. For I would not have offered to bring you along with me to this place unless I was glad that you acted as if you cared, and unless I cared, too."

Peter drew her close.

"Forgive me for the wicked things I've done, Dear. God helping me, I will live for Him and you."

"Yes, Peter, of course, I forgive you. I believe in you, Peter. I love you, too."

"Then what would hinder us from getting married right here in God's cathedral?"

"Peter!"

He lifted her hands to his lips.

Regina turned to her father, her mother, Hans, then to Johann Ferlinden. "You heard," she said. "What shall we do?"

"It is all right with us, Dear," her father consented.

Regina's face shone as she ran to kiss her mother and bury her head against her neck. "We will kneel on the same spot where we were all baptized," she said smiling happily through her tears. "Come, Father and Mother, stand beside us

"My Peter! My dear new transformed Peter!"

"Yes, Dear, I will be your own." Peter drew her arm through his and helped her kneel.

Johann Ferlinden clasped the hands of the happy pair as they knelt together.

"And now may yours be a beautiful perfect love," he prayed, "a love which knows no diminishing, but grows stronger and deeper with each new day. May your love for God be the key to all your happiness. And as it has brought you together, may it keep you close together all your days. Amen."

"And, Peter," said Ferlinden with a smile after Peter had helped Regina to her feet, "now you will be going to Austria with the rest of us."

"Yes," Peter answered. "Thank God! Thank God forever!"

"And, Peter," added Ferlinden, "if this little prisoner you set free will always help you spiritually as she has today, she won't soon let her guard escape from the Lord's leading, will she?"

Regina was radiant. Her face, aglow with joy, had never been more beautiful.

"No," mused Peter. "No." He kissed Regina softly. "Not my Regina."